MW00465652

THE
WOMAN
AT MY
WEDDING

BOOKS BY L.G. DAVIS

THE LIES WE TELL SERIES

The New Nanny

The Nanny's Child

BROKEN VOWS SERIES

The Missing Bridesmaid

Liar Liar

Perfect Parents

My Husband's Secret

The Missing Widow

The Stolen Breath

Don't Blink

The Midnight Wife

The Janitor's Wife

THE
WOMAN
AT MY
WEDDING

L.G. DAVIS

bookouture

Published by Bookouture in 2024

An imprint of Storyfire Ltd.
Carmelite House
50 Victoria Embankment
London EC4Y 0DZ

www.bookouture.com

Copyright © L.G. Davis, 2024

L.G. Davis has asserted her right to be identified as the author of this work.

All rights reserved. No part of this publication may be reproduced, stored in any retrieval system, or transmitted, in any form or by any means, electronic, mechanical, photocopying, recording or otherwise, without the prior written permission of the publishers.

ISBN: 978-1-83525-309-0
eBook ISBN: 978-1-83525-308-3

This book is a work of fiction. Names, characters, businesses, organizations, places and events other than those clearly in the public domain, are either the product of the author's imagination or are used fictitiously. Any resemblance to actual persons, living or dead, events or locales is entirely coincidental.

PROLOGUE

THE WOMAN

The salty breeze tugs at the woman's hair as she crouches behind a swaying palm tree, hidden from view.

Brynn is standing on her cozy porch, leaning over its cream fence, her silhouette framed by the sun's bloody, dying rays.

The woman isn't close enough to make out the expression on Brynn's face, but she can imagine it's as tranquil as the turquoise ocean that stretches out in front of her. There will be a self-satisfied glint in her eyes; the peace that only someone with so much privilege and luxury is able to feel.

Brynn is wearing a flowing white dress, much like the one she will wear down the aisle in a few short weeks, when she will be surrounded by loved ones as she steps into a future that does not belong to her.

Despite how much it hurts, the woman's mind conjures up a clear image of Brynn a few years in the future. She will be in this picture-perfect oceanfront home, surveying her stunning view with Nathan by her side. The woman can just imagine Brynn's laughter ringing out, light and carefree, carried on the wind. She sees the two of them watching the apricot sun setting on the horizon with their arms around each other.

Perhaps they will have a baby, and Brynn will be soothing the child to sleep, rocking slowly back and forth on the swinging seat, with the sound of the waves gently caressing the sand.

Shaking her head, the woman tries to rid herself of these cruel images that threaten to take root in her mind. But bitterness surges within her, a relentless tide. Her knuckles turn white as she digs her fingers into her palms, unable to look away even as the poison within her grows deeper and stronger.

After a while, she fidgets around in the sand, trying to find a more comfortable posture. Her lower back is starting to ache from crouching for so long. She knows she should leave. She should remove herself from this deeply painful situation. But she can't find the strength. She can't look away. It's as though she needs to etch every detail of this moment into her memory, to carry it around with her like a scar.

Finally, with one last lingering look, the woman walks a little further away, the white sand crunching beneath her feet. The only way for her to stop this torture is to bring an end to Brynn's happiness. The happiness she doesn't deserve.

And the only way she can do that is by making sure Brynn's wedding never happens.

Reaching into her bag, she pulls out Brynn's wedding veil along with a small blue plastic shovel. The veil flutters in the wind, and she smiles, slowly. Then she digs a hole just deep enough to bury half the fabric, which she knows cost more than any clothes she's ever owned. And as she covers it with sand and weighs the rest down with shells, she takes time to be mindful with every sweet movement, letting the sensations soothe the searing burn from the poison inside her. It feels so good to *do* something, to regain some sense of control.

She just hopes that when Brynn finds the buried veil, she will understand the message. But if she doesn't, well, the woman can't be held responsible for what happens next.

Brynn doesn't deserve this warning.
But for now, the woman will be generous.

ONE

BRYNN

30 Days Before the Wedding

It's the day of my wedding dress fitting, and folds of tulle and lace cascade down my hips and pool around my feet like the white frothy edges of the ocean. As if it's drawn to the warm glow in my heart, golden sunlight spills into the master bedroom of our new house, wrapping around everything it touches.

While I peer at my reflection in the full-length mirror, I get an unsettling feeling of déjà vu. It's as if I've already lived this moment, breathed in this air, and felt the silky softness of this exact dress against my skin.

I often feel this way, and I think it's because my life has been so fragmented. It might seem like I have it all, everything anyone could hope for. But there are many memories from my childhood that my mind has smudged or buried, to protect me from the pain. The luxury I now enjoy is new to me, and I would never take it for granted.

Long before I met Nathan, my husband-to-be, I fought and strived to get where I am. I hustled hard, working my way up from the bottom into what became a lucrative career in the art world. Before moving to this little town of Stoneview, Florida, I was an art gallery manager in Tallahassee, with my own small but successful art consultancy business on the side. I offered my services to clients who wanted to understand the value of their artworks for resale or auction purposes, and I loved my work even when the hours were long and I felt stretched in all directions.

Perhaps it's because there was so much ugliness and deprivation in my childhood, but for as long as I can remember, nothing has ever captivated me quite like gazing upon a beautiful piece of art that hides precious layers of meaning for me to slowly unwrap and treasure. Growing up, whenever I could find it, art was my escape from the harsh reality of life. So, I pursued my career with all the passion, determination, and single-mindedness I could muster, a trait I inherited from my mother. I'll always be proud of what I achieved, because at one point in my life, I'd never have thought it possible for someone like me.

However, moving to Stoneview gave me the opportunity to take a badly needed break. As much as I enjoy it, my career can often be very taxing. It's a vocation, not just a job, and I do tend to put a lot of pressure on myself in ways that aren't always healthy. But I will go back to it soon. I'm actually thinking that further down the road, I might open my own gallery here, in this lovely town I've come to call home.

So, yes, I'm pleased to say I worked hard to create the life I wanted; I wasn't born with a silver spoon in my mouth. But all of this? My handsome, intelligent fiancé, our cozy home overlooking the ocean, the dream wedding day we're going to have... it's far better than even my wildest dreams.

I know I'm lucky. But I can never rid myself of the fear lingering in my chest. The voice that says one day it will all be snatched away from me. I guess, deep down, I don't believe I deserve such happiness.

Turning away from the mirror, I distract myself from my anxiety by taking in the calm blue hues of our master bedroom and sipping from the fizzing glass of champagne in my hand. A gentle breeze wafts in through the open balcony doors, carrying with it a heady scent of salty sea air mingled with the sweet fragrance of the white roses, my favorite flowers, that sit inside a round glass vase on my coffee table.

I inhale a soothing, long breath, and smile, listening to the waves as they sweep the shore before retreating out to sea, only to come back again with renewed, steady energy. It's the perfect soundtrack to my life right now, I tell myself firmly. Everything is unfolding just as it should. All is calm and peaceful, steadily washing away my memories of darker, stormier days. Nothing is going to go wrong. I'm safe.

"You've got your head in the clouds today, Brynn." Hannah, my maid of honor and my wonderful florist, rises languidly from the bed's crisp cotton sheets. She walks over to the coffee table in the lounge area to top up her glass. "Is it that beautiful dress or the view that's got you so lost in thought?"

Wearing her maid of honor dress, a light mint-green chiffon gown that brings out her striking almond eyes and contrasts with her sun-kissed skin, Hannah looks utterly gorgeous. But, honestly, she could pull off a sackcloth and still look stunning. Her tight brown curls are pulled back into a messy bun, and, as usual, she looks effortlessly elegant.

The dress we chose for her is a strapless number with a flowing skirt that reaches just above her knees. Crystals embellish the sweetheart neckline and the waistband, catching the light and adding a touch of glamour. Hannah had been hesitant about it at first, worried that the strapless style wouldn't flatter her. But when she tried it on, her eyes lit up and she twirled around in delight like a child.

"I hope you're not worried about the dress." Elena, my dear friend, and wedding planner extraordinaire, lifts the hem to make sure it's the right length. "There's no need to be. Everything is coming together perfectly." Her nimble fingers delicately smooth over the folds of my wedding gown, and it seems to shimmer with its own kind of magic.

I smile at her. "I'm not worried about the dress at all. I couldn't be happier with it. I was just lost in my thoughts and enjoying the moment, that's all."

Elena steps back to admire me and nods in satisfaction. "Good. You're going to look breathtaking on your wedding day."

Elena is a petite woman with jet-black, short-cropped hair, and a warm smile that puts everyone at ease. Even though she costs a fortune, Nathan, my fiancé, said we should go with her since she's such a force to be reckoned with in the wedding industry. Her reputation is flawless: she's known for her calming presence, her intuition, her excellent taste, and her attention to detail.

Nathan is a successful lawyer, and unlike me, he comes from money. What to me are still enormous sums—like the money we're spending on Elena's services—are small fry to him. Our beach house here in his hometown was one of his many spur-of-the-moment purchases. I'd always wanted to live by the sea and to be able to hear the waves from my home. Ever the romantic, Nathan surprised me with it after we got engaged eight months ago, and it was love at first sight.

I have moved around a lot in my thirty-seven years, often settling in places where I knew no one, so it was a pleasant change to move to Stoneview. It's a small, close-knit place and I was grateful to have a warm, welcoming community already here, waiting for me. Hannah, Elena, and Nathan know each other from years ago. It was actually Nathan who introduced Hannah and me, and we soon became inseparable. It's been wonderful living near her and being able to go for coffee, lunch, or strolls down the beach whenever we like.

We only moved into the house two months ago, and it's just

me here for now. Nathan stayed behind in Tallahassee, where he's working on preparations for a high-profile murder trial. It's his biggest case yet—so much so that it could transform him from a very successful lawyer to a world-famous one. He's putting everything he has into it, and I'm really proud of him.

Even though the trial will probably be ongoing, I know that come what may, he'll be there to meet me down the aisle on our wedding day. He's promised to take some time off afterwards for our honeymoon, just as soon as he can. I don't mind that he's not with me in our home yet, because this is the reality of our life together; he's often going to be away for work. We also thought it could be quite romantic, in an old-fashioned kind of way, to be apart from each other in the lead-up to the big day. And I don't feel lonely, not really; I'm keeping myself busy by helping out Hannah with some of her contract florist work.

"Looks like we're out of champagne." Hannah shakes the empty bottle of Veuve Clicquot in the air. "Should I run out for another?"

"Yes, good timing. I need to step out for a bit as well," Elena says. "Silly me, I brought the wrong underskirt for the dress, so I need to nip back to my studio. Let's take a pause and reconvene in an hour."

As well as her successful wedding planning business, Elena works as a seamstress, and she's as talented at this as she is with everything she puts her mind to. She gathers up her sewing kit, and as she moves, her emerald-green dress, with delicate pleats across the bodice, sways elegantly. It's a vintage number; Elena is fascinated by anything to do with the past.

"Sounds good to me. I'll stop by a café and pick us up some lunch, too," Hannah chimes in, already changing back into her favorite black skinny jeans and a white off-the-shoulder blouse that highlights her toned arms. Ever the wellbeing fanatic, Hannah goes to multiple strong yoga and Pilates classes a week, working hard to keep her thirty-six-year-old body in top shape.

Even though she keeps trying to get me to join, anything that makes me feel like I'm punishing my body is not my cup of tea. I'd rather walk for hours down the beach than sweat it out in a power yoga class, ashamed of my inability to touch my toes or contort my body into the impressive shapes of the limber yogis beside me.

I glance at the clock on the wall. It's already past noon, and I've been standing in the same spot for almost an hour. "Yeah, that's good for me, too. I need a break. My feet are killing me. Thanks so much for getting the champagne and lunch, Hannah, I'm absolutely famished. How about some sushi? My treat. There's some cash in a tin on the kitchen counter you can grab on your way out."

Standing on heels for long periods of time has never been my forte, so while Elena and Hannah head out, with great relief I slip off my cream stiletto pumps and massage my aching toes. These ones are just for trying on the dress: the shoes I'll be wearing on my wedding day have not yet arrived from Italy. I've been checking on the delivery updates constantly, and I just can't wait to see them. They are custom-made by a designer in Milan, with intricate embellishments and real artwork on their soles. They'll arrive at Elena's store, so I can try them on there with the wedding dress and she can make any necessary adjustments. Our first fitting is here at my home, because we thought we'd make it really special and spend the day together, but going forward we'll be at Elena's boutique.

I love Elena's taste, and, more importantly, as I've gotten to know her, I've appreciated having someone to talk to about fashion and style. It's not about being superficial or image-focused; to me, fashion is another form of art. How I dress is a way of expressing myself, and I love to pick up items from thrift stores and independent shops, pairing colors and patterns with my mood and my intentions. Aside from a few suits for work, I've never felt the need to splurge on designer items. But for my wedding, I decided to push the boat out. These shoes will be something I treasure for the rest of my life, a reminder of just how perfect life can be when you design it yourself and pursue your dreams.

Releasing my wavy auburn locks from their twist at the base of my neck, I decide to go downstairs and out onto our covered porch by the living room, which is one of my favorite places to be. As I walk through the house, barefoot but still in my wedding dress, I admire the fresh, sweet smelling flowers that brighten its corridors and corners, and the neutral decor I chose. The house has a modern minimalist aesthetic, with pops of color in all the right places, and I'm very proud of how it looks. The living room porch is calm and inviting, decorated with plush furniture and throw pillows in the colors of the sea and sky. It's so tranquil out here, and I savor this moment of solitude. I wish I could sink into the oversized swing-seat covered in cushions, but I don't want to wrinkle my dress.

I'm about to perch on the edge when the doorbell's brash chime shatters the silence. The living room is at the back of the house, facing the ocean, and the front door is on the opposite side where we have a beautiful garden and a long driveway to the main road that takes us into Stoneview. So, I can't see the front door from the porch, and I know there's no way Elena and Hannah could have returned already. I rarely get visitors here, as I'm still getting to know people in the local community. Could it be a delivery for the wedding, perhaps, something I ordered and forgot about?

Gathering the hem of my dress, I take swift steps through the house across the glossy wooden floors, each movement making the fabric rustle with a soft whisper. When I reach the door, I make a mental note to get the doorbell camera set up. I hate not being able to see who's on the other side.

I turn the handle, realizing as I do so that I'm still in my wedding dress. This reminds me of a scene from my favorite comfort sitcom, *Friends*, and I'm chuckling to myself as I open the door.

When I see who is standing there, on my doorstep, my smile vanishes immediately and my heart leaps into my throat as I inhale sharply. She's here.

Looking as if butter wouldn't melt in her mouth, in front of me stands an older woman wearing a bright-blue floral dress. Her silver hair is coiffed in thick, graceful waves, her face is powdered, and her lipstick is immaculate. She's wearing large, round sunglasses that obscure her piercing blue eyes, but I can sense her critical gaze scanning me up and down. A bouquet of white roses bridges the gap between us.

"Well, hello, Brynn, my dear, how wonderful to see you," she says in a saccharine voice, her Southern accent as strong as ever. "And what a lovely dress that is. It'll be just perfect once you've taken it out a bit. A little tight around the middle, isn't it? Bless your heart. And you must be comfortable on your wedding day." She laughs lightly, a tinkling girlish laugh that grates against my very core.

In the space between us, a dance of unspoken words and shared memories—mostly bad—plays out like a movie reel. Her scathing, judgmental remarks are all too familiar to me, delivered wrapped in a disguise of kindness and generosity.

Clearly not much has changed since I last saw her. She always was passive-aggressive and snide. It's one of the things that drove a wedge between us. I can't abide the feeling of being manipulated; it triggers me like nothing else does.

My stomach lurching, I find myself frozen, words caught in my throat.

Finally, my voice emerges hoarsely, and I curse myself for sounding weak. "W-what are you doing here, Debbie?"

"Oh, my invitation must have been lost in the mail. Y'all would never have just not invited your mother-in-law to your wedding! Not to worry, I'm here now, and I'll help in any way I can. I'll make sure your big day is everything you deserve."

And with that, she sweeps in, dragging a giant shiny pink suitcase along with her and shoving the roses into my arms.

I take a shuddering breath, my bare feet frozen to the ground.

The heady sensation of peace and safety I felt just hours ago is shattered. I knew it was too good to be true.

Everyone who meets Debbie thinks she's the loveliest, sweetest person. Nobody has a bad word to say about her.

But if anyone knows how much danger can lurk beneath calm waters, it's me.

TWO

I follow Debbie inside, and she goes straight down the hallway into the living room at the back of the house, removing her sunglasses and placing them on the glass coffee table as confidently as if she's been in here before. My mind racing, I take a tall white vase out of one of our cabinets and place the roses inside, pouring in some water from a glass I'd left on the coffee table earlier. Debbie surveys the room, humming to herself with a smile playing across her lips.

"Very *modern*, isn't it? I must admit I prefer things to be on the cozier, more traditional side. I'd love to help you make it feel a bit more homely while I'm here. Just take the edge off, a bit more color and softness. A wife should make sure her husband is happy too, you know. She shouldn't just run the household according to her own taste!"

I grit my teeth and reply as calmly as I can, "Actually, Debbie, we both like it just the way it is."

Debbie waves dismissively. "Oh, I'm sure he goes along with whatever you say. But anyway, darling, I'm very happy to see you." She lowers her suitcase to the floor and wraps her arms around me in a cloud of musky perfume. I stiffen, my chest tightening, and my arms trapped awkwardly by my sides.

After a few seconds, I pull away. "I'm sorry, Debbie, please excuse me for a moment. I need the bathroom. I'll be right back." I quickly make my way out of the room, feeling immediate physical relief as soon as there's some distance between us. I close the bathroom door behind me and lean my back against it before taking several deep, slow breaths.

Why is she here?

Staring at my reflection in the framed mirror, a deep line etched between my eyebrows, I wonder what on earth possessed Debbie to turn up on our doorstep. It's been a while since we last saw each other, and our relationship has always been strained, to say the least. We are very much not in touch anymore; we're far from a happy family. And yet she's acting as if nothing happened. I just don't know what to say or do. She's up to something, clearly. But what game is she playing? Could she really think reconciliation would be this easy? That we could just ignore what happened as if it were some simple Thanksgiving argument?

My mind reeling, I splash some cold water on my face and breathe slowly, attempting to pull myself together, and summoning all my strength before heading back to the living room.

"Debbie, I'm sorry, but you really can't stay here. It's just not a good time."

Debbie looks at me calmly and raises one thin, shaped eyebrow. She's perched on the edge of one of our beige leather sofas, acting as if it's the most uncomfortable thing she's ever sat on. "Don't worry, my dear, I won't get in the way. I'm just here to help! I know how stressful a wedding can be, but you'll see, I'll make your wedding planning a breeze. After all, we're family."

I feel the muscles in my stomach coiling into a tight knot. I don't want Debbie anywhere near me, let alone helping to plan my wedding.

I shake my head and force a smile. "Look, Debbie, I appreciate your offer, really, I do, but it's not necessary. We've got everything under control. We have a wedding planner who's taking care of it all."

Debbie's expression darkens for a second, but she quickly plasters on another bright smile, her white teeth gleaming. "Oh, well, not to worry, I've come all this way to see you, and now we can just take the time to catch up. I'm sure there are plenty of things we can talk about." She gives me a small wink, her eyes razor-sharp.

I swallow hard and run a hand through my hair. "Um... Sure, I'd love to catch up. But I have a lot to do today, so—"

Suddenly, without warning, Debbie clutches at her chest and sinks back onto the couch. She looks like she's in agony, and I rush to her side.

"Debbie, what's wrong? Are you okay?"

She shakes her head, her eyes bulging from the effort to breathe, veins pulsing in her neck. "No, I think I might be having a heart attack."

Panicking, I remember my phone is all the way back in my bedroom, and I tell Debbie to stay calm while I go and call an ambulance. But she grabs my arm tightly, her fingers pinching into my skin. "No, please don't call 911. I don't want to make a scene. Just help me to my room and I'll rest for a bit. I think the pain is fading; it must just be my nerves."

She gets up unsteadily, and I help her slowly through the living room and over to the sunny guest room next door with a large bed and a direct view of the sea.

Clearly, she isn't having a heart attack, but it did truly seem like she was in pain. Perhaps it could have been a panic attack of sorts? Nobody acts that well, not even her. I look around the room nervously, pleased to see that everything seems perfectly tidy. I was keeping a lot of wedding things in here before, and it was becoming quite cluttered, but Elena took most of them to store for me in her boutique a few days ago.

Debbie is never satisfied with anything, but even she should find this room soothing. From the large French windows, with a chair next to them for the view, we can see the waves crashing against the shore and hear the seagulls flying overhead. She doesn't thank me or say anything complimentary though, of course. I help her onto the bed, and she lays there, still panting heavily.

"Thank you, dear. I think I just need to rest for a while. But maybe a glass of water would help?"

I head to our large, modern kitchen, which faces our garden at the front of the house, and, moving in something of a daze, I pour a glass of water and add some ice cubes, trying to untangle my thoughts.

I've never been very trusting. And as the minutes go by, I'm growing increasingly convinced that Debbie is manipulating me with her little panic attack drama. She just wants to stay here, with us, for what is undoubtedly some malicious reason.

I put down the glass, and my hands are shaking a little as I lean them on the kitchen surface. I'm annoyed with myself for this display of anxiety.

I can handle Debbie, can't I?

Grabbing my phone, I call Elena. There's no way I'm continuing with the dress fitting. Not until I've gotten rid of Debbie.

Elena picks up on the first ring, her voice cheerful and bubbly. "Hey, hon, I was just about to head back to you. What's up?"

"I'm sorry, Elena, I'm afraid I need to cancel the dress fitting—"

"Oh no, is everything okay?" she asks, immediately full of concern.

"Yeah, I'm just not feeling too well. I have a migraine that refuses to go away, and I think it's best if I get some rest. I'll let Hannah know too, and we can rearrange, okay?"

"Of course, sure thing, sweetie. Feel better soon."

I've barely dialed Hannah's number before she answers.

"Hey! I've got the food, enough sushi to feed an army. I'm nearly back at yours now. Do you need me to pick anything else up?"

I pinch the bridge of my nose and try to calm myself. "Hannah, I'm so sorry, I need to take a raincheck. I've canceled the dress fitting with Elena. I have a migraine and need to go and lie down. Maybe you could share the sushi with your housemate tonight? I'll call you when I'm feeling better and I have a new date for the rest of the fitting."

Hannah hesitates for a second before saying, "Sure, that's no problem. Take care of yourself, honey. We'll talk later."

I wonder if she knows I'm lying. I've never had a migraine before, and Hannah knows me well. Maybe better than anyone, except of course for Sam.

Sam is the only person who has known me through all the darkest and the best parts of my life, who knows just how far I've climbed and how hard I've fought. Sam would know exactly what to do about Debbie. And while I accept that people drift apart in life, I can't help but wish we were closer right now, not only for Sam's support in handling this whole Debbie situation, but also in the lead-up to my wedding day.

Steeling myself, I return to the guest room with Debbie's glass and find her fidgeting as if the pillows behind her head were made of straw.

She takes the water from me with an exaggerated wince. "Thank you, dear. You're such a caring soul. You couldn't plump up these pillows for me, could you? They're a little stiff."

I smile thinly and give one perfectly soft pillow a perfunctory smack. "Are you feeling better? Are you sure you don't want me to call a doctor?"

Debbie shakes her head and lays a French-manicured hand gently on my arm. "Absolutely not, there's no need to trouble anyone. I'm feeling much better now. It's my nerves, you see, it's happened before. I'm sure you can imagine the last few years have been quite difficult for me. I'm sorry for causing you so much trouble, and truly I'm grateful that you're letting me stay." She reaches for a tissue from the bedside table and dabs at her eyes. "Not having my son in my life is just so difficult. You'll understand one day, when you're a mother. There's nothing like the relationship between a mother and her son. Nothing could ever compare to it. So, I'm very grateful for your kindness."

Something sharp twists in my gut and I take a step back. "That's okay, Debbie," I say. "You should rest now. I'll come back to check on you in a while."

As I turn to leave, her grating, girlish voice stops me. "Brynn, I forgot to tell you. There was a little package on your doorstep. Maybe it's an early wedding gift?"

"Okay, thanks for letting me know. I hope you get some rest."

Still trying to calm my nervous system by regulating my breathing using the techniques Hannah taught me from her years of yoga, I slowly change out of my wedding dress. I'm very grateful that there's no corset or complicated buttons, so I can take it on and off myself. Craving comfort, I slip on some leggings and an oversized t-shirt before pouring myself a big glass of crisp white wine.

My stomach is growling, so I rustle up some wholemeal sourdough and tomato sandwiches and a fresh green salad, putting a plate aside for Debbie when she's feeling better. I settle down at the kitchen island to eat, but as I take my first welcome bite, I remember what Debbie said about the package and curiosity gets the better of me. I head over to the door to pick it up.

Outside, the pleasant early summer warmth greets me. I would normally take a moment to stand there, appreciate the day's beauty and enjoy the sounds of the bees buzzing around the flowerbeds, which are radiant with the vibrant colors of June. But not today. Debbie's presence has already sapped the joy out of everything.

I look down and pick up the parcel at my feet, feeling its weight in my hands. It's not very heavy, but it's bigger than a shoebox. It's addressed just to me in typed letters, with no return address. If it were an early wedding present, surely it would be addressed to both of us?

Could it be from Sam?

I head back to the kitchen and I'm just about to open the parcel, with my food and wine waiting in front of me, when I'm interrupted by Debbie calling me from the guest room.

As I enter, she's sitting up in bed with a small, pursed smile on her face. "I'm sorry to bother you again, dear, but I was wondering if you could make me some iced tea and a bite to eat? It's very stuffy in here, isn't it? Lovely photo, by the way," she says, pointing at the silver-framed photograph on the bedside table, of Nathan and me kissing on the beach at sunset. "He looks like he's very happy there, doesn't he? Although I'm sure life is more stressful for him now, what with that big trial he's working on in Tallahassee. I heard all about it in an interview he did with CNN. He said he would be getting married while the trial is still taking place and meeting you at the aisle. It'll be a lovely surprise when he sees me there too, won't it?"

I swallow hard. Nathan. What on earth is he going to say when he finds out Debbie is here? If I tell him, I honestly think it could jeopardize his chances of success at the trial, it would stress him out so much.

Perhaps if I really can't get rid of Debbie before then, I can at least try to keep her arrival secret until the big day. Then I can ask Hannah to keep her away from Nathan at the ceremony as much as possible. Hannah knows how complicated families can be; she'll understand.

But of course, she doesn't know what happened with Debbie. And I'm not about to let her find out.

"Debbie," I say slowly, "I'm not sure exactly why you've come. But if you're going to stay here, I need to know I can trust you to keep my secrets. Remember, I know one or two things that you wouldn't want to go... public."

"Of course, dear." She smiles, as casually as if we were talking about the weather.

But while outside the ocean is calm and the breeze is gentle, the air feels humid and sticky.

A storm is expected tonight, and I can already feel it stirring.

THREE

It feels strange to leave Debbie alone in my home, but I honestly can't cope with being around her for a moment longer.

When I brought her a tray with lunch and iced tea, she didn't even thank me. She just complained that I didn't use Duke's mayonnaise in the tomato sandwiches, nor did I season them to her liking. Before I said something I'd regret, I headed back to the kitchen, took a big gulp of wine, grabbed my sandwich, slipped on my sandals, and went out for a brisk walk down the beach.

The exercise and fresh air soon help me to feel calmer, and after a while I slow my pace and focus on my senses. Elena meditates every morning, saying it helps her to gain a sense of perspective and to stay grounded whatever the day throws at her. And while I struggle to focus for as long as she does, I am trying to learn from her example, to be more "present" in my body and in the moment. It really helps, and once again I'm reminded of how lucky I am to have strong, genuine, balanced women in my life who inspire and motivate me. Women who are the very antithesis of Debbie.

When I get home hours later, after walking on the beach

and going on a long drive around town, I'm frustrated to find Debbie making her way down the stairs. There is simply no need for her to go upstairs: her bedroom has an ensuite. So, I ask her if she's looking for something, and she says she's just having "a little explore."

As if that's a normal thing to do in someone else's home without their permission.

Nobody could ever accuse me of being a pushover, but it's vital I don't upset Debbie; I simply can't risk angering her so much she'd reveal my secret. Thanks to the time I just spent restoring my self-control on the beach, I rein in my impulse to snap at her, and instead I tell her I'm pleased she's feeling better.

Hoping to avoid more of Debbie's catty remarks about my cooking, I order in Mexican food for dinner, and we eat it out on the front porch. But, of course, that isn't good enough for her either; she says it's too spicy and that she prefers "home-cooked" meals. Thankfully, she retreats to her room early, saying she's still not feeling well.

Shortly after nine, I finally settle back in the kitchen, feeling as tired as if I've run a marathon. I'm normally the kind of person who speaks my mind. But this situation with Debbie is unchartered territory. It's like she's a ticking time bomb. And I can visualize the future I'm building exploding and cascading down around me like sand through my fingers.

I feel calmer now I'm alone in the kitchen. It speaks to everything I crave in a living space: soothing, neutral colors and a sense of order and cleanliness. A large island with bar seating takes center stage, while modern range and industrial-style fixtures provide an upscale look. The tiled floor gleams with light from the chandelier. Every detail has been lovingly crafted to provide a space exuding comfort and peace.

Nursing another glass of white wine—it's been a trying day

—I see the box that was left on my doorstep earlier, and realize I'd completely forgotten about it.

I tear off the brown paper. Inside there is a plain white box, and I lift its lid to see a dark-blue satin bag. This contains smaller boxes nestled within the folds, a black and a white one. Feeling pleasantly curious, my fingers brush against the black lacquered material and I open it to reveal a miniature wedding cake topper.

It's an exact likeness of Nathan in a custom-made tuxedo with a silver tie and black cummerbund. His mischievous grin and sharp blue eyes are exquisitely recreated. I can even make out the slight curl in his hair that falls across his forehead.

Then I reach for the white box. Inside, as expected, there is a miniature bride, a brunette like me, holding a bouquet of delicate white roses. She's wearing a simple, elegant, flowing dress with lace detailing that matches mine.

But there's something wrong. The bride is gruesomely disfigured.

Half of her face is smashed in.

What in the world is this?

As I hold the shattered bride in my frozen hands, fear gathers into a heavy ball in my stomach and sits there like a stone.

I desperately want to brush this off as an accident that occurred during transportation. But all the packaging and care taken over the boxes, and the perfect condition of the groom, make me doubt that theory.

No, this feels deliberate. My thoughts trip over each other in a panic as I stare at the disfigured bride. Is this a twisted joke?

Who would do something so horrible, so macabre?

My mind races with possibilities, but none of them make sense.

My fingers shake as I turn the bride over in my hands. And then I notice it.

There's a small note tucked inside her hollow body.

My stomach churning, I carefully extract the piece of paper and unfold it, scanning the spindly cursive handwriting.

It's going to be the perfect day. For me, anyway. For you, my darling, it will be your worst nightmare.

A chill breeze sweeps through the room, as if the temperature has suddenly dropped. I glance around me, half expecting to see someone lurking behind the curtains or hiding in the shadows.

But I'm alone.

Blood draining from my face, I read the note over and over again, trying to make sense of the words.

One thing is for sure: whoever sent it wanted to scare the hell out of me. But why?

Dropping the broken bride next to her groom, I fumble for my phone so I can call Nathan, but it goes straight to voicemail. My heart pounding, I redial his number repeatedly. But there's no answer. And after a few minutes I slow my breathing, gather myself, gulp down some more wine and try to calm down.

I don't know who is trying to threaten me. But whoever it is, they don't know who they're messing with. Nobody is going to ruin my wedding day.

I channel my inner Sam, marshalling all the strength, courage, and determination I have.

Sam would tell me to fight fire with fire.

It simply can't be a coincidence that Debbie turned up at the same time as this note. Maybe this is the first hand she's playing in her twisted game, a clumsy attempt to frighten me.

I know she's never liked me. She always resented the relationship I had with her precious son.

Prickling with rage, I march over to her door and rap until she calls for me to enter.

"Hey there, sweetheart," she drawls, her voice dripping like honey. She has changed out of her floral dress into some blue flannel pajamas with a white collar. "Is everything okay? You look a little... flushed."

"Debbie," I say, trying to keep my voice in control, "that package you said you saw on my doorstep, with the wedding cake toppers inside. Was it from you?"

"What? No, don't be silly. Of course not." Her eyebrows shoot up in surprise, and her blue eyes are wide and innocent.

But I'm certain that's a smile playing around her lips.

I hold up the bride and groom silently, watching her reaction.

She whistles. "Oh no, whatever happened to the little bride? She looks like she took a bit of a... tumble."

Something angry and dangerous unfurls itself in my chest. "Debbie, I know it was you who sent these, along with that horrible note. What are you playing at?"

Debbie's smirk drops, and she clutches a hand to her chest. "What are you talking about? What note?"

I step back, thrown off balance. She's so convincing.

Maybe it wasn't her?

I've always thought of myself as a good judge of character, and I can usually tell when people are lying to me. Debbie's hiding something, that's for sure. But right now, her eyes are filled with what looks like genuine confusion and concern.

I lower the figurines and exhale slowly. "Never mind. It's fine."

"Nonsense, of course it's not fine." She steps toward me and reaches out to tuck a strand of wayward hair behind my ear. "You look awfully upset." To my dismay, she suddenly pulls me into another awkward hug, stroking my hair as if I were a little girl. "Don't go borrowing trouble, dear Brynn. Everything will turn out just all right, you'll see."

Pulling away quickly, I head back to my room, where I sit

on our king-sized bed for a long time, staring through the window as the night sets in.

The forecast was right. It's a powerful, stormy evening, and the wind is howling outside, the rain lashing against the windows. The sound of waves crashing against the shore is deafening. The sea is angry and turbulent, a reminder of just how volatile nature can be, turning from peaceful stillness to a voracious energy within hours. It's both amazing and scary at the same time. Through the rain and the darkness, I can just about make out the moon as it struggles to shine through the thick clouds, only managing the weakest of glimmers.

As I sit there, I can feel the vibrations of another kind of storm rising up inside me.

One that would consume everything, if I don't get it under control.

I'm not exactly sure how much time passes with me stuck in my thoughts, but the ringing of my phone brings me sharply back to reality.

It's Nathan. And as soon as I hear his steady voice, a wave of relief washes over me.

"Hey, baby. Sorry I couldn't answer your calls. I was in the middle of a meeting with a potential witness. Are you okay?"

"A meeting, so late in the evening?"

"My love, you should know by now that us lawyers never clock out. It's the only time the witness could do, and it was urgent. You sound tense, is everything okay?" he repeats. His baritone voice is soothing, and I feel a smile tug at my lips despite the tightness in my chest and the frustration that it took him so long to call me back.

I hesitate before responding. I can't tell him Debbie is here, and I realize now that I don't want to tell him about the threatening note either. It would cause him so much stress at this crucial time.

No, this is something I'll have to handle on my own.

"Yeah, I'm okay. I just had a long day. And I miss you."

"I miss you too, Brynn. I can't wait to see you on our wedding day. I know it's going to be perfect. How is all the preparation going? Anything I can do from this end?"

"It's all going really well. And no, don't worry about a thing. I've got this. There's a lot to do, but I'll manage."

Nathan chuckles on the other end of the line. "You always do. I wish I could help you with it all, though."

He has been working tirelessly on this murder trial for months, and his determination and dedication have really impressed me. It's something we have in common. When we set our sights on something, we put our blinkers on, and we fight for it with everything we have. It's what makes him such a good lawyer, and it's one of the things that drew me to him.

He's the defense attorney for Amanda Lane, a woman accused of murdering three of her wealthy husbands in cold blood. She has been dubbed by the public as the "Black Widow Killer," and the media frenzy around the trial has been intense, bordering on obsessive.

"Don't worry about me, honey. I can handle all the wedding stuff. Just put all your attention on winning that case. I believe in you."

"Okay but promise me you'll take care of yourself, too. I don't want our wedding to be stressful for you; it's supposed to be a happy time. Delegate as much as you can and remember this is what we hired Elena for, to take the burden off you."

"I will, I promise." I pause to prop myself up higher against the pillows. "Speaking of our big day... have you decided if you're inviting your mother to the wedding?"

Silence falls between us and Nathan inhales sharply.

"No, I really don't want her there. She's toxic, you know

that, and I don't want her ruining our special day." His voice is firm, but I know him, and I can hear a hint of sadness in his tone.

"I understand, baby, I really do," I say gently. "It's just that Elena was asking if she should add her to the list. She's the only guest we haven't confirmed yet."

"Right, well, Elena can go ahead and take her off the list. I don't want her there."

"Okay," I say, my voice soothing. "I'll do that. Nathan, I can't wait to be your wife."

Nathan's voice softens as he answers, "And I can't wait to be your husband. Now, I must get back to work, I'm sorry. I'll call you tomorrow. Sleep well, my love."

"You too. Love you."

I hang up the phone and massage my temples. I wanted to take a break from my stressful career, but, if I'm honest, I really miss being surrounded by art and doing something I'm so good at. I'm not cut out for all this wedding planning and the lack of routine in my life. But still it's nothing compared to the pressure Nathan is under with the trial.

Before I fall asleep, I turn on my computer and pull up a video of Amanda Lane's latest interview with a local news station. She calmly denies any involvement in the murders of her husbands, claiming that she loved them and would never harm them.

She's so convincing, tears coming into her eyes at just the right moments, her pale face appearing vulnerable and ordinary.

But the best liars? The most dangerous people? They're the ones you'd never suspect.

FOUR

THE WOMAN

The woman sits by the window, her eyes fixed on the storm simmering out at sea, today's paper crumpled in her lap. Thunder rumbles in the distance, echoing the tumult within her mind.

Ever since she found out about Brynn and Nathan's engagement, she has been consumed by thoughts of derailing the wedding. A gnawing certainty lingers in her gut. Brynn is not the right woman for Nathan.

But, of course, she can't tell him that. One thing she knows about Nathan is that when he makes up his mind about something, he is as stubborn as a mule.

Sending Brynn that aptly broken bride figurine felt like a stroke of genius, and she is rather proud of it. She recently came across an advert in a magazine for personalized wedding gifts, and the idea had struck her like the lightning flashing on the horizon. Wedding cake toppers; a perfect resemblance of the happy couple. With a quick email to the company, she ordered a pair and submitted photos of Nathan and Brynn.

Less than a week later, the cake toppers arrived. They cost her a fortune, but she justified it as a necessary expense. After admiring their likeness, she took great pleasure in smashing the bride's head with a hammer. Next, she tucked the note inside the hollow remains of the body. Satisfied with her handiwork, she imagined Brynn's expression when she received her little gift— it could not be a clearer message, surely?

But now, as the storm outside worsens and fat raindrops pelt against the windowpane, the woman's confidence wavers. She wonders whether she has gone too far. What if Brynn goes to the police and reports the harassment? Panic begins to rise inside her, but she quickly squashes it down. She has thought this through, hasn't she? She was careful not to leave any identifying marks on the figurines. Yes, she has covered her tracks well.

She continues to stare out of the window to the tempest outside, which has now fully arrived in all its fury. Her heart races as she thinks about what will happen if she fails. The image of Nathan walking down the aisle with Brynn after they exchange their vows burns beneath her skin, a fire that refuses to be extinguished.

Her eyes drift down to the daily paper in her lap. Next to the wedding announcement, a photograph stares at her: the smiling faces of handsome, renowned defense attorney Nathan and that self-satisfied cow.

The Stoneview Gazette often uses color to emphasize certain parts of the paper, or call attention to important events, with Nathan and Brynn's upcoming wedding being one such occasion.

Nathan looks dapper in his black suit, with a tie to match the almost navy-blue color of his eyes. His arm is wrapped around Brynn, who is wearing a creamy satin dress, her auburn hair cascading in waves down her back. Her dark-brown eyes look up at Nathan adoringly. *Nauseating.*

Even though it tortures her, the woman rereads the article for the umpteenth time:

In July, 39-year-old Nathan Howard, son of esteemed Florida judge Robert Howard, will be marrying 37-year-old Brynn Powell in a lavish ceremony in the small town of Stoneview, Florida, his hometown, where the couple will spend their happy-ever-after. Nathan is highly respected in the legal community for his dedication to justice, and Brynn is a successful businesswoman with a passion for art and philanthropy. They met one year ago in Tallahassee and have been inseparable ever since.

With her teeth clenched so tightly that her jaw aches, the woman snatches the paper and hurls it into the wastepaper bin, only to fish it out again. Suddenly, she gets up and marches over to her handbag, pulling out her pencil case and selecting a red marker pen. She pops off the cap with unnecessary force, and the pungent scent of the marker floods her nostrils.

Sitting back down by the window, she smears the red ink across Brynn's smiling face, transforming the joyous bride-to-be in the photograph into a chilling figure with a bloody, scarlet smear across her features.

She studies her work, and the sensations of satisfaction and vindication mingle and soothe the flames inside her. Then she pushes back her chair and stands, leaving the paper behind as she watches the storm.

A storm that will pale in comparison to the one she is about to unleash on Brynn's perfect life.

Brynn will soon learn that Nathan doesn't belong to her.

FIVE

BRYNN

29 Days Before the Wedding

It's a little after eight in the morning, the day after Debbie's arrival, and I'm standing at the kitchen island, slicing into a juicy orange, and savoring the fragrance while my coffee brews.

Despite that horrible package arriving yesterday, I woke feeling unusually calm, and before coming down to the kitchen, I stood for a little while on the balcony and took in the ocean view, as I always do when I wake up.

Early mornings are my favorite time. There's something so uniquely special about the way the ocean and sky blend together in a fleeting blaze of color as the day wakes up.

The view from this house at sunrise reminds me of a painting of the ocean that I once sold at a New York art exhibit. The colors were breathtakingly vivid and alive. I never thought that one day I'd live in a house that offered a seascape view as beautiful as that painting. The bidding was fierce, and the painting ended up being sold for a staggering amount of money. But as I soak in the natural beauty before me, I know that no piece of human art could ever come close to capturing the beauty of the natural world. To me, nature is art in its ultimate iteration.

Now, I lick the sweet orange juice from my fingers, feeling the steady breathing within my chest, and enjoying a sense of stability and peace I always try to cultivate, but that has been badly disturbed over the last twenty-four hours. Being inside my kitchen often helps me to feel more myself. I can't say cooking is my favorite thing, but I've always been a kitchen person; I gravitate toward it in every home I've ever had.

Reaching for another orange, I take my time to enjoy the rhythmic motion of the knife as it cuts through the peel.

Debbie's lurking presence in my home has been plaguing me all night, so I barely slept and while I'm starting the day well, I know I'm moving more slowly than usual. It's going to be a many-coffees and a lot of self-care kind of day.

I sigh, squeezing the juice from half an orange into a glass and arranging the remaining pieces on a plate with some blueberries, two slices of toasted sourdough, and a scoop of creamy avocado.

I love my little rituals, such as eating the same thing at roughly the same time most mornings. I've tried to keep some routines in my day while I'm not working. It's comforting to me; the familiarity, the sense of order. I like to take my breakfast out onto the living room porch and eat it slowly there, and when I've finished, I drink my coffee and say a mantra out loud as I look out over the ocean. That's another wellbeing trick Elena taught me, and I love starting my day this way. Today, my mantras will be:

I'm strong.

I've been to hell and back, and I survived.

My future is bright.

Just as I'm about to carry my breakfast to the porch, my sacred me-time is disrupted by the sound of approaching footsteps and a little "ahem." My heart sinks. Debbie.

I'd really hoped she'd sleep in for a little while longer. But while I'm still in my pajamas, she's already dressed in a black and cream tunic with loose linen trousers, her silver hair pinned to her head in an elegant yet casual updo. She looks flawless. As always. And she's carrying grocery bags; she must have already gone out shopping.

"Oh, Brynn." She lets out a sigh. "I was fixin' to cook you a proper Southern breakfast, as a little thank-you for letting me stay with you. And I'd love to show you how to cook it, too. Every wife should know how to cook a good breakfast for her husband! It's a chance to fuel the body and start off on the right foot. Now, I know cooking isn't your forte, but it's hardly your fault, with your mother passing when you were so young."

I can feel my cheeks flush, but I force a gracious smile onto my face. I'm not going to let her get to me. "Thank you, Debbie, that's very kind of you, but, as you can see, I've already fixed myself something."

Debbie ignores me and walks around my kitchen, opening cupboards and drawers and peering into them, before pulling out various items and ingredients from her grocery bags. "Dear, this is such a lovely kitchen. You simply must make the most of it."

Before I realize what's happening, she reaches for my plate and heads for the trashcan. I watch with a mix of utter disbelief and fury as she dumps my lovingly prepared breakfast.

"Debbie, what on earth are you doing?" I ask incredulously.

"Don't worry," she coos. "When you taste my breakfast, you'll never look back. I'll feed you until you're fuller than a tick on a big dog. I may have moved around a bit over the years, but the art of Southern cooking never left me."

Clenching my fists, I try my best to regain my composure. Debbie is utterly infuriating. She's honestly the most rude, arrogant person I've ever met. I can barely stand to be in the same room as her.

But she knows she can get away with acting like this. She has power over me, after what happened. And I don't know what her game is yet.

I have a feeling that if I do anything to upset her, it will only make things worse.

So, for now, I push down my fury and try to play along. I need to at least buy myself some time to figure out my next move. Maybe I can even force myself to be nice enough that she might reconsider whatever she's planning.

Before long, Debbie has located one of my aprons, which she puts on with a flourish. Then with pans clanging, ingredients sizzling and, of course, her non-stop instructions and criticisms, soon we're cooking up an elaborate breakfast. It's a feast fit for a whole family: buttermilk biscuits, sausage gravy, blueberry muffins, pancakes, crispy bacon, and scrambled eggs.

She even instructs me to pull out napkins and my fanciest tableware, setting the island with an unnecessary flourish. Finally, we sit down together to eat, and she smiles at me brightly after saying grace. "Now, there we have it. A proper breakfast, don't you think?"

I manage a weak smile and nod.

Digging in, I must admit that the food is absolutely delicious. The biscuits are flaky and buttery with just a hint of salt, the sausage gravy is rich and comforting, and the blueberry muffins melt in my mouth with a bright pop of lemon zest. I can't help but enjoy every single mouthful, digging in as if I haven't eaten for days.

There's another reason why I have so many rituals, particularly around preparing and savoring food. When you've known what it's like to starve, food will never just feel normal again. Sometimes I find myself restricting my intake, to the point where I'm often hovering around being underweight. It's like my mind is still convinced it's in famine, even when the reality is that I don't have to go hungry anymore. So, all food tastes delicious to me; I just can't take it for granted anymore and it's never far from my mind. And a luxurious home-cooked breakfast like this? It's bliss. I let out a satisfied moan as I take a bite of the soft scrambled eggs, and Debbie glances at me, a smirk playing at the corners of her lips.

"Glad you're enjoying it," she says, taking a sip of her coffee.

To my surprise, right now I'm kind of enjoying her company. She seems genuinely pleased to have been able to cook with me, and she was good fun in the kitchen even though she was a little patronizing and controlling. It was nice to see her in her element.

As we eat in companiable silence, it's almost easy to forget the things that happened between us. The past that neither of us have properly confronted since she arrived. At least, not yet.

When we're done eating, I begin to clear the plates and take them over to the sink, but she stops me.

"Oh no, don't worry about the clean-up," she says, waving her hand dismissively. "I'll take care of it; this was my treat. You just relax and enjoy the rest of your day, dear."

I watch her gather the dishes, ignore the dishwasher, and fill the sink with hot soapy water as she hums a tune under her breath.

Maybe having her stay will have its perks.

One thing I've learned about life is that what would once have seemed impossible sometimes does happen. You can go through the worst possible things and then find yourself living the life of your dreams. You can see the worst of people and then find yourself surrounded by love and friendship. Thanks to Nathan, the cynicism I once had about human nature is fading just a little, and I'm starting to think that it's possible for people to change. So maybe Debbie isn't up to something sinister. Maybe she really is just trying to connect with me. She's lost her whole family, after all. It's her nature to be controlling and manipulative, a habit cemented over years of practice, but maybe deep down she doesn't mean any harm. Or perhaps it's just her delicious food that's softening me toward her.

As she sings and dips her hands into the steaming, sudsy water, I find it hard to believe she would be capable of sending me that horrible note. It's so dark, so obvious, so *direct*. It's just not her style.

But then who else could it have been?

"Thank you so much, Debbie," I say, after a final gulp of strong, milky coffee. "Breakfast was lovely, I really enjoyed it. I'm going out for a bit, but I should be back before lunch."

We've rearranged yesterday's unfinished dress fitting to take place at Elena's studio. I didn't want to do it here anymore, not with Debbie watching and trying to interfere.

As I turn to leave the kitchen and get ready for the day, her hand on my arm stops me in my tracks. "I hope you know, dear Brynn, that I only want the best for you. I really do. I just hope we can put the past behind us and start fresh. That's all I want."

"Yeah... Me too. Thank you, Debbie," I repeat, conscious of a cold edge in my voice as I pull my arm free and try to stop myself from pushing her forcefully away.

I cannot stand it when people invade my space, grab hold of me, restrain me. It's just not something I can tolerate, even when they don't know the impact they're having. And I particularly can't handle it from Debbie. She should know better.

I'm convinced her eyes are following me as I walk away, and I only feel calmer once I've disappeared around the corner, heading upstairs to take a hot shower.

I really want to believe her, that she's genuinely keen for us to start anew. But that strong grasp on my arm, and how instinctively I reacted to it, remind me that the past is never far behind.

And deep down, I can't shake the feeling that it's going to catch up with me.

SIX

As I drive through Stoneview on my way to the fitting, I remind myself to enjoy the moment, taking in the narrow streets that weave between gorgeous homes with vibrant flower boxes and comfortable porches, all bathed in the soft rays of the sun. It's a stunning, blue-skied day, the air cleared of its humidity and pressure after last night's storm.

Stoneview is the kind of place that radiates with nostalgia, its warmth and charm reminding both visitors and residents of simpler times. The proud trees that line the streets burst with emerald leaves, and I can't wait to see how they'll transform into stunning hues of gold and red when we move into fall, my favorite season.

But even now in early summer, as I drive into the center, the town is bursting with character. Shops with weathered signs boast their wares, and there are stalls of fruit and vegetables spilling out onto the cobbles. Stoneview is well-known for its antique shops and its quaint independent cafés; and for being one of those very rare places where there are no chain shops to be found. It would be hard for anyone to come here and not feel immediately at ease.

But today, I can't ignore a niggling voice that tells me not to settle in too much, not to let myself feel as happy and content as I want to be. Because then it'll just hurt even more if all of this is taken away.

Anyway, as much as I would like to stop somewhere and take in the scenery, I need to hurry if I'm going to get to Elena's wedding studio on time.

The Bridal Bliss is nestled between an art gallery and a chocolate shop on Main Street. It has wide glass windows adorned with delicate lace curtains, and the door is decorated with a wreath of lavender and baby's breath. I park my car and step out onto the street next to a sleek black Lamborghini. Suddenly feeling tired and in need of another boost of caffeine, I lift out the bag carrying my wedding dress from the back, and on the short walk to Elena's shop, I remind myself: *You can do this. You're safe. You're strong. You're allowed to be happy.*

The scent of rich coffee from a nearby café is too tempting to resist, but just as I'm heading out of it, clutching my steaming take-away cup, a little girl with pigtails and a chocolate-brown dress skips past me, knocking into my leg and causing me to spill some of my precious caffeine fix.

Fortunately, I'm carrying my dress on my other arm, so it remains unscathed.

"Oops, sorry!" the girl giggles, before continuing on her way.

As she disappears down the street and I lick the coffee off my hand, I can't help but feel a twinge of sadness. I never knew that kind of blithe joy as a child; happiness only came to me in small doses, and even then, it never lasted long. But something about the girl's smile also sparks a flickering hope inside me.

Maybe one day I will let go of the past and be as carefree as her.

Maybe I really can have a happy ending.

Just as I reach the Bridal Bliss, I drain my coffee, wishing I'd asked for an extra shot. But as I enter the studio, I'm greeted by an invigorating explosion of colors and textures. Elena has sectioned her studio according to her two talents as both wedding planner and seamstress. On one end, there are towering shelves stocked with bridal magazines, wedding planners, and fabric samples. And the opposite side is a workshop, complete with sewing machines, mannequins, and racks of dresses in various stages of completion. A waiting lounge with plush couches sits between them. All of Elena's furniture is from the antique store her parents used to own, where she fell in love with everything that carries stories from times gone by. She's a whimsical, authentic soul who, like me, appreciates beauty and individuality. It would be hard for anyone not to love her.

"Morning, Elena," I call as I spot her at the far end, dressing a mannequin in an elegant lace gown. She turns, her eyes lighting up when she sees me.

"Hey, you." Her voice is a balm, and I find myself relaxing and feeling more awake and alive in her company already.

Elena is the kind of person who always seems to radiate with genuine kindness. While some people need to be in a relationship to feel complete, she thrives on her own. She says she's happy being single as she recently got out of a serious relationship, and she needs some time for herself. Even though she's turning forty next year, she seems to be in no rush to settle down. But I have no doubt that when she's ready, she will have no problem finding someone who appreciates her for who she is.

She's a truly wonderful person, who balances a successful and busy career while also taking care of her father who is suffering from Alzheimer's. His condition deteriorated rapidly after her mother passed away from a long illness five years ago, and Elena won't allow him to be sent to a nursing home. When she's not at home herself, she pays for a top-notch caregiver to look after him, even though it's costing her a fortune. She also sends money to her sister in New York, who has been out of work for a little while. So even though she's always working hard, I know she must count the pennies to get by. It's a real testament to her selflessness and dedication to her family, and it's one of the many reasons why I admire her so much.

She's sporting a bohemian vibe today, wearing a flowy maxi dress in shades of green and brown. On her head is a headband adorned with beaded details, a typically Elena touch that complements her short black hair and adds a hint of vintage charm to her look.

"Wow, you look incredible," I say admiringly.

Elena laughs and walks over to give me a hug. "Thank you, lovely. You always know how to make a girl feel good in her skin."

As she pulls away, the bell above the door jingles. It's Hannah, right on time, and she rushes over to give me a warm hug. As always, she's dressed simply, this time in jeans and a loose black t-shirt, but she looks as chic as ever. In her hand is another bottle of champagne.

I've never met anyone who loves bubbly as much as Hannah does. She's all about balance: she loves her rocket yoga flows and her kickboxing, and she keeps herself in great shape. But she also knows how to have a good time, saying that life is too short to deprive yourself of the things you enjoy.

I couldn't agree more. Life *is* too short; it can be snatched away from you in an instant. Which is all the more reason to fight tooth and nail to get to where you want to be.

When Nathan first introduced me to Hannah, she was a little wary of me, since he had just come out of a messy break-up. But we soon bonded over our mutual love for travel, good food, and the adrenaline buzz we get from a trashy scary movie or a rollercoaster ride. Just as my relationship with Nathan was a whirlwind, so was my friendship with Hannah. Two months after we met, we even flew to Greece for a week-long girls' trip.

We became close so fast that when it came to choosing a maid of honor, I knew it had to be her.

"How are you feeling?" Hannah's voice is gentle and steeped with genuine concern as she gives me a peck on the cheek.

Elena places a hand on my shoulder. "Oh yeah, how are you today? Feeling better?"

"Yes, it was just a migraine," I say lightly, giving them a bright smile. I'll never take for granted having such caring people around me. Friendships like these are precious beyond words. "I feel much better today."

But Hannah's gaze is perceptive, her eyes searching mine. "Are you sure you're okay, honey? You look a little pale."

I nod. "Absolutely, I'm just a little tired. Thank you both for being so understanding, you guys. I'm sorry we had to rearrange."

Elena taps a deep-purple nail against her chin, her expression thoughtful. "You know, sometimes stress can trigger migraines. Are you feeling okay about the wedding?"

I grin, determined to keep any lingering anxiety from my eyes. "Of course. How could I be stressed when I have you to help me with everything?"

"That's right. I never want you to feel overwhelmed." She turns to look at Hannah. "We're here for you every step of the way."

Like Hannah, Elena feels like someone I've known forever. The kind of friend I want to keep for the rest of my life.

"Exactly," Hannah adds. "Never forget that. We've got you. We want you to be fresh and relaxed on your big day, not a bundle of nerves."

"Thank you both so much. I couldn't do this without you."

Elena smiles. "It's my pleasure. And honestly, I'll make sure everything runs smoothly. They don't call me the Queen of Weddings for nothing."

Hannah laughs as she walks over to the side table where Elena keeps champagne glasses and complimentary chocolates. She opens the bottle of champagne she brought like only an expert would, carefully twisting the wire cage until the cork pops with a satisfying bang.

"I don't know about you two, but I could sure use a glass of this right about now. Anyone else? I know you'll probably say no, Elena, but how about you, Brynn? A little bubbly might chase away any jitters."

I shake my head. "You know what, I think I'll pass. As much as I want to, it's probably not the best idea after the killer migraine I had."

"True," Hannah says. "Well, then, all the more for me!"

"So," Elena begins as Hannah pours herself a glass, "Brynn, let's get to work finishing your wedding dress, shall we? Go on over to the dressing room and change into it, and I'll be along in a minute."

"Sure." My wedding dress bag still dripping from my arm like a waterfall, I retreat to the dressing room.

A wave of exhaustion hits me as soon as I'm alone. Suddenly, my head is pounding for real. I take a deep breath, trying to compose myself and push through the pain. I pride myself on being prepared and organized, and I usually carry a small bottle of painkillers in my purse, along with the mandatory EpiPen. My nut allergy is severe, so much so that it has nearly killed me on several occasions. I reach for the bottle and swallow two painkillers, taking a moment to sit and collect myself.

As I slowly unbutton my faded jeans and climb out of them, my palms feel a little sweaty. Maybe I am nervous about the wedding, not just about Debbie and that horrible package. It's a big deal after all, this moment I've been waiting for since the day my eyes met Nathan's.

We were in Tallahassee, in front of a popular coffee shop

across from the Smithson and Associates office, a firm he helped build from the ground up. Sipping on my flat white, I had just left the coffee shop and I was on my way to a nearby art gallery when I saw him.

My eyes couldn't just brush over him like all the other passersby; he was so tall and handsome in his tailored charcoal suit, and he had an energy about him that was somehow irresistible. We locked eyes for just a moment before he disappeared into the law firm's entrance, but I knew we would meet again, I just knew it.

And we did, a week later, at a restaurant close to both our places of work. I was sitting nearby, and I still remember the way his blue eyes crinkled when he smiled, the deep, relaxed sound of his voice as he ordered his food. It was like everything around us faded away, and it was just the two of us.

He had been having lunch with his colleagues, but I could feel him watching me throughout their meal. Before they left, he slipped a napkin with his number on it onto my table, and I knew then that we were destined to be together.

Our first date was unique and unforgettable. He took me to a small airfield, where he had arranged for us to take a private plane ride over the city. And as we soared through the sky, I felt like I was on top of the world. When we landed, he took me to a rooftop bar, and we danced under the stars until the early hours of the morning. It was like being in a movie, and I could hardly believe it was happening to me. Over the next few weeks, we were inseparable, bonding over our shared passion for art, diverse food, and travel.

And now here I am, about to become Mrs. Brynn Howard.

I lift my hand and study the engagement ring on my finger. It once belonged to Nathan's grandmother, and it is a one-of-a-kind ring, with a glittering large diamond that sits atop a platinum band, surrounded by smaller gems.

I slide into the dress, as carefully as I can, but something snags the delicate lace and my heart sinks when I see a small tear.

"Elena?" I call out and she hurries into the room.

"What's happened?" she asks, taking in my distraught expression.

I lift my dress to reveal the hole in the lace. "I tore my dress. I'm so sorry."

Elena takes a closer look and nods. "It's okay, it's just a small tear," she says calmly. "I can fix this easily, then you can try it on again." She helps me out of the dress, being careful not to worsen the tear, and disappears to her workstation.

While I wait for her, I slip my clothes back on and head to the lounge area, where Hannah is sitting on the sofa, leafing through a bridal magazine. She looks up and gives me a warm smile. "Hey, how come you're not wearing your dress?"

"There was a small tear in the lace, but Elena is fixing it."

Hannah nods, but her expression is troubled, her eyes narrowed as she says, "Brynn, is it just me, or does something feel... off?"

"What do you mean?"

Hannah shrugs. "I don't know. I just have this feeling that something is not right. Like there's something you're not saying, a weight on your mind that's troubling you."

I sigh and sit next to her, and she puts a comforting arm around my shoulders.

"What's going on? You can tell me."

Can I?

Even though we're close, there are some things I keep from Hannah. Sam is the only person in my life who I've never kept anything from. As much as I crave companionship, and no matter how much I yearn to let my new friends in completely, there are things that I simply can't reveal to anyone else.

But perhaps there are some things I don't have to carry alone.

"I was thinking about something I found on my doorstep yesterday. It was a gift box, but I don't know who sent it."

Elena walks into the lounge at that moment, and her voice is intrigued as she chimes in, "A mystery gift? How exciting."

Hannah's curiosity is piqued as well. "What was inside?"

My fingers tangle together, but it's a relief to get this off my chest. "Okay, well, promise not to freak out, but the box contained a threatening note along with some wedding cake toppers. The bride's head was smashed in. It's probably nothing, but it was kind of scary. I've no idea who could have done it or why." I pause for a second and pull in a jagged breath.

Hannah's eyes widen in surprise. "A threatening note? Oh my god, Brynn! What did it say?"

I reach into my bag and retrieve the note, handing it to Hannah. I'd brought it with me, part of me thinking I might want to share this with them, although I wasn't totally sure I would until just now.

Hannah's eyes skim over the words and widen in horror. "*It's going to be the perfect day. For me, anyway. For you, my darling, it will be your worst nightmare,*" she reads aloud, her voice full of anxiety. "What the...? What kind of sick person sends something like this?"

Elena peers over her shoulder. "What the heck? That's so chilling. Brynn, you poor thing, that must have been really scary. Are you going to report this to the police?"

I shake my head as Hannah hands the note back to me. "No, I don't think the cops can do anything. I wasn't hurt and they're busy with much more important things." I fold the note and slip it back into my bag. "It's probably some kind of twisted practical joke. I guess I just need to be a little careful and watch out for anything suspicious."

Hannah and Elena want to continue talking about the note, but it's making me so uneasy that I soon steer us back to the wedding dress and all the things we still have left to plan.

. . .

A short time later, I'm back inside my car with my dress and veil. Elena offered to keep them with her, but I know trying them on again at home will cheer me up if I'm feeling stressed or down later. I had planned on going for coffee with Hannah, but she had to cancel because Ed, her new boyfriend, took the day off and wanted to spend it with her.

As I start the engine, my phone buzzes inside my purse with a text message, and I wait until the next traffic light to read it.

How are things going? I need updates, please! xoxo Sam

My fingers dance over the buttons, trembling a little as I reply:

Coming back from a dress fitting. The dress is lovely.

Sam responds almost immediately.

Good to hear it. But don't get too caught up and stressed by all the wedding details.

The smile on my face disappears as I write back.

Of course, Sam. Don't worry about me. How's India?

A few seconds later, Sam's response comes in.

The heat is unbearable this week. But forget about me. Focus on what matters.

Before I can write back, the traffic light turns green and the car behind me honks impatiently.

"Okay, okay, hold your horses," I mutter under my breath as I accelerate, glancing at the frustrated driver behind me in the rearview mirror.

I find a parking space near the post office and take a deep breath before getting out of the car.

But the moment my sandals touch the ground, a shiver runs through my body from head to foot. Hannah, who is often superstitious, would say it's because someone is walking over my grave.

Is someone watching me? I look around, trying to see if there's someone there, but there's nothing out of the ordinary. Just the regular hustle and bustle of small-town life.

And yet the feeling won't let go of me; a nagging sensation that something isn't right. That gift box and its menacing contents are lurking in the back of my mind.

Is the sender around here somewhere? Are they following me? I shake my head, trying to clear away the paranoia. I'm just being silly. It's probably just nerves, with the wedding coming up and all.

I'm safe. The past is gone, and I have a bright and beautiful future ahead of me.

I won't let anyone steal my happiness.

SEVEN

I told Debbie I'd be home by lunchtime, but instead I treat myself to a giant, comforting bowl of parmesan-covered pasta in a homely Italian café. Afterwards, I linger over a cappuccino and enjoy people-watching from my red gingham-covered table in the town square. Everything is normal. There are no suspicious glances or familiar faces from my past; just warm smiles and greetings from locals, and innocent people going about their chores.

My anxiety slowly eases, and I pull out my Kindle for a while, escaping into the simple, happy life of the main character in my latest romance novel. The afternoon falls away quickly, and by the time I leave the town center and pull into my driveway the sun is casting long shadows on the front lawn. With the sky growing darker by the minute, my chest grows tight, and I get that unsettling feeling again. Like someone is watching me.

When I enter the house, I call out for Debbie, but I'm greeted only by silence.

My heart flutters with hope. Maybe she left? Maybe my life is going to go back to normal.

But no. Now I can hear the low murmur of the TV drifting toward me.

I walk toward the sound, my footsteps echoing on the wooden floor. The closer I get, the more I can make out the words coming from the TV. It's some news report on a burglary in the area.

I find Debbie sitting on the beige chaise lounge I fell in love with at Elena's favorite local antique store. Nathan, Elena, Hannah and I had been spending a pleasant Saturday afternoon mooching around Stoneview, and Elena saved the best part of her tour until last: a treasure trove of a shop oozing with history and memories. I'd already bought the new leather sofas for the living room, but when he saw me admiring the chaise lounge, Nathan insisted we had to have it, despite its hefty price tag. It's made from a rich, soft fabric decorated with intricate patterns and embroidery, with a curved back, long, slender arms and firm cushions that are now tossed onto one of the sofas on the opposite side of the room.

Debbie is hunched over a photo album with her reading glasses perched on the end of her nose. She reminds me of a stern librarian, her eyes focused intently on the pages before her. Then she looks up at me and the light from the fireplace and lamp casts uneven shadows on her face.

"You're back." She flips over an album page. "I was beginning to worry."

"Sorry, I had a lot of errands to run today. What are you up to?"

Her lips curve in a smile that doesn't quite reach her eyes. "I've been working on something special for you, dear... gathering some little ideas for your wedding."

"Oh, Debbie, I appreciate the effort, but I promise you that everything is already taken care of. And I don't really like surprises."

She closes the album, her fingers absentmindedly tracing

the embossed cover. That's when I notice that it's not actually the photo album I thought it was. It's a scrapbook. From where I'm standing, I can see it's full of fabric swatches, magazine cutouts, and photos of everything wedding-related. And from the thickness of it, it looks like she's been working on it for some time.

"Of course. I understand," she says calmly, pausing to mute the TV. "I just wanted to help, to make sure you're both happy."

Her words are innocent, but there's something calculating about the way she's watching me, searching for something on my face.

"We are happy, Debbie," I reply firmly, with a tight smile, as I try to quell my rising unease. "Nathan and I are really excited about the wedding."

Her smile wavers for a second, almost imperceptibly, before returning to its previous brightness. "I'm glad to hear that, dear. It's just that, well, I've been through this process before, and I thought I could offer some insight. Weddings can be rather stressful."

My discomfort is growing by the second, like a noose tightening around my neck.

"I know you mean well," I say evenly. "I really do, but I promise you I have everything under control. Elena, our wedding planner... She has been amazing."

Her smile widens, but it's one of her forced ones, the kind that twists her features into something almost grotesque. "Of course, Brynn. I'll leave the planning to the professionals then. After all, we wouldn't want anything to go wrong, would we now?"

She walks out, closing the door softly behind her. I'm left alone in the room, my only company the TV flickering softly in the background, a silent witness to the uncomfortable exchange that just took place.

For a while I stare at the screen, not really seeing it as my mind whirs.

What is Debbie doing here?

The tension is suffocating, wrapping around me.

But I can't afford to panic, not when everything is finally coming together for my dream wedding day. I remind myself that I have to keep my cool, no matter what. I will not allow Debbie to ruin this.

But her last words linger in the air; I can almost see the smoky outline of their letters.

With a sigh, I move to the living room window, gazing out over the porch to the beach beyond, with our private path leading down to the sandy shore. I can see the moon's reflection dancing on the water's surface. It's a view to die for.

But I can't find the peace I'm looking for, and I stand there, lost in my thoughts. Then suddenly, I hear a soft voice behind me. I jump, clutching my hand to my chest.

"Brynn, dear, I didn't mean to startle you."

I spin around to find Debbie standing in the doorway, her presence casting a shadow against the hallway.

"It's all right." I force a smile onto my face. "What can I do for you?"

She steps further into the room, and her eyes are darting around, as if she's looking for something. "Well, I couldn't help but notice... I think there might be a small issue with the faucet in my ensuite. It's been leaking. You might want to call a plumber."

"Oh no, I'm sorry. Thank you for letting me know. I'll take care of it right away." Walking out of the living room, I head to Debbie's bathroom to investigate.

Turning off the water supply, I crouch down to inspect the faucet, then I look up at Debbie, who is watching me intently, making me feel self-conscious and irritable.

"It's not too bad, I should be able to fix it myself." I stand up and brush my hands off on my pants.

Debbie's eyes narrow. "You know how to fix a faucet?"

"Among other things."

"Well, color me impressed," Debbie says, a smile playing at the corners of her lips. "You really are a woman full of secrets, aren't you?"

"A woman should know how to take care of herself, don't you think?" I bite back. "I'll go and get the tools."

I head to the garage, feeling Debbie's eyes on me still. When I return, she's sitting on the edge of the tub, and I can't help but chuckle as her eyes grow wide when she sees the toolbox.

"It's... pink," she says.

I smile. "Yeah, when Nathan found out about my DIY skills, he thought it would be funny to get me a pink toolbox. I'm not a typically 'girly' person and he assumed it would irritate me, but I loved it. The tools all match, too." I lower it to the ground and open it up, pulling out a wrench and a pair of pliers. "Now, let's see about fixing that faucet."

Debbie watches me closely as I work, and she genuinely seems interested as she asks how I learned to do this.

I glance up, sitting back on my heels. "I had a great teacher. My grandfather was a very handy man, and since my mother was sick a lot, I spent a lot of time with him. He always said that I should never depend on a man to get by, and that included knowing how to fix things around the house."

Debbie nods. "Well, it's certainly a valuable skill to have. Although, you know, in my day, women would never be doing work like that."

I roll my eyes and then with a final twist of the wrench, the leak is fixed.

Debbie applauds lightly. "Well done, Brynn. You've saved yourself a plumber's bill. And I suppose with all the money you're spending on the wedding, every penny saved counts.

Especially if afterwards you want to stay home and take care of your husband and children."

I raise an eyebrow but choose not to comment. I'm not going to explain to her that I'm only taking a break from work and will start again in a couple of months. I have also never really thought much about having children. My work has kept me so busy, and the idea of staying home all day is daunting. I'm not sure I could cope with it; I already miss my job so much. And there's no chance Nathan would take a break from his career, at least not anytime soon.

Debbie's traditional beliefs and my independence are always going to clash, and I'd be a fool if I let it bother me too much. Life is too short.

She watches me quietly as I wipe my hands and clean up the tools. When I'm about to leave the room, she offers to take the tools back to the garage for me. I pass her the keys as she says, "By the way, I rustled up some dinner for you and left it in the oven. I wish I could join you, but I'm used to eating early, and I have some calls to make."

The kitchen smells wonderful: of garlic, herbs, and buttery pastry. But Debbie has opened the windows wide, perhaps because of the heat from the oven, and I feel exposed somehow. I've never felt unsafe in this home before, but now I can't stop looking nervously over at the darkness in the garden on the other side of the glass.

So, I heap up a plate with chicken pot pie and take it to my room, glancing behind me. I know I'm being ridiculous. It's not as if someone is chasing after me inside my own home. But I feel safer once I've closed my bedroom door and cozied up under a blanket on my armchair, relishing every delicious mouthful of Debbie's food. She really is a wonder in the kitchen.

Soon after I've finished eating, I'm resting my eyes a little when my phone rings. It's Nathan. He'll be wanting to know how my day went. I plaster on a smile before I pick up, and hope it translates in my voice.

He mustn't know anything is wrong. He needs to focus on his case; there's no need for him to know what an anxious wreck I'm becoming. What he doesn't know won't hurt him.

And if there's anything I'm good at, it's keeping secrets.

EIGHT

28 Days Before the Wedding

It's Debbie's second day waking up in my home, and there's no sign of her leaving anytime soon. She takes a morning stroll while I'm finishing my breakfast, and I'm just savoring my last bite of toast dripping in honey when she comes back in and pours herself some coffee.

As she sits next to me and stirs in her cream and sugar, she offers to teach me how to crochet.

"I'm sorry, but I have so much to do today," I decline politely, hoping she won't push the matter. I don't think I have the patience for crochet, nor do I relish the idea of spending quality time with Debbie.

She reaches out for my arm. "Brynn, dear, you look as tense as a coiled spring. Crocheting can be incredibly calming. You should take a break and unwind. Trust me, it's a great stress reliever."

I take a deep breath and pull away, trying to keep my composure. "Honestly, I'm fine. I just really need to tick some things off my to-do list."

Debbie smiles sweetly and replies, "All right then, but if you change your mind, I'll be in the living room."

As soon as she leaves, I let out a sigh of relief. But a little later, as I sit down at my desk in our bedroom and pull out my checklist of action points for the wedding planning, my mind keeps wandering back to her offer. It actually would be nice to relax for a while, to learn a new skill and do something creative.

Without thinking, I find myself getting up and walking to the living room. Debbie is already settled in on the leather sofa by the French windows that lead onto the porch, her fingers flying over the crochet hook as she works on something bright pink. Next to her is another ball of yarn and crochet hook.

She must have known I'd join her.

Saying nothing, I pick up the spare crochet hook and sit down next to her, even though the air between us is thick with unspoken words. She smiles brightly at me, clearly genuinely pleased, and I try my best to return the gesture.

"What made you change your mind, dear?"

"I guess I have a weakness for any opportunity to learn something new," I admit with a shrug. "I don't like not knowing how to do something."

She nods in understanding. "I've been crocheting since I was a little girl. It's a wonderful way to keep your hands busy and your mind at ease. Turning yarn into something pretty and useful doesn't hurt either." As she speaks, she takes my hand and adjusts the way I'm holding the crochet hook, guiding my fingers through the first stitch. Her touch is gentle, and I can feel the warmth radiating from her skin to mine. For a moment, I feel like pulling away, but this time I don't. "We'll kick things off with a simple chain stitch."

It's awkward at first, but as I get the hang of it, I find myself getting lost in the repetitive motions. Debbie is right; it is relaxing. And before I know it, I've crocheted a small square.

"You're a natural," she says with a smile, and I can't help but feel a sense of pride.

As we continue to work on our projects, the tension between us begins to dissipate. Debbie shares stories of her childhood and how she first learned to crochet.

"My mother taught me when I was just five years old. She'd sit with me for hours, guiding me through each stitch till I got it right. Crocheting has been my anchor through many a rough patch, especially on days when I'm thinking about my son." A dark cloud sweeps across her features before it clears again. "If you ask me, it's better than spilling your soul to some stranger on a therapist's couch."

I shift slightly, suddenly feeling uneasy.

Noticing my discomfort, she places a hand on my knee and meets my eyes. "Are you all right, Brynn?"

"Yes... I just... Should I get us something to drink?"

"Sure, that sounds lovely," she replies kindly, withdrawing her hand from my knee.

In the kitchen, I take a deep breath, leaning against the counter and looking out of the window, focusing on the towering sunflowers in the garden to steady myself. Then I open the fridge, grabbing a bottle of water and pouring a glass. I take a sip and savor the sensation of the cool liquid soothing my throat. I'm slightly nauseous and my head is buzzing, but I pull myself together and return to the living room.

Debbie is no longer crocheting. She's standing at the mantel over the fireplace and clutching a photo of Nathan and me. Pausing at the doorway, I notice a faint tremor in the hand holding the photo. She turns around and sees me there, her demeanor softening.

"Oh dear, I didn't realize you were there." She places the photo back on the mantel a bit too quickly, causing it to topple. With that tinkling laugh of hers, she rights it again. "I was just admiring this picture of you and Nathan. Y'all look so deeply in love."

Her words stir a pang in my chest, but I force a smile and sit down, hoping she'll come back and join me. "Thank you," I say, striving to keep my voice steady. "We... we are. Should we continue?"

She nods, but then her expression turns to a frown. "I thought you were going to get us something to drink."

Staring at my empty hands, embarrassment washes over me, but I try to brush it off with a laugh. "Oh no, I got a bit distracted, didn't I?" I say, feeling my cheeks flush. I stand up, but she waves me back down.

"Don't worry about it, we can have a drink later. I'll make us some lemonade."

We work in companiable silence for a while, the only sounds being the soft click of the crochet hooks and the occasional rustling of yarn.

"I can sense you have a lot on your mind," Debbie observes eventually, breaking the silence. "I hope my presence isn't causing any discomfort. Given the circumstances—"

"No," I interject. "It's not you. It's just... all these wedding preparations. There's a lot to think about, that's all."

But I'm lying; it's Debbie who is plaguing my mind. Everything was fine before she turned up. I'd insist on her leaving, but I'm not stupid. We both know what's at stake here; it's like our very own Cold War. One wrong move from either side and everything will come crashing down.

So, I push aside my discomfort and try to forget about it all. As we begin to make casual conversation, I even find myself unexpectedly enjoying her company. She's witty and funny, full of anecdotes that make me splutter with laughter.

But then she turns the topic back toward me, and the spell is broken.

"You've never been one to share much about yourself,

Brynn. You're like a locked chest, ain't you? I feel like I've barely scratched the surface of who you are."

I swallow hard. "There's not much to tell, really."

"Oh now, there's always something worth sharing," Debbie pushes. "Come on, tell me something about yourself that I don't already know. I've already yapped on about my love for crocheting. Why don't you tell me about the things you love to do?"

"Art," I say without hesitating, since surely that's a safe topic to talk about. I loop the yarn around my crochet hook, trying to sound relaxed and breezy. "That's why I studied art history. My dream was always to work in art galleries or museums, to be surrounded by beautiful paintings and sculptures all day."

I smile to myself as I think of my plan to own my very own gallery right here in this beautiful town of Stoneview. This is just the place for it, with all the tourists who flock here to soak in the atmosphere of the historic town, and the local business owners who form a supportive community.

"It must be nice, to be able to use your little hobby to make a living. I've always been more of a practical person myself; home economics was my forte. I never had much time for art." Debbie's tone is light, but a hint of condescension lurks beneath.

I bristle at the insinuation that art is somehow less valuable than home economics, and that my career isn't a lucrative one, which is completely untrue. My hands tighten around the crochet hook.

"Art is useful," I say sharply. "It's not just about pretty pictures on a wall. It's about culture and history and expressing yourself when words would fall short." I also draw and paint quite well myself when I make the time for it, so I know the power that art holds for processing trauma and for easing a busy, strained mind. I think that if more of us found time to express ourselves creatively, the world would be a much happier place.

Debbie halts her crocheting and looks at me, her eyes wide.

"Oh dear, I seem to have upset you. My mother used to warn me that my tongue would get me into trouble someday."

I feel slightly mollified and shake my head. "It's fine. I just... I'm passionate about art, that's all. Just like crocheting helped you through tough times, for me, it was art that—" I bite my tongue and stop talking.

"It's all right dear, you can talk to me. I've got a good ear for listening," she says gently. "You said your mother was ill a lot when you were growing up. Did art help you cope with that?"

I nod, my thoughts scrambling to come up with a way to end this conversation.

"And, if you don't mind me asking, was it an illness that took her... your mother?"

I freeze, my heart thudding. I never intended to reveal this much about my past to Debbie. Now it seems like I've walked into a trap.

"I... I don't really want to talk about it."

"That's okay, I understand. How about your father, then? Is he still alive?"

Normally I'd be angry at her prying; I've always been a closed book about my past. But all I can see in her eyes is kindness, and despite myself I feel tears burning in mine.

I shake my head. "No, he passed away as well."

She offers a sympathetic nod. "I'm sorry to hear that. Losing a parent, or anyone you love, is never easy. It's like having your heart torn from your chest and trampled. I'd love to see your artwork, Brynn, perhaps you could share it with me sometime. I haven't seen any of it about the place—do you keep it hidden away somewhere? Maybe you could show it to me on a little tour of this place; you still haven't given me one yet. I'd love to see it all, maybe give you some ideas for how to decorate it and really make it a home? I'm sure your mother would have helped you if she were here. But I'll do whatever I can to help."

That's quite enough for me, and I stand up abruptly. "This

has been lovely, but I have some calls to make, I really must get on. Thanks for teaching me how to crochet, Debbie, it was very kind of you. I'll see you in a little bit." I offer her a tight smile before turning and practically bolting out of the living room.

Back inside my bedroom, I lock the door and lean against it, breathing heavily as I slide to the floor.

I need to be more careful. The last thing I need is Debbie poking around in my personal life and reopening old wounds that have never fully healed.

Even after my breathing returns to normal, I stay on the floor, staring at the slightly open balcony doors, where a faint breeze flutters the curtains.

I could have sworn that when I left the bedroom this morning, the doors were closed.

NINE

THE WOMAN

Brynn is peacefully asleep, her room lit up by the soft moonlight streaming through the thin balcony curtains. The woman moves silently around, before being drawn to the walk-in closet.

What she is doing is risky. Brynn could wake up at any moment and catch her in the act. But it's irresistible, and she's getting bolder. She knows that Brynn is a deep sleeper; she's tested the ground by watching her sleep from the balcony, and little noises don't seem to make her stir at all. Unless a nightmare startles her awake. No surprise there, though. All the messages she has been sending have planted fear and paranoia deep within Brynn, and it is to be expected that they will manifest in her dreams.

The closet is like a room of its own, indeed it has a large window overlooking the beach. And since the curtains have not been drawn closed, she can see everything inside.

The walls of the closet are lined with shelves full of clothes, shoes, handbags, and hats. The floor is covered by a soft, cream rug, and the ceiling is framed with intricate molding. A large, ornately carved dressing table stands against one wall, surrounded by mirrors, and lined with neatly arranged bottles of perfumes and cosmetics.

Beneath the floral notes of Brynn's perfume, she detects the pleasant scent of suede and leather from her expensive bags and shoes. But the woman is not interested in those.

Holding her breath, she scans the hanging rails, her eyes finally landing on the garment bag she's looking for. She carefully unzips it to reveal the beautiful white dress. A dress Brynn will never wear down the aisle, not if she can help it. The woman's fingers graze the soft tulle fabric as she reaches inside. But she does not remove the dress this time. Instead, she zips up the bag again slowly, inch by inch, careful not to make any noise, then takes a step back. She reaches to the back of the closet and brings out the box with the veil.

As she lifts it out of the box, she can't help but imagine Brynn walking down the aisle with the veil flowing down her back.

Just the thought of it makes her muscles tense. She had thought her note and the wedding cake toppers would put a stop to all this, but they haven't been enough.

Lifting the veil up higher, she watches it sparkle under the light, and then she plucks one of the crystals from the fabric and slips it into her pocket. It's a small, inconsequential act, but it feels like a victory somehow. It makes her feel like she's taking control of the situation. Before she can take another breath, another crystal finds its way into her pocket, and then another. She can't stop herself.

In the end, she decides not to return the veil to its box. Another idea has come to her, and it makes her heart race with mingled excitement and fear. She exits the closet and tiptoes closer to the bed, the veil clutched tightly in her hand as well as an album she grabbed impulsively on her way out.

She reaches out, her fingers hovering over Brynn's face. She wonders how it would feel to have her fingers wrapped around her throat, to feel her struggle for breath.

Or even better, strangle her with her own veil... now that would make headlines.

Can she really be having thoughts like this? What is happening to her? She shakes her head, pulling herself together, and then she leaves the room reluctantly, silently, via the balcony window once more. It's quite easy to climb up and to drop down onto the sand from there since there's a convenient lattice for her to grab hold of. Once outside, a walk along the beach will do her good.

There are other ways to make Brynn suffer. If she's smart, if she knows what's good for her, she will end things with Nathan.

And then maybe the woman won't be forced to go any further.

But oh, that adrenaline rush is addictive. And she can't wait to feel it again.

TEN

BRYNN

26 Days Before the Wedding

I wake up suddenly, feeling both cold and sweaty. I can't explain it, but I feel certain someone was in my room, watching me while I slept.

It would be completely dark in here if it weren't for the moonlight seeping through the curtains. I rub my eyes, trying to shake off the fear that clings to me like a second skin.

I sit up in bed, scanning the space and seeing nothing but the dim outlines of the furniture. But when I switch on the bedside lamp, I notice that the door is slightly open, and my heart skips a beat. I always close it before going to bed. I feel like I'm losing my mind.

Since finding the balcony doors open the other night, I've been constantly on edge, terrified that someone might be breaking into my home.

Swallowing hard, I swing my legs over the side of the bed, and reach for the lamp, wielding it above my head as I approach the door, my heart pounding rapidly.

I reach the door and push it open slowly, trying to make as little noise as possible.

My breathing is shaky and shallow, and all my muscles are tense as I step out into the hallway.

But it's empty; there's only silence and shadows.

The steps creak under my feet as I move downstairs and head toward Debbie's room. When I reach the door, I stop and just stand there, the lamp dangling at my side.

"You can come in, dear," Debbie's voice comes from inside the room, light as a feather.

I freeze.

How does she know I'm here? And why is she still awake? The bedside clock had read 2 a.m. when I woke up.

Lowering the lamp and putting it down on the floor, I step inside.

The past few days with Debbie have been bearable; in fact, they have been far less uncomfortable than I could ever have predicted. We sat down to crochet again yesterday, and I even found myself doing it on my own when she was not with me. She has also helped quite a lot around the house, and I've appreciated the flowers and herbs she's brought in from the garden and all the weeding she's done out there. Besides her talent for cooking, she also has a green thumb, and she even brought her garden tools with her.

But there were still times when I caught her watching me, her expression hard and unreadable. Now, in the softly illuminated room, she's sitting up in bed in her nightgown, the covers pulled up to her waist and her gray hair in curlers. Next to her are a bunch of newspapers.

As soon as she sees me, she reaches for the remote and flicks off the TV that was playing at low volume. I wonder what she was watching.

"How did you know I was outside?" I ask awkwardly.

She gives me a small smile. "I heard the stairs creaking, and I could see your shadow through the crack under the door."

I nod, and I don't even try to explain myself. I'm too anxious to think up excuses.

She dips her head to the side. "Is everything okay? You look like you've seen a ghost."

"I... I was just wondering if you heard anything strange tonight," I ask, trying to keep my voice steady.

"No, not really. But then again, I was so engrossed in my movie that I might not have noticed if there was any noise outside. Not until I heard you, that is. Why do you ask? Is something wrong?"

"I found my bedroom door open, so I was worried that someone might have come into the house."

Debbie sits up straighter. "Oh dear, that's quite concerning. Are you sure you didn't leave the door open yourself, darling? Did you check to see if anything was missing?"

I shake my head. "I didn't think to."

"Well, you should have a look, just in case." She swings her legs over the side of the bed and stands. "I'll come with you."

Before I can say no, she walks past me, grabbing her robe on the way.

Together, we leave the room and head back upstairs toward my bedroom. As we walk, I can feel Debbie's hand on my shoulder, and to my surprise, I find it comforting.

But when we reach my door, I suddenly feel uneasy about her or anyone else entering my personal space, so I stop in my tracks. Debbie notices my hesitation and looks back at me.

"It's all right," she says softly. "I won't go in if you want to check on your own. I'll just go and check the doors and windows downstairs to make sure they're all locked."

I nod gratefully. "Thanks, Debbie."

When she walks away, I step into my room, closing the door behind me.

The room is just as I left it, but something feels off. I can't quite put my finger on it, but the air feels heavy with an invisible presence that makes me shiver. I look around carefully, and in the end, I walk back out to where Debbie is waiting and tell her that everything seems to be in order.

"That's good. I didn't see anything strange downstairs either. It must be that you just forgot to close the door properly before you went to sleep, don't you think?" she suggests as we walk back down to her room.

"I don't think so. It's never happened before," I say, and my voice sounds scared and childlike, unfamiliar. *What is happening to me?*

Debbie nods, her expression thoughtful. "Well, there's a first time for everything. It's probably nothing. Maybe it was just a draft from the window. But you still look a little shaken up, darling. How about you come in with me and we watch a movie, something to take your mind off things?"

I want to say no, but to be honest, I'm too scared to go back to my room. I feel like a child again, and the fear pulsing through me is even greater than my reluctance to appear vulnerable in front of Debbie.

"Okay, that sounds good," I say gratefully.

As she searches for a comedy on Netflix, I ask why she's awake at such a late hour.

"I have a hard time sleeping in new places," she admits with a small smile. "I also had a bit of a bad dream earlier. Perhaps there's something in the air tonight. Here, how about this one?"

I read the description of a comedy about a group of bored housewives who decide to become nuns to escape their family obligations. It sounds ridiculous, but I'm willing to give it a shot if it means a distraction, and above all not having to be alone.

Debbie invites me to sit next to her, propped up by many pillows and cushions, and I accept awkwardly, although I can't quite bring myself to snuggle up under the comforter with her.

"Here." She covers me with a thick quilted blanket. "You look like you could use a little extra comfort."

I feel unexpectedly safe in this room, with her, and I begin to relax a little. But as the movie starts, I remember that she has a habit of predicting every twist in the plot. Gradually her constant nattering becomes too frustrating, and I can't take it anymore. I'm too tired to be patient.

"Debbie, you're kind of ruining the movie for me," I say, trying to sound playful.

Her face falls slightly, as if she's disappointed in herself. "I'm sorry, I didn't realize it bothered you. I just get excited when I think I know what's going to happen next."

For the next ten minutes, she says nothing, but I can tell she's struggling because every few seconds her hands clench and unclench on the bedspread and she keeps glancing over at me.

"Look," I say, smiling in spite of myself, "it's fine. I'm just being silly. Tell me what you think will happen next."

As though I flicked a switch, her face lights up and she starts again. Instead of getting annoyed, I find myself getting caught up in her enthusiasm. We laugh at the silliness of the plot and cheer on the nuns. Her predictions are always accurate, and I find myself enjoying the movie much more than I thought I would.

When it ends, she turns to me with a grin. "See, wasn't that fun?"

I can't help but return her smile. "Yeah, it was. Thanks for watching it with me. I feel much better now." I push away the blanket and get to my feet. "I should catch a few more hours of sleep."

"I guess I should do the same," she says. "Goodnight, dear. Don't worry, you're safe. It's just you and me here."

I nod weakly and leave the room with a quick goodnight

and a strained smile. I climb the stairs slowly, and when I'm back in my bedroom, I close the door firmly and look around.

I've never missed Nathan as badly as I do now; I know I would feel safe if he was nearby. I used to love this room so much, but now it feels cold and lonely, and far too big for one person. I crawl under the sheets, but even though I'm exhausted, sleep eludes me. So, I switch on my phone and head to the Safe Haven Sisters Facebook group, a support group for women, where I like to offer advice and share uplifting messages with members who are going through a hard time. Helping others has always been therapeutic for me, especially when I'm feeling anxious myself.

I scroll through the posts, liking and commenting on a few before coming across a message that catches my attention. It's from a woman named Sarah, who is struggling to leave an abusive relationship. My heart sinks as I read her words, then without hesitation, I start typing out a message of support and encouragement. I tell her that she's strong and capable of making the change she needs to live a life free from fear.

But after I switch off my phone, I'm still not relaxed enough to sleep. So, I get up again. I know something that always lifts my spirits.

My walk-in closet is like something out of a movie, and I know many women would dream of having one like this. It's still hard to believe it's mine. The decor is a blend of modern and vintage, with a crystal chandelier hanging from the ceiling. There's even a set of comfortable velvet chairs in the corner, where a flat-screen TV is mounted on the wall. And it has a wonderfully cozy feel thanks to the cream shag rug and the soft beige curtains that cover the windows. Scented candles line the shelves, perfuming the air even when they aren't lit with the calming aromas of lavender and vanilla.

I open the bag containing my wedding dress, but instead of trying it on, I just run my fingers over the soft fabric, dreaming about the day when I will be wearing it down the aisle. With a contented sigh, I turn away from it and reach for the flat box nestled in the corner of the closet.

But when I lift the lid, I find nothing but an empty box.

A sinking feeling settles in my stomach.

Where is my veil? Could I have misplaced it? Did I forget it at Elena's studio the day of the fitting? I was so sure I took it back with me in case I wanted to try it on again. But I've been forgetful recently, my nerves causing me to be careless and clumsy. I need to give her a call in the morning. That'll be it, surely.

But something feels off.

Walking back out of the closet, my eyes land on the now closed bedroom door.

I think back to my movements in the evening, and even though I wish I was wrong, I couldn't be more certain. I remember closing the door, leaning back against it briefly before I went to change into my pajamas.

It *was* opened during the night.

And that means somebody was in here while I was sleeping.

In an instant, fear seeps into every fiber of my being.

I need you, Sam.

Somebody knows. Someone is coming for me.

ELEVEN

21 Days Before the Wedding

With forensic precision, I drive the nail into the dining room wall, positioning it between the two tall windows that offer a view of the garden. It's only 9 a.m., but it's already a gloriously sunny day, and I've opened up both windows to let in the fresh air.

As I slam the hammer against the head of the nail, the rhythmic thud of metal against drywall echoes through the house.

Finally, I carefully hang up a canvas abstract painting I created a few years ago. It fits brilliantly, and the bold colors bring a burst of life into the space. I don't often use the dining room, preferring to eat in the kitchen, but I'd like the place to feel more personalized and inviting so I can have people over and host dinner parties.

Debbie's words the other day struck a chord with me, too. I hadn't yet put any of my artwork around the place as I found it too hard to choose.

But selecting my own pieces to display around the home

brings me comfort and makes me feel more in control even while my nerves are still frayed. Our dining room has the ideal light to let this painting shine. We have a beautiful long wooden table, and I can just picture it laid with candles, napkins, and fresh foliage from the garden.

As I step back to admire my handiwork, my phone buzzes from a window ledge. I pick it up and glance at the screen, my heart skipping a beat as I see Elena's name.

Days have passed since I asked her if I'd left my veil at her studio, and she said she hadn't seen it. I know it's unlikely that she'd miss it, as her store is so organized, but since then every time she calls, I can't help but hope it's to let me know that she found it.

I guess I don't want to think about the alternative; that someone went inside my room, into my closet while I was sleeping, and took the veil away.

I press the pickup button. "Hello?"

"Brynn, sweetie, I'm so sorry to call you early." Her voice is uncharacteristically serious and tinged with concern, and I brace myself instinctively. "I just found out that you canceled the venue, and I wanted to ask why. I'm a little confused. I thought it was your dream wedding location."

The words hit me like a punch to the gut. Our venue, the Glass Parlor, has panoramic views over the ocean from its hilltop location above Stoneview, and a fragrant, picturesque rose garden. It's an exquisite place, down to the finest detail. But above all, when Elena took me to see it, I fell head over heels in love with the way the light dances through the stained-glass windows in the main room where the wedding ceremonies are held.

I have visualized every detail of our wedding in that setting, from the white roses to the jazz music, to the way the sun would set behind us as we exchanged our vows. My artist's heart is also drawn to the dance floor, which is decorated with an abstract painting, an intricate design of swirling colors that come alive under the lights. It's like it was designed for me.

"The venue... canceled? I don't understand. What do you mean?"

Elena pauses for a moment before continuing. "You're not aware of it? I thought... Well, I just called them to ask about hiring extra staff for the reception, and they informed me that our booking has been canceled."

"I don't understand," I repeat. "We've had the reservation for months."

"I know. But they said you canceled it."

"Me? How...? What?" Sitting down slowly on one of our dining room chairs, I struggle to make sense of what she's telling me. "Elena, I never canceled anything. I've been so looking forward to having the wedding there. It was our first choice. There must be some mistake."

"Yeah. I know you were so excited when we got the reservation, and they're very in demand. We were lucky to get a spot at all."

"Exactly. It doesn't make sense. I would never cancel it," I say, my voice rising with frustration.

"That's what I thought, too." Elena pauses. "Do you think that maybe Nathan would have done it?"

"Definitely not," I say firmly, getting up from the chair again to pace up and down by the windows. "He knows how much that place means to me."

"Okay, okay," she says calmly. "Maybe it's just a mistake or a miscommunication. I'm sure there's a logical explanation for all this. Let me call them again and see what I can find out."

Tears threaten to spill from my eyes, and I grip the phone tightly. "This can't be happening, Elena. It was perfect. Everything was falling into place."

"I know how much it means to you to have the wedding there, Brynn. I promise I'll do everything in my power to try and get the reservation back. Or find an equally amazing alternative."

I nod, even though Elena can't see me. "Thanks. Please, do whatever you can."

"I will. I'll call you as soon as I have any updates."

After we say our goodbyes and I hang up, the weight of disappointment and confusion bears down on me, and I sit down at the table again. I bury my face in my hands, letting the tears flow.

It's not like me to cry like this, my whole body heaving with sobs. And I know it's not just about the venue; it's everything. First Debbie arrived, then I received that horrible broken bride figurine and the note, then my veil went missing, and now this. I desperately want to pretend like everything is going to be okay; I'm trying so hard to hold it together, but the truth is I feel like I'm falling apart.

After a while I lift my head and blink back the tears, then I stand up unsteadily and walk upstairs to my bedroom, stepping out onto the balcony. In the distance, I spot Debbie on the beach, a mug in hand, looking out at the ocean. Her serenity contrasts sharply with the turmoil inside me.

As if she knows I'm watching her, she turns, and my heart stutters as our eyes meet.

For a moment, it's as if she can see right through me.

Could she have had something to do with this?

She lifts a hand and waves with a smile, but I don't wave back. I feel like my arms are frozen to my sides. I didn't even talk to her about the wedding location. But what if she found out where it was, and did this to hurt me?

And if she didn't do it... who else could it have been?

I throw on a robe and head out of the house toward her.

Debbie glances up as I approach, her face lighting up with a warm smile. "Brynn, darling, isn't it a beautiful morning? This view really is something special."

"Actually, I came to talk to you about something," I say slowly, my voice sounding strained and unfamiliar.

"Of course, dear. What's on your mind?" She wraps both hands around her rose-pink mug. "You look upset. Is everything okay?"

I take a deep breath, my fingers tightening into fists by my sides. "The Glass Parlor, my wedding venue—it's been canceled."

Her expression doesn't change one bit. Not a flicker. "I'm so sorry to hear that. That's rather unfortunate, to have something like that happen so close to the wedding day."

I nod, steeling myself. "Debbie... do you happen to know how it came to be canceled?"

Debbie's smile drops. "Now why on earth would I have anything to do with it?"

I stare at her, but she remains calm and composed, and I feel a surge of anger and desperation. I take a step closer. "Debbie, this venue meant everything to me. If you did this, please just tell me. I need to know."

She shakes her head, her eyes sad and pleading. "Brynn, I honestly had no hand in this. As hard as it may be to believe, given our history, I want you and Nathan to be happy." She pauses. "Darling, is there someone else who wouldn't want you to be happy? Someone from your past, perhaps?"

The question catches me off guard, and I stumble over my words. "No, I... no, I don't think so."

But Debbie gives me that piercing look again, as if she's searching for something in my eyes. "Are you completely sure of that? You know, sometimes we go through life thinking the past is behind us. But it has a way of catching up when we least expect it."

Her words stick to me like grains of sand as I shake my head. "No, there's no one I can think of who would do this."

"Well, I can't give you any answers, I'm afraid. I honestly

just hope you get what you deserve, Brynn. If you ever need someone to talk to, you know I'm always here."

With that, she turns and walks back toward the house.

She really does seem sincere, and the truth is, I'm not certain she was behind the cancellation. Even if she was, what could I do? She knows she has power over me. She could take everything away from me in a heartbeat if she chose to do so.

So, I can't make her leave. I certainly can't get on her bad side even more than I already am.

I need her close by, where I can keep an eye on her.

I'm about to follow her inside when my phone rings again, and I answer Elena while walking aimlessly along the beach, my bare feet sinking into the sand with each step.

"I'm so sorry, Brynn. I called the Glass Parlor back, but they insist that the reservation has definitely been canceled and there's nothing they can do."

"Were you able to rebook again for the same date? Please tell me you did."

"No, I'm sorry. They're fully booked for that date now. They have a long waiting list and as soon as your reservation was canceled, someone else took it. I'm really, really sorry, but I'm afraid we'll have to find another venue, or think about postponing."

I sigh, utterly deflated. "Okay, thanks so much for trying. I'll have a think about it and let you know where we could go instead."

After ending the call, I continue walking in silence, my head throbbing and hot tears burning behind my eyelids. Without the Glass Parlor, the wedding simply won't be the same. It was the ideal venue, with its stunning views and elegant architecture.

But I remind myself that the most important thing is marrying Nathan. A venue is only a small part of the celebration, not the be-all and end-all. I know what Sam would say: *Don't sweat the little things.*

I need to focus on what truly matters.

I haven't been walking for long when I spot something fluttering on the ground. This is a clean beach, so anything that doesn't belong here is easy to spot, and it's near the palm tree where I love to meditate or just sit and stare out at the ocean. I come here most days to do that, although since my veil went missing, I have been too on edge to even think about trying to meditate or enjoy my favorite spot on the beach.

As I approach it, I realize it's a piece of fabric that's half-buried in the sand, with some shells pressing it down so it can't blow away. Curious, I bend down and tug.

Then I realize it's not just any fabric.

My hands are shaking as I watch the dirty veil slowly unravel from the sand.

My wedding veil.

The crystal-encrusted comb should glitter in the sunlight. But the crystals are missing, plucked out one by one, leaving behind gaping holes.

The significance of the veil being buried is very clear. Whoever did this must know my past.

They know what I've done.

This is a message, a warning.

I should run. I should call Sam, and get as far away as I can.

But I can't.

I've tasted what it's like to have the life of my dreams. And even though it's completely irrational to stay put given the danger I'm in, I can't bring myself to give it all up now.

Despite everything, a determined voice inside me still believes that as soon as I walk down the aisle and into Nathan's arms, everything will be okay.

I just have to make it there.

TWELVE

It's ten at night when I finally flop down onto my bed, my thoughts spiraling, catastrophizing, pulsing through my mind. From the canceled venue to the buried veil, today has been a nightmare, and I'm equal parts scared, exhausted, and angry. No, that's not right. I feel more anger than anything else.

I toss and turn under the covers, knowing that sleep might bring me some peace and clarity, but I simply can't settle. While I'm still stuck in my thoughts, my phone lights up on the nightstand. It's Nathan, and I quickly answer, needing his voice to ground me. I've been trying to reach him all day without success.

"Hey, love. How has your day been?" he says brightly.

"It's been... Honestly, it's been quite a day." I massage the space between my eyebrows, unsure how I can manage to put into words everything that's happened without breaking apart.

Nathan hates it when people beat around the bush, preferring directness and honesty. So, after a brief pause, I tell him about the venue, blurting out all my feelings—my frustration, confusion, and anger—in one go. But I don't tell him about the veil. It's just too weird, too scary. I wouldn't want him worrying about me. I wouldn't put it past him to cancel everything, quit the trial and come home to protect me. He'd ruin his career because he loves me that much.

I haven't even told Elena or Hannah about finding the buried veil yet. I will, but I'm worried they'll try to get me to call the police again.

And no matter how afraid I might feel, I can't afford to do that.

When I'm finished talking about the Glass Parlor, there's a brief pause on the other end before Nathan speaks, and his normally steady voice sounds bewildered and concerned. "Canceled? Why, what the heck? We paid the deposit, didn't we?"

"We did. I don't understand either, and neither does Elena. She asked me if you canceled it, and I told her you'd never do that. It must have just been some kind of mistake, but there's nothing we can do about it now, our slot has gone. I'm just... Oh, Nathan, I'm so disappointed. I really loved that place." My voice cracks, and I press my teeth into my lips to try to curb the flow of tears.

Nathan's response is immediate, gentle, and full of reassurance. "Hey, it's going to be okay, Brynn. We'll figure this out, I promise. We can still have the wedding of our dreams. It will just be in a different location. A venue is not what's going to make our wedding special anyway; it's us, our love for each other. You and I forever, until death do us part. Remember that."

The tightness in my stomach softens a little. Nathan always knows how to calm me down, with his unwavering clear mindedness and sense of perspective. "I know, I know. You're right. It's just that we had everything planned out for the Glass Parlor, and I'm disappointed. I don't even know where to begin looking for a new location and I guess I'm freaking out a little."

"Okay, well, listen to me. Take a deep breath. We'll take

care of this together. We'll make it work, no matter what. I promise."

Obstacles never seem to faze Nathan; he always finds a way to make things work. He lives by the motto that wasting time on what went wrong won't fix anything, so it's better to focus on finding a solution instead. And right now, I need that mindset more than ever.

I just wish I could tell him everything.

Well, not *everything*. That can never happen.

I sigh, twisting the bedsheet in my fingers. "What are we going to do, though? The wedding is three weeks away and most venues need to be booked months in advance. Time is running out and the guests and other vendors need to be informed of the change in location."

"I know that, but I wonder... Maybe we don't have to book another venue. I have a bit of an idea. What happened might actually be a good thing."

I sit a little straighter against the pillows, feeling a flicker of hope. "What do you mean?"

"Well, how about celebrating our wedding in our very own dream home on the beach? Isn't that even better, even more *us* than the Glass Parlor would have been?"

It turns out, he's absolutely right. I hadn't considered it before, but the idea of having our wedding in our forever home, the most beautiful place I have ever lived in, seems like a lovely, intimate way to celebrate our union.

I feel better than I have in days, and a soft smile tugs at the corners of my lips. "You know, you might be onto something. I never even thought of it, but it does sound amazing. We could have a beach wedding at sunset."

I can just imagine the sun setting in a blaze of purple and gold, accompanied by the soothing melody of rushing waves as we exchange our vows.

He chuckles softly. "Yes! Exactly. And we could have a big

bonfire on the beach after the official reception. I'm sure everyone would love that."

"Nathan, that sounds magical. We could hang lanterns from the palm trees and string up fairy lights." I can feel my heart swell with excitement.

"You see, there's always a solution to every problem. We can transform our home into our own magical wedding venue. Not many people can say they got married on their own private beach, right? We'll make it perfect. Just like us," he says affectionately.

I nod, feeling giddy with excitement and relief. "Exactly. We'll make it unforgettable."

Finally, my body begins to fully relax. I'm so grateful for Nathan's unwavering positivity. He always knows how to turn a situation around and make it better. I can only imagine how many times he's had to think on his feet and come up with a solution in the courtroom, and frankly if it were me on trial, there's nobody I'd rather have defending me.

We spend the rest of the time on the call brainstorming ideas. Nathan suggests using the living room porch for the wedding buffet. It has steps leading down onto the beach, and the guests can enjoy their meals on tables and chairs on the sand.

"You're incredible, you know that?" I say, putting him on speaker and jotting down his ideas in the Notes app on my phone. "I don't know what I would do without you."

"You don't have to worry about that. I'm here for you, always." His voice deepens. "I can't wait to marry you, Brynn. You're the best thing that ever happened to me."

"Same here. I can't believe how lucky I am to have found you."

After we say our goodnights, I settle into bed and think about my life to come, my heart full of hope and gratitude. Everything is unfolding beyond my wildest dreams. I'm no longer so worried about things going wrong, but now I'm kept awake by excitement. I've never been the most patient person and I wish I could just grab a remote and fast-forward to our wedding day. Thankfully, I only have to wait just a little longer before I get to marry Nathan.

But the intense anxiety of the last few days hasn't completely gone away, because when I finally relax enough to fall asleep, I tumble into a recurring nightmare; one that has been plaguing me for a few nights now. It's my wedding day, but it's taking place in the middle of a dark forest.

Twinkling lights are everywhere, hanging from the trees and illuminating the path leading to the altar. Instead of my maid of honor, there are multiple bridesmaids. They're standing on either side of the aisle smiling at me. And as their faces come into focus, I start to recognize some of them. Hannah, Elena, Debbie. But the rest are strangers.

As I walk down the aisle, my bare feet are scratched by the pine needles on the forest floor, and my dress is itchy and too tight.

I'm overcome by a sense of absolute dread; something terrible is going to happen.

The air is thick with a heady, dirty scent, like rotten flowers. I look down at the white rose bouquet in my hand and see that the flowers are wilting and decaying. The petals are turning black and are falling off with each step I take.

My chest tightening, I look up and notice that my groom is not Nathan. It's a stranger with a face I can't quite make out.

I try to stop in my tracks, but my feet keep moving forward, leading me closer and closer to him.

Finally, as I stand in front of my groom, I realize that he's not even looking at me. He's staring past me, his eyes fixed on something in the distance. I turn around to see what it is.

That's when I see her.

A woman, dressed in all black, with long, stringy hair

hanging in front of her face. She's standing at the edge of the clearing, just out of reach of the light from the twinkling bulbs. She starts slowly making her way toward us. Her steps are heavy on the ground and her hollowed eyes are fixed solely on me.

When she's close enough for me to hear her breathing, I try to run. But my feet are rooted to the spot. As she gets even closer, my fear intensifies. I feel as if I'm going to suffocate.

But just as she's about to reach me, I wake up.

For just a few moments, I know who that woman is.

But then the name, and the face, fade away from my mind.

THIRTEEN

I sit up in bed, sticky with sweat, my nightgown clinging to my skin. Running my fingers through my damp hair, I try to reassure myself that I'm safe, I'm here in my bedroom; the woman in my dream can't hurt me. The echoes of her footsteps still resonate in my mind, but I push them away, focusing on reality.

To calm myself down, I practice the Pranayama yoga breathing techniques Hannah taught me. I count slow, soothing breaths until the room feels safe again, a sanctuary where the woman can't reach me. But my fingers still tremble as I reach for the glass of water on my nightstand. Taking a long gulp, I glance at the clock on the wall. Its numbers beam in the darkness; 1 a.m. It's late, and the world outside is quiet.

With a shaky exhale, I swing my legs over the side of the bed and plant my feet on the floor, focusing on the sensation of the soft carpet beneath me. Then I make my way to the window, where I pull the curtains farther apart to allow the moonlight in. And there she is—the vast expanse of the ocean, her dark waves whispering secrets to the night. Pressing my hand to my chest, I can feel the steady thud of my heartbeat beneath my fingertips.

It wasn't real, I tell myself. The fear, the abject panic, those terrifying images—they were just a product of my imagination, formed from fragments of my memory and the thought processing of my subconscious mind.

As I return to the bed, I draw the covers close around me, and the soft fabric is a comforting embrace. I close my eyes and allow the residual adrenaline to ebb away. But after trying for a while, I know I'm not going to fall asleep again. So, I decide to do something productive.

I head to the Safe Haven Sisters Facebook group, and after spending a little while there scrolling through the posts and offering words of comfort and advice, I text Sam. An update will be badly needed after my frantic message about the canceled venue.

Hey. You won't believe what Nathan just suggested. We're thinking of having the wedding right here in our dream home. What do you think?

Almost immediately, my phone buzzes with a response.

I love it! Now stop stressing so much. Everything will work out just fine, future Mrs. Brynn Howard. Ignore the hiccups along the way.

I smile and tap on Elena's number. She'll see my message first thing in the morning before she calls around in search of a new venue.

Elena, problem solved. We'll have the ceremony and reception at our home. Please call me when you wake up so we can discuss. Thanks, Brynn

I try to rest again, but it's soon clear that sleep is going to be impossible at this point. So, I curl up with my Kindle, craving the comfort and escape of my light, heartwarming romance novel, and I'm only a few chapters away from the end when the first fingers of daylight creep through the curtains.

Stretching my aching limbs, I get out of bed and make myself some strong coffee, taking the mug out with me onto the beach where I sit with my toes curling into the sand.

Even though I'm exhausted after so little sleep, I feel surprisingly positive and energized for the day ahead. *Everything is going to be okay.* We're going to have the wedding right here, on the beach by our lovely home. I have a wonderful fiancé, friends who love me, a golden future stretching out ahead of me. And today is going to be a good day, starting with coffee and a catch-up with Hannah before I help her out with a flower-arranging workshop she's running at a local hospice.

A few hours later, I walk into my favorite Stoneview café, Honeywood.

Honeywood's pastel-colored walls glint in the sunlight, and the potted plants along the windowsills are thriving in bursts of green and yellow. The café is filled with soft seating areas along with wooden tables, each one decorated with a small vase of wildflowers. All along the walls there are shelves displaying vintage china and artwork depicting Stoneview and the local beaches, and the beams that crisscross the ceiling are entwined with foliage. But best of all, there's a counter covered in mouth-watering cakes; glass jars filled with homemade cookies; and plates of pastries of all kinds, bursting with plump dried fruit, chocolate, crème pâtissière, and marzipan. The rich aroma of coffee and freshly baked treats is irresistible, and I defy anyone to feel stressed or despondent here.

Hannah is already sitting at our favorite table, absorbed in her journaling, and nursing what I know will be her usual chai latte. I order myself a flat white and give her a warm hug.

Time flies by when I'm chatting with Hannah, and it always feels like we've put the world to rights. We get stuck in with our catch-up, and she's very concerned about the last-minute change with the wedding venue. She knew how much I loved the Glass Parlor, and she thinks we should hold out until it's free again. But I soon convince her that the last thing Nathan and I want is to postpone the wedding by at least a year, just to get a reservation there again.

And soon we move onto other topics, such as the yoga teacher training Hannah is going to be starting soon. She wants to get some supplementary income, alongside her floristry work. One day, she hopes to have enough to be able to open her own store again.

Listening to my best friend talking about her plans and dreams reminds me that as soon as the wedding is over, I need to start putting together a business model for my own art gallery. I do feel a little guilty when I think about how easy it will be for me to purchase real estate here in Stoneview and set up my gallery, compared to Hannah who will need to save for years before she can afford to open another florist shop. But I know that it's a bad idea to mix money and friendship, so I haven't offered to support her financially. And she's never asked. I help in other ways, though, particularly now I'm not working. Elena has been amazing, finding lots of clients for Hannah, but since Hannah can't afford any staff, she needs all the help she can get with her contracts for local events.

This workshop at the hospice today, though, is purely charitable. We're going to be using flowers left over from Hannah's most recent job, a wedding anniversary party, and helping the patients to arrange bouquets which they'll then be able to take back to their rooms. It was all Hannah's idea. She has such a generous spirit, always looking to give back to the community and focusing on how she can help others, no matter what she has going on in her own life.

It blows my mind that she's been so unlucky in love, given how beautiful she is inside and out. I haven't met her latest boyfriend, Ed, as they've only been dating for a few weeks, and I probably never will, just like I never met the last one. Hannah's relationships don't last for long: either she doesn't feel a "spark" with them, or she senses something about them that sends up warning signals. She says it doesn't bother her when she's single, that she's happy with her own company. But I know there's hurt lying beneath the surface. Somewhere in her history I'm certain she was damaged by some idiotic man who couldn't see or respect how precious she is.

Several coffees later, Elena interrupts our heart-to-heart with a quick phone call to kick-start our new plans for the wedding venue. I hang up, my mind positively bursting with hope and excitement, and I grin at Hannah as she heads to the bathroom before we leave for the workshop. Still smiling, I see a newsflash pop up on my phone, and open it to read a new article interviewing Nathan about the trial.

I know I'm lucky to have a man like him, and I'm reminded of this every time I chat to Hannah about her love life. But even Nathan has another side to him. He stays so calm most of the time, and I've never seen him explode. But occasionally his buried emotions rise to the surface and his veneer of control slips just a little bit. That comes across a little in this interview, where the journalist is asking if he feels guilty about defending someone like Amanda Lane after all the terrible things she's done. He's polite enough, but he gets increasingly snappy and frustrated in his responses.

I wonder what would happen if he lost the case after

pouring so much of himself into it. How would he cope with it? Would he manage to keep his emotions in check?

The thought makes me uneasy.

From what I've heard about Nathan, even if I've never seen it myself, he really doesn't like to lose.

FOURTEEN

THE WOMAN

The room is draped in shadows as she sits alone in her bed, listening to the humming of the air conditioning unit. In her hands, she cradles an album that once belonged to Brynn, filled with memories of her and Nathan. Carefully she opens its glossy pages, revealing a collection of moments frozen in time.

Her fingers trace the smooth surfaces of each photograph, and she slowly picks up a pair of scissors from her bedside table. Then she begins to trim away at each picture, meticulously cutting Brynn out of every single one, before chopping her into tiny little pieces.

The woman stands up languidly and stretches, cradling the pieces in her hands, before she makes her way to the bathroom. She drops the pieces of Brynn into the toilet bowl and flushes them away, watching them disappear into the swirling water. Some resist, clinging to the porcelain, but she continues flushing until they are all gone.

Returning to the bedroom, she sits back down on the bed, surrounded by a collage of images, which finally just have Nathan's face. She picks up one of them and whispers words she wishes he could hear: "I will never let anyone take you away from me, Nathan. Never. I've got your back."

Her mind then drifts to a distant memory of elementary school. She remembers a doll she used to love. One day during class, a vindictive little bully called Lauren Singer had snatched it from her bag and cut off its head and limbs. She has never forgotten the feeling of helplessness and anger that consumed her that day.

But she didn't shed one tear, because she knew she would pay her back. And she did.

Lauren crossed a line, and the woman delivered a swift and brutal revenge. She pushed Lauren from one of the highest slides, causing her to break her arm. Then she blamed it on another girl who stood nearby, and everyone believed her, as they always did. They didn't see the woman smile when she saw the blood dripping from Lauren's nose.

That sense of taking back power and control was addictive.

The woman still loves that feeling today.

She knows in her core that she is a good person, fiercely protective of her friends and of those she loves.

But she also has a powerful sense of justice. She is unstoppable in her determination to get what she is owed and fight her corner.

And nothing feels better than revenge.

FIFTEEN

BRYNN

The gentle hum of the dishwasher plays in the background as I meticulously scrub away the remnants of dinner, washing the dishes that could not fit inside the machine. The scent of coconut and lemongrass from the detergent mingles with the leftover aroma of pan-seared salmon and roasted vegetables, and I find myself smiling, enjoying these simple pleasures.

After the last pot finds its place in the drying rack, I head to the laundry room with a basket of clothes under my arm. When I've finished, I'm washing my hands at the deep laundry room sink and I notice that I don't have my engagement ring on. I always take it off before washing the dishes, so I assume I must have left it in its usual glass bowl by the kitchen sink. It's not like me to forget it, but I haven't been myself lately. I make my way back to the kitchen.

But the bowl is empty.

My heart sinks. I can't have lost my ring.

I just can't handle this, not now.

Debbie left after dinner to answer an urgent call upstairs. In fact, since she arrived, she has never answered a phone call in front of me, and sometimes when I walk in on her on the phone, she hangs up.

Anyway, I need to ask her about my ring. Part of me wonders if she has picked it up, for some reason. Or at least she may have seen where I put it. I don't want to accuse her of taking it and ruffle her feathers, but this ring has been in Nathan's family for generations; I simply can't lose it.

When I reach Debbie's closed door and hear that she is still talking on the phone, I'm about to walk away when the muffled sound of my own name catches my attention, and I hesitate. But the rest of the conversation is too garbled to make out. I'm tempted to press my ear to the door and eavesdrop, but I resist the urge and head back to the kitchen, where I settle at the table with a cup of chamomile tea and distract myself with my Kindle. I'll see her before long; Debbie never goes to bed without saying goodnight.

It seems like ages pass before I hear her footsteps, and I turn to face her.

Her eyes sweep the tidy kitchen, then she smiles at me. "My oh my, you have been quite busy, haven't you?" she says breezily. "I'm sorry for not helping clear up tonight."

I squeeze my hands around the mug. "That's quite all right," I say coolly, looking her squarely in the eyes.

Debbie's smile falters. "Is everything okay, Brynn? You're looking troubled."

"Yes, I'm fine. But I was just looking for my engagement ring," I say, trying to keep my voice calm, and playing with the dangling string from the teabag. "I left it in the bowl by the sink, and it's not there anymore."

"Oh, dear, that's not good," Debbie says sympathetically. "Let's look for it together, shall we?"

I hesitate before I agree, plastering a smile onto my face. "Okay, thanks, that would be lovely."

Debbie and I search the kitchen and the laundry room, but there's no trace of the ring. While I'm looking rather desperately under the washing machine, Debbie calls me, and I head back into the corridor. She's at the bottom of the stairs with a broad grin and an outstretched hand.

"Found it! It was in one of the kitchen plants, the one next to the sink. You must have dropped it in there by accident."

I look down at the ring, then back up at her face. "How odd. I could have sworn I left it in a bowl by the sink. I always do."

Pressing the ring into the palm of my hand, she shrugs. "Well, accidents happen. Just be more careful in future, with such a precious piece of jewelry. Perhaps you have a better place you could put it when you take it off? A safe, perhaps, or a locked cupboard?"

I'm about to snap at her, but then I change my mind and thank her instead. I'm just relieved to have the ring back. As I slide it back onto my finger, Debbie wishes me goodnight with a squeeze on the arm and heads toward her room.

Before she reaches her door, my curiosity gets the better of me. "How did your phone call go? Is everything okay? It seemed urgent."

She waves it off with a casual smile. "It was just my sister, Rose. Nothing important. Goodnight, Brynn." She turns away quickly.

I go back to the laundry room and sit on a cushioned stool, my mind whirling like the clothes in the machine in front of me.

A sister?

Debbie is an only child. She must have forgotten I know that about her.

Why would she lie?

SIXTEEN

14 Days Before the Wedding

The doorbell rings just as I'm finishing a call with Nathan. The trial started this morning, so I was pleasantly surprised that he took the time to call me on his lunch break.

"Babe, sorry, I have to go," I say with a sigh. "Someone's at the door. But best of luck at the trial. You've got this! I'm so proud of you. I'll call you this evening." I get up from my seat at the kitchen island, hurrying to the front door before Debbie gets there first.

We ate lunch together earlier, and afterwards she headed to her bedroom for one of her sacred afternoon naps. But I wouldn't put it past her to rush to answer the door and introduce herself. And if anyone in this little town finds out she's here, it won't be long before Nathan knows, too.

As I open the front door, I'm taken aback to see Laura from Delicakes, holding a cake covered with a glass dome. Behind her on the driveway is her assistant, who is opening the back of their van, and the two women are wearing white chef jackets with the company logo embroidered on the front pockets. They look smart and professional, and I feel embarrassed by my leggings and oversized gray sweatshirt. Cursing myself internally, I realize that I've completely forgotten about our cake tasting appointment.

The Glass Parlor worked with an in-house caterer and baker, so we lost the cake along with the venue when our booking was canceled. But thanks to Elena, Delicakes stepped in at the last minute. Laura is lovely, an old friend of Elena's, and while she is very busy and I know she doesn't really have the time for new clients right now, she said she was delighted to be able to help.

We were originally going to have a giant Black Forest cake, Nathan's favorite. But since we'll be having a beach wedding now, I decided to go for a completely different cake. I'm not sure what flavors it will be, but it will be stunning: three-tiered, with white fondant frosting and edible mother-of-pearl shells that glisten in the light. Simple but elegant, with a touch of beachy charm. I'm excited about it, and I can't really complain about having to start over with the cake: after all, it's an opportunity for another cake tasting.

"Hello, Brynn! As promised, I've brought an assortment of cakes for you to try," Laura says cheerfully. She's a small, pretty woman with a bubbly personality, fiery red hair, and eyes the color of emeralds. "It's today we agreed on, right?" she asks, a hint of concern in her voice, and I realize I've been standing there silently for an awkward few moments, lost in my thoughts.

I nod. "Yes, it is. Please come in." I open the door wider and step aside to make way for them.

Within a few minutes, Laura and her assistant have brought trolleys laden with cakes into the kitchen, and they spread them out on the island.

I'm admiring her handiwork as Laura reassures me, "I know we discussed this on the phone, but just so you know, there's not a trace of nuts in any of these."

"Great, thanks so much." I smile.

Soon Hannah and Elena arrive, and as we gather around the kitchen island, Laura talks us through her tantalizing creations. It's going to be hard to pick. Among many others, there's a classic vanilla with layers of delicate buttercream, a rich chocolate ganache cake, and a delicate strawberry shortcake adorned with fresh berries.

Elena is in her element, engaging in animated discussions with Laura, and Hannah, who has a sweet tooth, is practically drooling. In the bright, positive company of these women, I'm distracted from my frustration at how forgetful I've been lately, and my ever-increasing anxiety that something is about to go badly wrong.

After the workshop at the hospice that Hannah and I ran a few days ago, we went out for dinner with Elena and, despite my best instincts, I finally told them about finding the veil, hoping that the shock would be softened after they'd had a few drinks. Elena, ever practical, immediately got on with ordering me a new veil, but both she and Hannah were even more worried than I'd thought they'd be. They tried to push me again to go to the police, and I talked them down eventually, but only by telling a little lie. I said I'd been sleepwalking lately with the stress of the wedding, and that I hadn't told them because I didn't want them to worry, but the obvious explanation is that I must have buried the veil myself.

So, it's a relief to see that my friends are just enjoying the cake tasting now, and none of us have mentioned the veil. I really just want to focus on the positives and escape all the worry for a little while.

I know I can't hide from reality forever, but the truth is that I've lived through so much pain in my life. So, whenever the opportunity for a wave of joy presents itself, I want to ride it and savor every moment. The thought of anything corrupting my unfolding dreams is just too unbearable for me to accept.

Hannah pours us all some champagne to accompany the cake, and my heart feels weightless and warm as I appreciate it all: the peals of laughter from my friends, the delicious food spread out in front of us, the safe walls around me. *It's all going to be okay*, I tell myself.

But just as we're about to dig in, Debbie walks in and announces herself. She's wearing a pale flowy dress that reaches her ankles, and her silver hair is pulled into a neat bun, her scarlet lipstick thickly applied as usual.

"Why, hello, everyone."

Go figure. If I hadn't forgotten about the cake tasting, I'd have asked Debbie to go out for a walk, making it clear that she wasn't invited.

We're still getting on well enough on the surface, all things considered. But if I'm honest I've been feeling increasingly uncomfortable around her, particularly after finding the veil buried in the sand. I don't know for sure that it was her, but I just can't think of who else it would be.

And then there was that strange incident with my missing ring, and her lie about her sister. I also keep finding her in odd locations around the house. And maybe it's just my paranoia, but I have an unsettling feeling of being constantly under observation, with her judgmental, calculating eyes following me.

I still haven't told Elena and Hannah that Debbie's here. Until now, I've found all kinds of excuses to keep them from coming to the house since she arrived, because I really don't want Debbie to have the opportunity to talk with them, given what she knows about me.

I'm still entertaining the hope that I can persuade her to leave before the wedding, and my back-up plan was to wait until the very last minute to introduce her to Hannah and Elena, asking them to keep her away from Nathan so we can avoid drama on our wedding day. There are enough people coming that it might just work.

But now the cat's out of the bag. I've been careless and forgetful, and I really can't afford to be. It's not like me at all; I'm normally meticulous with my planning and forward-thinking. Sam would tell me to pull myself together, and I know I need to get a grip on this situation urgently.

I think fast and try to keep my tone casual. "Oh, hi Debbie, I thought you were asleep. This is Elena, our wedding planner, and Hannah, my maid of honor. Elena, Hannah, this is Debbie."

Elena and Hannah offer polite greetings, but I can sense their curiosity, and Hannah frowns slightly as she nods at Debbie.

To my relief, Debbie excuses herself to walk over to the fridge on the other side of the kitchen and pours some iced tea from a jug, having politely declined Elena's offer of a glass of champagne. I exhale a breath I didn't realize I was holding.

As I turn back to Elena and Hannah, I notice that Hannah is looking at me with a quizzical expression.

"Who is Debbie?" she asks in a hushed tone, pushing a stray chestnut curl of hair behind her ear.

I hesitate. "She's... Nathan's mother."

Before I can say more, Debbie returns. "Well, now, doesn't this look like a wonderful spread. You and Nathan must have spent so much on all of this, Brynn! You are a lucky girl, aren't you?"

Hannah looks at me, and she must see the annoyance on my face because her eyes narrow, and she studies Debbie for a moment before saying, "So, Debbie, will you be joining us? It's nice to meet you; I didn't know you were visiting."

Debbie clears her throat, her gaze flicking toward mine for the briefest moment. "Yes, well, I'm staying with Brynn for a little while. She needs all the help she can get with this wedding."

Elena and Hannah exchange glances, clearly surprised, and

I'm still flustered, not sure what my next move should be. Sensing my discomfort, Elena switches on an upbeat playlist and insists we get started.

With Hannah topping up our fizzing glasses and our friendly chatter beginning to flow once more, I start to relax a little as we sample slice after slice, and it's all delicious. Even Debbie compliments Laura on her baking skills.

But while Debbie and Laura are discussing the benefits of different kinds of butter, Hannah leans in closer to me, and whispers, "I thought Nathan's mother wasn't coming to the wedding?"

"Yes," Elena whispers, "you told me to remove her from—"

Before she can finish, the latest cheesy song ends on the playlist and our conversation halts in the pause before the next one begins. A few minutes later, I motion for Hannah to follow me into the living room.

"Look, Hannah, please don't mention to Nathan that Debbie is here," I say urgently. "He's dealing with so much right now, and his mother is the last thing he needs. We didn't invite her. And I don't want to burden him with their relationship troubles while he needs to focus on the trial."

"Sure, okay. I'm really shocked that she's here, to be honest. I know their relationship has been dead in the ground for a long time. She was already out of the picture before Nathan and I met."

"Yeah, he doesn't talk about her very much, but I know their relationship is strained."

"Strained?" She laughs. "That's the understatement of the century. Growing up, Nathan never even kept a single photo of her around. It was almost as if she didn't exist."

"What exactly happened between the two of them when he was little?" I ask. "He told me she was a terrible mother, but he's never really gone into much detail."

"That woman walked out on him and his dad when he was

just five. She's tried to be in touch a few times over the years and I think there was a brief period recently when they saw each other. But he never forgave her for leaving them, and he always said she was toxic." She shakes her head. "So, he has no idea that she's here and she's coming to the wedding? That's going to get complicated, isn't it?"

I sigh. "I know, but I don't want to worry him. The Amanda Lane trial could be such a career-changing opportunity for him, and I don't want anything distracting him from it."

"True, but won't he find out at the ceremony? And then it'll be even worse for him because he won't have had time to prepare himself emotionally." Hannah leans her back against the living room door, her eyes full of worry.

"Well, I was thinking that maybe you and Elena can help separate the two of them to prevent any potential drama."

Hannah nods slowly. "I got you. Consider it done. But what about you? Are you okay with Debbie being here?"

I shrug. "I'm fine. She's only here for a couple of weeks. I can handle it."

Hannah reaches out to squeeze my hand, and her next words are so characteristic of her perceptiveness and empathy, they almost make me cry. "Honey, I'm so sorry you lost your own mother at such a young age. I can't even imagine how it must feel to be getting married and not having her there. And now you have to handle this stressful situation with Nathan's mother, too, while he's busy with his trial."

I swallow hard, trying to keep my emotions in check. "Yeah. It's tough, but I know my mother will be with me in spirit."

"She definitely will." Hannah flashes me a bright smile. "Now we better get back to those cakes before the others start wondering where we went. Don't worry, I won't breathe a word to Nathan. And I'll explain the plan to Elena after the tasting."

I let out a deep sigh of relief, grateful as ever for her endless understanding and support. "Thank you so much, Hannah. I really appreciate it. I just want everything to go smoothly."

I'm feeling calmer now. I'll make sure Debbie doesn't have much time alone with Elena and Hannah in the lead-up to the wedding, and I know they'll do everything they can to keep her away from Nathan on the big day.

Honestly, it's a relief to have one less secret to keep from my friends.

But as I get back to the cake tasting and dig into a delicious lemon sponge, I just can't get myself to fully relax. There have been so many disturbing incidents now, and even though I'm trying to ignore them and keep going, I can't shake off the feeling that there's more to come.

Something far, far worse.

SEVENTEEN

The vanilla and lemon cake is exquisite. Each morsel dances on my tongue before leaving behind a trail of sweet and sour.

"Brynn, you really must try this chocolate ganache cake. It's to die for... absolutely sinful," Elena purrs, her voice low as she licks the frosting from her lips.

Smiling at her enthusiasm, I reach for a slice of the chocolate cake and take a bite, savoring the smooth texture as it melts in my mouth like snow on a bright winter's day.

"You're so right," I say between bites. "This is incredible."

Nathan is a chocolate fan and I know he would love this one. But my favorite so far is definitely the lemon and vanilla, and I think it matches the vibe of our beach wedding best.

I turn to Laura with a sigh. "You're really making it hard to choose. They're all so delicious."

Laura chuckles. "That's the point, my dear. A wedding should be an indulgent celebration of love with a feast for all the senses." She waves a hand around the table. "Don't forget that your cake will have several tiers and each layer can have a different flavor. You don't need to settle for one!"

Debbie allows her fork to drop into her plate, lifts a napkin to her lips and dabs her mouth delicately before saying, "Brynn, dear, can I have a quick word in private?"

"Sure, Debbie." I excuse myself and follow her out of the kitchen, already bristling. I can tell that she's about to criticize me passive-aggressively for something or other.

But when we're in the living room, she smiles sweetly and takes my hands. "Brynn, I wonder if you would allow me to bake your wedding cake. Pardon me for saying this, but those in there are absolutely full of artificial flavors and preservatives." She lets my hands go and clasps her own in front of her, her eyes pleading.

I'm quite impressed; I can't believe how convincing she was, complimenting Laura on her baking all this time. This woman really is fake, through and through. I shake my head in amazement as she continues, "That strawberry shortcake... it didn't taste like it was made with real strawberries, or proper butter. I think she uses that cheap margarine to cut costs, no matter what she says about only using quality ingredients. I'm sorry, but I just think you and Nathan should have the best."

"I understand your concern, Debbie," I say patiently. "But Laura is a professional and has been in the business for years. She knows what she's doing. And I can assure you everything is homemade and organic."

"But she's a businesswoman, darling." Debbie plucks a piece of lint from my dress. "She'll always tell you what you want to hear to make a sale. And you're not exactly a baker or very gifted in the kitchen, are you? You wouldn't notice the poor quality of her cakes like I can. But if you tasted what I can rustle up with a bit of real butter and sugar, you'd immediately know what real baking should be like. And that's homemade with love and care put into every ingredient. Also, I'm sure she's charging you a king's ransom, and Nathan works so hard for that money. I would do it for free, of course. I'll just need access to your garage, I can set up a space to work on the sugar flowers in there, and I can keep all the little decorations hidden away as a lovely surprise for you on the big day."

I cross my arms. "Like I said, everything in Laura's cakes is fresh and carefully sourced. She's a great pastry chef. She takes pride in her craft and would never compromise on the quality of her ingredients."

Debbie nods, but her expression remains skeptical. "I know you believe that, and I'm sure she's a very nice woman. But there's just something about homemade cakes that can't be matched. It's never the same when you get it from a bakery, even a professional one."

I sigh, my exasperation finally rising to the surface. "Look, Debbie, I really need to get back to my guests. I appreciate your concern, but I have made my decision and I trust Laura."

"Very well, dear. I trust that you know what's best for your wedding. I just hope nothing goes wrong." She gives me a small smile before turning her back on me and heading to the kitchen.

We're soon finished, and Debbie offers to make us all some coffee. As she starts bustling around and grinding coffee beans, Elena leans over to me and places a hand on my arm.

"Is everything all right?"

"Yes," I whisper. "All fine."

As we drink the coffee, we finalize the details for the wedding cake. I'm going for multiple flavors as Laura suggested, and I think Nathan will be pleased with everything I've chosen.

I'm just pouring myself another steaming mug when I notice that Hannah doesn't look well at all. Her face has gone pale, and she has a hand on her stomach, her face twisted uncomfortably.

"I need to... excuse me." She stumbles out of the room, and I follow her into the hallway where she hunches over, clutching her belly.

"Hey, are you okay?" I place a hand on her back.

"No," she croaks. "I think I'm going to be sick."

"Okay, it's okay. Let's get you to the bathroom."

The moment we enter, she rushes to the toilet and starts vomiting.

I rub her back gently, trying to offer her some words of reassurance, but I'm filled with worry.

Her sickness eventually subsides, and I help her to her feet, her slender frame trembling and weak.

"Do you want me to call a doctor?"

"N-no." She rinses out her mouth and shakes her head. "That's not necessary. It's probably just something I ate yesterday. Look, I know we were going to hang out this evening, but I think I should head home and rest for a bit."

"Of course," I say, trying not to convey how concerned I am. Hannah never gets sick. "I'll drive you home in your car and take a cab back."

She's about to protest, but I hold up a hand. "I won't take no for an answer. Come on, then. Let's go."

She grips my arm tightly as we make our way back to the kitchen to grab her things.

"Is everything all right?" asks Debbie, rising from her seat.

"I'm just driving Hannah home; she's not feeling so good," I say quickly. "I'm sorry to cut this short, Laura, but we need to head out. Elena can finalize the last details with you. Thank you so much for everything you've done. I really can't wait for the cake."

Laura nods understandingly. "My pleasure. I hope your fiancé likes your choices too, but just let me know if you want any changes. Otherwise, I'll begin working on it."

"Feel better, Hannah," Elena calls as we step out of the house.

Hannah lives in a two-bedroom townhouse that's only twenty minutes away. Her floristry business in Tallahassee took a major hit after an article mentioned that she had been Amanda Lane's florist. So, she moved back to Stoneview to live in the house she grew up in. She's lucky it was left for her, but money is still tight, so she rents out the other bedroom to a Spanish exchange student for extra cash.

When we pull up outside the house in her car, I turn to her. "Do you want me to come up with you or are you okay on your own?"

She hesitates before shaking her head. "I think I'll be okay. Thank you for driving me home, though. I really appreciate it."

"All right. But if you need anything, please just call me."

"I will," she promises, giving me a fragile smile. "Don't worry about me though, I'm sure I'll be fine after a bit of sleep."

I give her a hug and watch her walk slowly up to her front steps.

As I head back home in a taxi, I get a call from Laura. She needs to leave soon, and she's wondering if I have a preference about the wedding cake toppers, or if I'm happy to go with the ones Elena has suggested. Thinking about figurines is the last thing I want to do right now, so I ask her to just go with Elena's recommendation.

"How's Hannah feeling?" she asks.

"She's a little better, thank you."

There's a pause before she continues. "I hope you don't think she got food poisoning from my cakes." Her voice is tinged with worry.

I really don't want to believe that, and I think it's unlikely given that we all sampled the same things. But if I'm honest, the timing of it does make me a little concerned. "I don't know, Laura," I say hesitantly. "It could be anything."

There's a moment of silence before she speaks again. "I can assure you that I take great care in my baking. I use only the freshest ingredients and I follow all the safety guidelines to the letter. Are you aware of any allergies that Hannah has?"

I shake my head. "No, she doesn't have any. That's just me."

"Well, I'm glad she's going to be okay. And Brynn, I promise you that for your big day, I'll double-check all the ingredients and take extra precautions, just to be safe."

I thank her and assure her that I'm not blaming her for anything.

But as the day draws on, my anxiety grows.

What if the cakes were contaminated? If they were, why was it only Hannah who got sick? I really do trust Laura, and it's so unlikely a reputable professional like her would prepare food in an unsafe way. Hannah must have an allergy she doesn't know about.

Or, what if someone tampered with her slice of the cake on purpose?

At this point, most people would cancel the wedding. But I can't bear the thought of doing that.

I'm determined not to let anyone destroy my happiness.

But how can I keep myself, and my guests, safe?

EIGHTEEN

13 Days Before the Wedding

The next morning over breakfast, Debbie and I are surrounded by unspoken questions and the atmosphere is strained.

Debbie finally clears her throat and lowers her cup of coffee to the table. "How is your friend? Do you know what happened to her?"

I clear my throat. "Actually, we think Hannah got food poisoning," I admit reluctantly. "But she's going to be okay."

"Oh dear." Debbie brings a hand to her mouth, feigning dismay as her blue eyes grow wide. "That's terrible news. And I suppose you suspect it was one of the cakes she ate yesterday?"

"Yes, maybe. But none of the rest of us got sick, so it's all very strange. Laura's cakes are safe, though. She only has amazing reviews and I know she's a stickler for hygiene. Perhaps it was a reaction to an ingredient, but then Hannah doesn't have any allergies that she knows about."

Debbie straightens her back. "Then what are you saying? That someone else could have tampered with Hannah's slices of cake? But why?"

I shrug and lift my rose-colored mug to my lips. "That's exactly what I'm trying to figure out." My eyes lock onto hers. "Debbie, there's something I need to ask you. Did you have anything to do with what happened to Hannah?"

"What? My goodness Brynn, how could you even think that of me?"

"I don't *want* to think it. But—"

"Certainly not." Her eyes well up with tears. "Brynn, I may have been outspoken with my opinions about the wedding cake, but I would never wish harm upon anyone, and certainly not you or your friends. I'm a good person."

I want to believe her. But I can't help but remember how convincing she was when she praised Laura's baking to her face, and then how she criticized it so cruelly to me.

If she did this, then I think I've underestimated her.

But if she didn't, someone else did.

And whoever it was, I'm increasingly terrified about what they might do next.

Later that morning, I drive to Hannah's place, and as soon as she opens the door, I wrap her in a tight hug, relieved to see her looking better. Her skin is still a little pale, but her eyes shine with their usual spark.

I pull away to take a good look at her. "How are you feeling?"

"I'm much better, thanks." She smiles weakly, and beckons me inside. It's a narrow hallway, but it opens up on the left into a beautiful living room with large windows that allow a lot of light to flood in. Since she moved in, she has filled the room with houseplants and rustic wooden features and painted the walls in complementary shades of damask rose and sage green. The effect is immediately soothing.

We settle on the couch, and she pours me some coffee from a French press but doesn't take any for herself.

"I'm a little suspicious of everything I put into my mouth now. It'll be just water and plain food for me for a few days, I think."

"Yeah, that's probably wise. Listen, Hannah... I'm worried. I know it might just be a stomach bug or an allergy you didn't know about, but part of me is worried that you got food poisoning. And since none of the rest of us did, and I know Laura has the highest standards... Well, this sounds crazy, but I'm worried somebody tampered with the slice of cake you ate."

Hannah's eyes widen in shock as she stares at me. "What? Why?"

I run my fingers through my hair and let out a sigh. "I don't know. Maybe I'm just being paranoid. But you're my maid of honor, and my best friend, and I feel terrible thinking that somebody made you sick because they're trying to get at me. I just want you to be careful. A few strange things have been happening, as you know, and I'm sure it's nothing serious but it wouldn't hurt for us all to keep an eye out, I think."

Hannah narrows her eyes. "Brynn, those wedding cake toppers, and that note you received... Did you find out who sent them to you?"

"No, I didn't," I sigh.

"Look, I know you said you might have buried your veil while sleepwalking. But if there's a chance it wasn't you, that's just very creepy. There's something really strange going on. I'm sorry, I know you don't want anything to spoil your big day, but I think we need to take this seriously."

Silence falls between us, and I lean back on the couch and close my eyes, trying to gather my thoughts.

"Hon, can you think of anyone you know who might want to ruin your wedding?" Hannah continues, gently.

"No. No, I can't. I just need it to stop. It's all so frustrating."

I decide to change the subject, feeling my body tense up. "Look, just for today, let's focus on your rest and recovery. We can watch some scary movies and take our minds off everything. I'll make you some nourishing noodle soup for dinner if you think you can stomach it."

We spend a restful day together, and when I leave, I'm reassured that Hannah really is on the mend. By the time I arrive at home the sun is setting, and I've been inside all day so I kick off my shoes and head onto the beach via the living room porch for a walk. The sand is still warm under my feet as I stroll along the shoreline, the sound of the waves soothing my mind.

Seeking some familiar reassurance and strength even from afar, I dial Sam's number.

"Sorry, I know you're busy... it's just... I need someone to talk to."

"Brynn, what's wrong? Is everything all right?"

I talk about Hannah's illness, and my growing certainty that someone is trying to sabotage the wedding.

"Did you tell Nathan about this?" Sam asks.

I hesitate. "No, I haven't told him yet. And he still doesn't know that Debbie is staying with me. I don't want him to worry."

There's a beat of silence on the line before Sam speaks again. "Good, that makes sense. But Brynn, you need to be careful. That woman is dangerous. Just promise me you'll take care of yourself and that you'll keep an eye out."

"I will," I reply, sounding more confident than I feel. "Anyway, how about you? Are you coping okay?"

"Yes, I'm okay. It's still very hot and I'm tired, but it's nothing I can't handle. Look, I need to go. Expect a call from me tomorrow."

We end the call, and I return to the house, feeling as if I'm carrying a heavy weight on my shoulders.

When I go back inside, I notice that the door to Debbie's

bedroom is slightly open, with the sound of running water coming from the adjacent bathroom. Almost as if my feet have taken on a life of their own, I enter as quietly as I can, and I begin to open drawers and cupboards, searching through her belongings.

Aside from clothing, yarns, and crochet needles, a dog-eared World War II novel, a stack of old newspapers and magazines, several crossword puzzle books, and bottles of medication with labels I don't recognize, there's nothing that stands out. But then I unzip her pink suitcase and tucked away in the bottom, I find a leather-bound journal.

I'm about to open it when I hear the sound of the shower getting turned off. My heart racing, I shove the journal back inside. But before I can zip the suitcase shut, I notice a small crystal glinting in one corner. I quickly tuck it into my pocket before running out of the room.

Shortly afterwards, a loud knock on my bedroom door makes me jump, and I open it to find Debbie standing there wrapped in a terrycloth bathrobe, her gray hair in two braids, her face looking pale and drawn without her usual layer of makeup. She's holding my house keys in her hand.

"You left these on my bed." Her tone is soft and friendly, but danger lurks under the words.

Reaching out, I take them from her, my cheeks burning. "Th-thank you."

She merely nods before turning away.

Feeling like a complete idiot, I watch her retreat down the hallway. What was I thinking? I should have known better than to snoop around like that. And then forgetting my keys? That's not like me at all.

Sinking onto my bed, I take a moment to catch my breath. Then I reach into my pocket and pull out the crystal.

As I hold it up to the light, the colors seem to dance and shift in the lamplight, so that it looks as if it's alive.

The more I stare at it, the more my stomach twists.

This is one of the crystals from my veil.

I'm about to go and confront Debbie, anger boiling inside me. But then I think about it a bit more, and I wonder if there could be an innocent explanation. Before she arrived, I kept a lot of my wedding stuff in that room; it was like a staging area. Elena took most of it to her boutique a few weeks ago, saying this would make it easier for her to be able to keep on top of everything we still needed. But I did once try the veil on in the spare room when it first arrived, before I took it to my bedroom closet. So, it's possible the crystal could have fallen off and then Debbie found it, or got it tangled up with some of her belongings by mistake.

That means I don't know for sure it was her who buried the veil.

But if it wasn't her, then who?

I move to the bedroom window and look out at the beautiful ocean, wishing it could tell me what it saw that night my veil was buried. Who it saw.

Whoever did it, if their plan is to drive me insane before my wedding day, I'm afraid to say they're doing a pretty good job of it.

I grab a comforter and go into my ensuite bathroom, lock the door, and do something that used to bring me comfort as a kid. Something I haven't done in years.

I climb into the bathtub, curl up into a ball, and pull the cream comforter over my head, my eyes shut to the world.

If I can't see the monsters, they can't see me.

NINETEEN

THE WOMAN

The room envelopes the woman in darkness, save for the flickering glow of the television screen that casts eerie shadows on the walls. It's the middle of the night, and she's alone. The scent of her steaming mug of green tea wafts through the air.

Her attention is fixed on the drama playing out before her; a trial that has captured the nation.

Amanda Lane stands accused of the murders of her three wealthy husbands. The first was believed to have died in a mysterious car accident, the second allegedly succumbed to a heart attack, and the third drowned in their swimming pool.

The prosecution alleges that Amanda was the mastermind behind all three deaths, having married each man only for his fortune before orchestrating his untimely demise.

As she sits in the courtroom, Amanda Lane flickers between poise and uncertainty. Her wavy brown hair frames her face in an almost ethereal manner, and the faintest hint of a smile plays at the corners of her lips. Dressed in a simple yet elegant black suit, she exudes a sense of dignity. Her posture remains composed, her gaze steady even as the details of her alleged crimes are discussed.

Her hands rest on the table in front of her, but periodically she picks away at her nails. It's in those small gestures that one might catch a glimpse of the woman behind the headlines. The woman who now finds herself at the center of a courtroom drama that will shape her fate. There is an air of mystery about her, something more to her story than meets the eye.

The evidence against her is overwhelming, the public opinion decidedly against her. Yet she is being represented by none other than Nathan Howard, a hotshot lawyer who is well-known for his ability to bend the minds of jurors to his will.

The woman is watching a rerun of the opening statements.

Nathan is a mesmerizing force, just like she knew he would be. The place buzzes with an electric energy as the proceedings unfold, and rows of polished wooden benches are filled with onlookers having hushed conversations. The courtroom walls are adorned with deep mahogany panels and the ceiling soars high above, decorated with intricate molding and ornate chandeliers that radiate light over the entire room.

In the jury box, there is an array of faces, and each person is a potential agent of justice. Their expressions are a mix of curiosity and focus. Then there is the judge's bench, an elongated platform draped in deep-green fabric.

The judge, a stern-looking man with a thick bushy mustache, presides with an air of authority, his unwavering stare enforcing order in the bustling room.

The woman's attention returns to Nathan. His presence is magnetic, his sharp tailored charcoal suit exuding professionalism. His dark hair is neatly combed, and his tie is knotted with precision. He is the kind of man who understands that every detail counts.

He stands at the lectern, his hands resting casually upon it, a picture of self-assuredness.

Nathan's eyes sweep across the courtroom, acknowledging

those who have come to witness the proceedings. As he speaks, his deep voice has everyone captivated.

When he starts walking around the room, his movements are deliberate, and his gestures measured. Leaning in to emphasize a point, his eyes lock onto individual members of the jury, inviting them into his narrative.

He is not just an attorney, thinks the woman; he is a storyteller with the power to weave a tale of doubt and possibility. And he has certainly mastered the game of crafting an alternative reality for those willing to listen.

Everything Nathan says and does is calculated to pack a punch and make an impact. The woman watches all his televised cases, and he shines in every single one of them. He not only has a way with words; he has style and panache.

"Ladies and gentlemen of the jury," he says, his voice like velvet, "I stand before you, not to deny the tragedy of these untimely deaths, but to remind you that the courtroom is where truth must prevail, and that our justice system is based on the belief that everyone is innocent until proven guilty. Our duty here is not to jump to conclusions," he continues, his attention never leaving the jurors, "but to keep our minds open, and ensure that every piece of evidence is examined with unwavering scrutiny."

The woman reaches for the remote and increases the volume, her eyes glued to the screen. She finds herself entranced by his every sentence. Through the screen, she can feel his energy, his conviction, as he weaves a story that sends the jurors dancing on the edge of empathy and doubt. Murderer or not, Nathan is about to turn Amanda Lane into someone the jury and everyone else in the courtroom will root for. By the time the trial is over, the woman is sure the whole country will be on Amanda's side.

"Ladies and gentlemen, we must not let ourselves be swayed by emotion or preconceived notions. The woman that stands before you today is a grieving widow. She is a fellow human being who should be treated with openness and empathy. This woman is not the monster she's been portrayed to be. She is simply a very unfortunate person who has lived a very difficult life. She did not kill her husbands. She is the victim of the cruel hand of fate."

A prosecutor with short, cropped hair stands up from her seat. "Mr. Howard, the evidence against the defendant is substantial. All three husbands died under mysterious circumstances, with the defendant as the sole beneficiary of their life insurance policies."

Nathan's response is steady and determined. "You may think you have a motive, but you have no evidence. There is simply no real evidence whatsoever to connect my client to these deaths. Because she didn't do it, and the media's persecution of her is nothing short of a witch hunt. I believe in our justice system: innocent until proven guilty. *Proven.* How can someone be proven guilty when there is no evidence of their guilt? Jurors, whatever you may think of her, if you have even a shadow of doubt that Amanda may be innocent, it's your duty to exonerate her."

Pride swells within the woman as she watches Nathan's strong, confident demeanor. He's a hero, someone who is not afraid to fight for the underdog. Her attention goes back to Amanda, who, like the rest of the room, seems to be entranced by Nathan's words.

When a diaper commercial comes on, followed by one about cat food, the woman switches off the TV and flicks on a soft night light, allowing it to bathe the room. She's sure that over the next few days, most news channels will be filled with coverage of Amanda's trial, and she will be watching diligently.

She retrieves a stack of newspapers, all chronicling every piece of news relating to the trial. Her fingers trace the headlines, and then armed with a pair of scissors, she carefully cuts out images of Nathan. Then she brings out an empty album, along with all the supplies she needs to create a scrapbook dedicated solely to him. Pasting her collection of pictures and articles onto the pages, her lips curl into a smile. When she's done, she tucks the album into her bedside drawer.

As she curls up in bed, exhaustion finally overtakes her. But she feels calm and hopeful too, because today she has been reminded that no matter how much darkness there is in the world, there are people who stand up for truth and justice with steadfast determination. She is proud to know that Nathan is one of them.

As her eyes close and she falls to sleep, her mind conjures up another image.

The face of the woman who is keeping her from Nathan.

Brynn.

Nathan deserves so much better.

And he will get it.

TWENTY

BRYNN

12 Days Before the Wedding

It's a little after eight in the morning when I make a quick stop at Artful Blooms. Hannah recommended them to me for the bouquets and boutonnieres, because while she's handling the rest of the flowers herself, with all her maid of honor duties as well, she will have her work cut out.

Artful Blooms make stunning arrangements; their bouquets are beautifully put together from wrapped wire, silk, dried flowers, crystals, and various unusual materials. The owner, Marianne, a tall blonde with a tinkling laugh, delicate features, and a whimsical sense of style, was more than happy to work with Hannah to make sure everything matches. Today is just a quick chat to go over any last-minute changes or additions we want to make to suit the new venue.

"To match the beach vibe you're now going for, the wire is going to be wrapped with pearls and tiny seashells, and I've used pastel-colored silk flowers to make it look like a mermaid's treasure trove." Marianne points to the small handle. "As you can see, the handle is made of crushed seashells and coral pieces, to give it a unique texture. And I've woven copper wire throughout the bouquet for a playful touch and to give it a more organic look. It'll match Hannah's arrangements of white roses. What do you think?"

I shake my head in awe, beaming. "This is wonderful, Marianne. I absolutely love it. I can't thank you enough for all your hard work. Sorry again about all the last-minute changes."

She waves off my apology with a smile. "Please don't worry about it. It's all part of the job. I'm just glad we could make everything work out for you." She pauses. "For the boutonnieres, I will be using some of the material your bouquet is made of, but I'll also be incorporating some sea glass and driftwood to give it a more masculine touch."

I nod in agreement. "That sounds lovely. You really have an eye for detail."

"Oh, thank you. As we agreed, I'll be delivering these to the venue at one p.m. on the day of your wedding. That should give us plenty of time to make any last-minute adjustments."

"Great," I say, getting to my feet. "I'll see you then."

When I step out of the shop, I'm hit with a sudden gust of wind that causes my hair to whip around my face, and I reach up to tie it back with the band I keep around my wrist.

Suddenly I feel absolutely certain that someone is watching me.

I scan the space around me, but there is no one suspicious, and I try to pull myself together as I head to my car and make my way to the jewelry store.

Inside, an elderly man in a pristine suit hands me the cream boxes containing the wedding rings. I open one and smile as the ring gleams under the bright lights. The diamonds catch the light and throw it back in a dazzling display.

"They have been polished and adjusted according to your specifications."

"Thank you so much." I snap the box closed.

With the rings safely stowed away in my purse, I step out again and sit down for a few minutes in a nearby café, nursing a cappuccino and enjoying a croissant stuffed with thick-cut ham and mozzarella. It's a mild day for June, and I wish I'd worn more layers as I keep shivering. I'm sure it's just the cooler weather.

By the time I finish my comfort food and drink and head to a vintage wedding dress boutique to buy a new veil, I feel more at peace than I have done in a few days.

Elena had ordered me another veil, the same one I had before, but I asked her to cancel the order. I want something totally different, so it doesn't remind me of what happened with the first.

Inside the boutique, the walls are adorned with delicate lace dresses from different eras, and the air smells of lavender and old books. A woman greets me with a warm smile. She has silver hair that's styled in soft waves and wears a sea-shell necklace that sits on her collarbone. She kind of reminds me of Elena.

"How can I assist you today?" she asks in a relaxed, gentle voice.

"I'm looking for a new veil for my wedding," I reply, returning her smile.

"Of course. Well, we have a lovely selection here. Is there a particular style you're interested in?"

"Something simple and elegant. No crystals or anything like that." My eyes scan the racks of veils in front of me.

The woman nods and guides me to a corner of the store where a few veils hang from hooks on the wall. I take my time examining each one, and in the end, I go for a classic fingertip veil made of delicate tulle with a subtle lace trim.

As I leave, the door chime tinkling behind me, the sun is high up in the sky and the rays of light shine down on me, welcome heat seeping into my skin. Clutching the bag containing my new veil, I feel like I'm sending a message to whoever took my old one. I'm showing them that they haven't won, and they won't win. I don't give up.

Driving away, I sing along to an empowering Spotify playlist, trying to absorb as much confidence and inner strength as I can.

But when I glance in the rearview mirror, a prickling sensation takes hold of me again.

My eyes scan the cars trailing behind, my heart hammering. My instinct that someone is there, that I'm in imminent danger, is really strong now, urging me to pay attention. I try to dismiss it as paranoia. But I'm still so distracted that I narrowly avoid a collision.

I chastise myself for letting my imagination run wild.

No one is following me. It's just nerves. And even if there is someone out there? Let them give me their best shot. I can take care of myself.

My last stop is the drugstore to get myself some cold medication. Last night, my nose felt so congested that I couldn't breathe properly, so I think I might have a cold coming on. It should be over before the wedding, but I'm going to try to nip it in the bud anyway. So, I grab a nasal spray and some vitamins before heading to the checkout counter.

When I get back home, Debbie isn't there to eat lunch with me; she left a note to say that she's meeting friends. I had no idea she had any friends in town, but I'm glad I have my house to myself.

I spend the afternoon resting, even getting out my sketchbook to do some drawing, which I haven't done in ages. And when Debbie is still not back by the evening, I order in Chinese food, which I enjoy on the porch while on a video call with Nathan.

"Hey, future husband," I say, grinning at him.

"Hey, beautiful. Miss me?"

I chuckle, leaning back in my seat to get more comfortable. "Always."

Our eyes lock across the screens, and in that moment, it's as if we're together, the miles between us fading into insignificance.

"How's your day been?" Nathan asks.

His smile widens as he listens to me recount my day, and I can sense his happiness and excitement for our wedding.

"And how about you? How was it in court today?"

His expression hardens, and he lifts a glass of red wine to his lips. "Unfortunately, it's not going so well. The prosecution has found some new evidence that's making things complicated."

"I'm so sorry you're stressed, babe. I wish I could be there for you."

He manages a small smile. "I know you're here with me in spirit."

We continue to talk, our conversation flowing effortlessly. It's as if the laptop screens disappear and we're in the same place.

As the sky darkens and the conversation draws to a close, Nathan's voice grows softer, more intimate. "I wish I could hold you right now, Brynn. I miss you so much."

I blow him a kiss. "I miss you, too."

He clears his throat, a hint of vulnerability in his eyes. "You know, even on the toughest days, it's thinking about you that gets me through."

"I'm glad I can help even from here." I dip my head to one side and give him one of my brightest smiles. "You're so strong, Nathan, and so talented. You'll get through this. I know you will."

"Thank you, my love."

Eventually we say our goodbyes and end the call, and I look over at the sky, which is dotted liberally with stars. The porch feels like a sanctuary, and I remain sitting there for a while longer as I watch the waves and the evening breeze doing their nightly dance.

I only head to bed after Debbie arrives home. She looks a little flustered as she says goodnight briefly before going to her room.

Even though I want to rest, I find myself unable to sleep. So, I send Nathan a text to see if he can chat again. After a few minutes he calls back and we talk about his case, with me offering him as much support as I can.

When I hear a sound at my door, I end the call and open it just in time to see Debbie rushing away down the corridor like a naughty child, disappearing toward the stairs.

I feel a familiar surge of anger. What right does the woman have to listen in on my private conversation? I haven't snooped on hers, no matter how suspiciously she's been acting, even after her lie about her sister.

In fact, I've been giving her a wide berth, avoiding confronting her because of the power she has over me.

But she's not the only one who holds the power.

Maybe it's time to fight back.

TWENTY-ONE

THE WOMAN

The trees lining the streets of Stoneview sway gently as the woman drives through them, their leaves a vibrant green canopy. Flowerbeds are bursting with life, showcasing a riot of colors while bees and butterflies flit from bloom to bloom.

In the distance, the town's gazebo is adorned with twining vines of ivy and bunting that dance in the breeze, and a local musician is strumming on a guitar.

She pulls up in the town square, and watches as elderly couples stroll hand in hand, while children run around playing games.

Coffee shops release the enticing aroma of freshly brewed coffee, and Stoneview's highly popular bakery has a queue of customers waiting outside it. She would treat herself to a pastry and a coffee herself, but she doesn't have much time before Brynn arrives.

Then she sees her, driving in her fancy white Porsche. Brynn, who threatens to steal Nathan away.

The woman follows behind and observes as Brynn navigates a maze of errands, including a stop at a jewelry store. It infuriates her that she still hasn't got the message. Clearly, she's still intent on going ahead with the wedding.

Later that night, the woman rifles through her carefully assembled collection of mementos, and she pauses over a baby photo of Nathan. His chubby cheeks and toothless grin are adorable. He looks so innocent and pure. She does not know how she will be able to bear standing in the audience, watching Brynn marrying him.

It's time to start thinking about the next stage in her plan.

Brynn has only herself to blame.

TWENTY-TWO

BRYNN

10 Days Before the Wedding

Nathan calls me at 7 a.m., his voice warm, but tinged with urgency.

"Babe, I hope I didn't wake you. I need you to do me a favor."

I stifle a yawn, exhausted after a night of tossing and turning as my sore throat kept me awake. "No, don't worry. I was already awake. Whatever favor you need, your wish is my command."

"I need some paperwork from my study. It's research that could help with the trial. It's in the box labelled case 121. Can you find it for me?"

"Of course. Is it something that might prove Amanda's innocence?" I ask curiously.

"Perhaps. As you know, as a defense lawyer I normally don't allow myself to have an opinion on the guilt or innocence of my clients. But if I'm being completely honest, as time goes by, I'm starting to lean toward Amanda's innocence. Let's just say there are some inconsistencies in the prosecution's case. And I think there's more going on here, things nobody has even thought about." He clears his throat.

"What do you mean?" I ask, my surprise clear in my voice.

"Well, if she really did do this, then I don't think she acted alone. Anyway, it goes without saying, but please don't mention this to anyone. Sorry to rush you, but I need you to find that paperwork this morning if you can."

I assure him I'll send it over immediately, and then I head straight to the study. I haven't been in there since Nathan left for the trial, and the moment I enter, the faint scent of cigars drifts into my nose, reminding me of his occasional indulgence.

The walls are the color of sand and are minimally decorated with a few framed certificates. A large wooden L-shaped desk sits in the center of the room, with a leather swivel chair behind it. Shelves all along one wall are filled with law books and legal documents, and there are boxes lined up neatly against the opposite wall. I cross the deep burgundy carpet and kneel down beside them.

Nathan is such a neat freak that all the labels face outwards, and everything is in order, so it's not hard to find the one I'm looking for.

There are two other boxes on top of it, and I move them aside before opening 121. It doesn't take me long to locate the folder Nathan needs.

But as I begin to close the box again, a small leather-bound notebook draws my attention. I flip it open to find that the pages are blank, but a photo falls out from between the pages. The glossy surface catches the morning light from the study windows.

And when I see the faces of the people in the photo, I feel frozen to the spot, kneeling like I'm facing my own executioner.

It's a group photo taken in what looks like a backyard. There are five people in it, three men and two women. They're all laughing, caught in the middle of some joke or funny anecdote.

And there are two I recognize. Nathan and Elena. Nathan has one arm around Elena's waist and the other is holding up a champagne glass. Elena is holding a glass as well, her fingers clutching the stem.

The ring on her finger holds my eyes captive.

My heart is thudding in my ears and my throat feels like ashes. It's my engagement ring. The ring that Nathan said had belonged to his grandmother, who, before her death, had gifted it to him to give to his future wife. It's right there, nestled on Elena's finger. And... what's Nathan's arm doing around her waist?

The room around me blurs and the photograph slips from my trembling fingers. I rise unsteadily to my feet and take a step back as a rising storm of emotions threatens to engulf me. I turn away from the photograph and collapse into a nearby chair.

It takes me some time before I can gather myself enough to dial Nathan's number. The seconds stretch painfully as I wait for him to pick up, fury and disbelief coursing through me.

He doesn't answer, and I'm left to navigate my whirlwind of emotions alone.

A long hour passes before my phone buzzes, his name flashing on the screen.

"Nathan," I say in a broken whisper.

"Brynn," he replies, his voice a mixture of urgency and weariness, "I'm in the middle of another court session. Oh, and I found a digital copy of those papers I asked you for. No need to send them over anymore." He exchanges a few hushed words with someone on his end, then he gets back to me. "Is everything okay?"

The tears pricking at my eyes fall freely down my cheeks as I reply, my voice trembling. "No, Nathan, everything is not okay."

"Baby, what's wrong?"

I swallow the lump in my throat. I can't believe this is happening. It's as if the whole world is spiraling away from its orbit around the sun, the universe out of control. "I found a photo. A photo of you and Elena. I had no idea you were a couple."

A beat of silence follows, and then he speaks slowly. "It's... It's not what you think."

"To be honest, Nathan, I'm not sure what I think right now. So, go ahead and enlighten me. I need the truth." I sigh and cover my aching forehead with my palm.

He's quiet for a long time, then he clears his throat. "Yes, Elena and I used to date. But it was a short relationship, nothing serious."

His words hit me like a tidal wave, leaving me gasping for breath. Until now, there was a sliver of hope in my mind, that he might have an explanation for me, something that would make all of this go away. "That's a lie," I gasp. "You... you were engaged to her, Nathan. You were engaged to Elena, our wedding planner. I saw the ring on her finger, the same ring you gave me."

He exhales heavily. "It was a long time ago, Brynn. Before I met you."

"I don't care how long ago it was. Why didn't you say anything when I told you I was hiring her?"

"I... I'm sorry." His voice is tinged with regret. "I just wanted you to have the wedding of your dreams, and Elena is the best wedding planner in town. I know she's trustworthy and dedicated."

"But you kept this from me. You lied. I can't believe you didn't tell me something so important."

"You're right. I'm so sorry," he murmurs again. "I've been wanting to tell you, but I was afraid you'd get upset."

The sharp feeling of betrayal cuts through me and I can't

stop my tears from falling. "Did Hannah know? I mean, the three of you have been friends for years. So did she know you and Elena were together?"

When he doesn't respond, I shut my eyes so tightly my eyeballs start to ache.

"So, you *all* lied to me?" My voice comes out in a choke, and I jam my fingernails into my palms. "I can't. I can't do this right now. I need time to process this... to think."

He blows out a breath. "Yeah, okay, I understand. Can we talk later, please? I promise I'll explain everything, okay? I love you so much."

For the first time ever, I don't say it back, and after the call I cry for what feels like hours. But then I pull myself together. I take a cold shower and paint makeup over my distraught face.

I'm not going to give up.

With trembling hands, I dial Elena's number and ask to meet her for a drink.

An hour later, I walk into Honeywood and spot her sitting at the back in a cozy armchair. When she sees me, she waves and smiles brightly.

"Hey, Brynn," she says as I take a seat next to her. She's wearing a flowy floral dress in the color of pale lavender, complemented by a camel wide-brimmed hat over her short black hair. Around her neck dangles a delicate silver necklace with a small opal pendant that catches the light as she moves.

"Elena," I reply in a clipped voice, "there's something I need to talk to you about."

In an effort to calm my nerves, I tightly grasp my wrist, feeling the cool silver tennis bracelet that Sam gifted me on my last birthday.

Elena's smile falters. "Sure. Is everything okay?"

"No. Not really." I clasp my hands on my lap and notice a

stain on my jeans. Compared to Elena, I must look like an absolute mess, my hair unbrushed and knotted, my eyes puffy and my clothes hurriedly thrown on without a care. "Earlier this morning, I found a photo of you and Nathan."

Her expression remains neutral, but I catch a flicker of panic in her eyes. "Brynn, it's not what you think."

"What is it then? Please don't lie to me, Elena. Nathan already told me about your history, your past relationship. I called him, and he owned up to it all."

Elena picks up the glass of water and takes a sip, her eyes downcast. "Okay, yes, Nathan and I used to be together. But that was a long time ago."

"How long ago?" I demand, my voice rising.

"Six years," she says quietly.

I let out a bitter laugh. "And you never thought to mention this to me?"

She reaches out as if wanting to touch my hand, but her hand hovers in the air before she pulls it back. "I didn't want to complicate things. Nathan and I are just friends now... And anyway, I honestly did not speak to him for ages, I only got back in touch with him because Amanda Lane, who as you know was my client for her weddings, needed a lawyer. I really did think she was innocent back then, so I asked Nathan to do what he could for her, and we chatted a few times since then. That's it."

I'm surprised to hear Elena mention Amanda Lane. I knew she was the wedding planner for all of Amanda's three weddings, but it's not something she's ever wanted to talk about. She just said it's too painful to think that she'd been in any way involved in Amanda's murderous plans, and that she's ashamed that she didn't see her for who she really is.

But Amanda's not the only one who has hidden her true nature. It seems I'm surrounded by people I can't trust. People I thought I knew.

Tears well in my eyes. "I don't get it. How could you keep this from me? It would have hurt less if you had just told me."

"I truly care about you, Brynn." Elena's voice is gentle. "I want the best for you and Nathan. I understand that this is a shock, but I promise you, it was just a fleeting moment in our past. You and Nathan have a long and beautiful future ahead of you. Why would I plan your wedding if I was still hung up on him?"

"I'm not an idiot, Elena. You two were engaged. This was more than just a fleeting moment. And I don't like being lied to."

With that, I rise from my seat and leave the café.

Inside my car, tears blur my vision, and my fingers shake as I type a text to Sam.

Sam is the only person I can trust. The only person who has never hidden their true nature from me.

Guess what? Nathan was engaged to our wedding planner. He lied to me.

The text is sent, a virtual cry for understanding and support.

Minutes later, my phone buzzes with a reply.

You're letting your emotions cloud your better judgement. Don't let a past relationship stand in the way of what you want. Let's talk tomorrow, okay?

I try to find reassurance and strength in Sam's words. But when I start the car and drive home, a very persuasive and unwelcome thought takes root in my mind.

What if Elena has been working to derail my perfect day from the start?

What if she's not over Nathan at all?

TWENTY-THREE

I'm stirred from my restless sleep by the persistent buzzing of my phone. My eyes are heavy from hours of crying, and my body aches with emotions I've never allowed myself to feel so intensely for a man.

The phone continues to vibrate, and I stare at Nathan's name on the screen. I'm not sure if I can cope with talking to him right now. But then the buzzing stops, and I pick up the phone, my finger hovering over the call button. I can't ignore him forever.

Holding my breath, I call him back and he picks up on the first ring.

"Brynn?" His voice is breathless.

I remain silent.

"I'm so sorry," he finally croaks. "I'm sorry we... I didn't tell you that Elena and I—"

"That you loved each other?" I interrupt, my voice full of bitterness. "That you wanted to spend the rest of your lives together? That none of you told me? That you gave her the same ring you gave me?"

I launch into a tirade, my words a torrent of pent-up emotions. I tell him about feeling betrayed, humiliated, and blindsided. Nathan tries to assure me that his heart only belongs to me, that he loves me without question. He tries hard to mend the cracks that have formed between us.

"Baby, I know I really messed up here. But I want you to be happy, and if letting Elena go as our wedding planner will make you feel better, then it's fine with me. I'll never talk to her again, I promise you."

I hesitate. The wedding is only a little over a week away. But I can't stand the thought of seeing Elena again, let alone fathom the prospect of working with her on the wedding now.

"Yes," I say decidedly. "We're not using Elena anymore."

"Should I... or do you want me to—?"

"I'll handle it," I say. "I'll let her go."

"Okay. I think it's for the best, anyway. I'm not sure she's the person I thought she was," says Nathan cryptically.

"What do you mean?"

"I can't say a lot right now, but you know Amanda was her client, years ago? Well, Elena told me soon after I became Amanda's lawyer that she wanted to distance herself from her. She said she'd read up about the case and she wasn't sure about her innocence anymore. But I was doing some digging last night, and I think she's downplayed her friendship with her. All I'm saying is, until this case is over, it might be best to keep a distance from her anyway."

"Are you saying she was involved somehow in—?"

"No, I'm not saying anything. Just, look, go ahead and fire her but try to keep things civil, and stay away from her."

As soon as we hang up, I dial Elena's number, and when she answers, her voice is calm and composed, as if she's been expecting my call.

"Hi, Elena. I... we need to let you go as our wedding planner."

There's a pause, then she sighs. "Yeah, okay, I understand."

"You... you do?" Her reaction catches me off guard, and I'm not sure how to respond. I had expected her to put up a fight, but instead, she's taking it all in her stride. I don't know whether this relieves or angers me.

"I understand that this situation has put you in a difficult position," she says, "and the last thing I want is to cause any trouble for you and Nathan. If me being your wedding planner causes any tension or discomfort, then it's the right decision for you to let me go."

"And what about the dress?" I ask, biting into my lower lip. I'd taken it over to her studio for some final adjustments, and I know she's put a lot of time into it.

"You can keep it, if you like. I'll arrange to have it and the shoes delivered to your place. I'll also contact you in a few days to discuss my payment for the work I already did."

"Right," I reply tersely, and say goodbye.

My jaw still clenched, I read through Sam's latest messages. They offer me a semblance of comfort, reminding me that I'm the woman Nathan chose to marry in the end.

With a deep sigh, I respond.

I fired the wedding planner. She won't come between us.

A few hours later, I've taken myself back into bed, where I'm nursing a mug of coffee and distracting myself with my book. Then I hear a gentle knock on the door, and I let out a low groan before calling to Debbie to come in. She stands in my doorway, her expression a mixture of uncertainty and something else I can't quite decipher.

"Brynn, darling," she says softly. Her voice carries a note of unexpected empathy.

I know I look a mess, my eyes still red-rimmed from crying, my skin pale from lack of sleep. "Hey, Debbie. What's up?"

She takes a cautious step forward and closes the door behind her. "I overheard your conversation earlier today," she admits. "I apologize for eavesdropping, but I couldn't help but hear what that awful wedding planner woman did to you."

"Don't worry about it. But if you don't mind, I'd really like to be alone right now," I say wearily. I don't have the energy for Debbie's games today.

She hesitates before walking slowly toward me, until she's standing by the edge of my bed. "Brynn, I know we haven't always seen eye to eye," she says, her voice gentle. "But I want you to know that I'm here for you. And that if ever you need someone to talk to, I'm willing to listen."

To my surprise, she lowers herself onto the bed and wraps her arms around me, pulling me into an embrace. I freeze for a moment, taken aback by her compassion.

Over my shoulder, she murmurs, "If I can give you one word of advice, it's that you mustn't throw away something good, just because of a relationship that happened in the past."

I stiffen in her arms. How dare she try to advise me? I almost respond with sarcasm, but I hold my tongue.

"Everyone has baggage, my dear," she continues. "Even you."

I come back to my senses and pull away. What a fool I was to think even for a second that she would care about me. I fix her with a cold, steely gaze. "Thank you for coming to check up on me, but I really want to be alone now."

"Of course, dear. If you need anything, you know you can just call." She pauses. "Also, I don't mean to overstep, but you've been looking rather poorly lately. Maybe you should go and see a doctor."

I just nod and say nothing. After she leaves, I pick up my phone and dial the number of a company that specializes in wedding photography and videography. With Elena no longer involved in our wedding, I need to take charge of the planning myself. When the call is answered by a woman with a nasal voice, I take a deep breath and clear my throat before speaking, making sure my voice is focused and business-like.

"Hi, this is Brynn Powell. I wanted to touch base with you about some of the details for my wedding."

I'm met with the sound of typing, before the woman speaks. "I'm sorry, Miss Powell, but we received a call that Elena Ward is no longer your wedding planner. Unfortunately, we only work with wedding planners, so we won't be able to provide services directly to you."

My heart sinks and I grip the phone tighter. "Yes, you're right. Unfortunately, Elena and I had to part ways. However, the wedding is still on, and I was hoping we could work something out. I'm sure you understand that last-minute changes like this can be quite stressful, so any help you can provide would be greatly appreciated."

Another pause. "Can I call you back in a few minutes?"

"Of course," I reply, my tone polite. "I'll be waiting for your call."

She calls back less than ten minutes later, and it's not good news.

"I'm so sorry, Miss Powell, but we won't be able to provide services for your wedding anymore. I hope you understand."

"I'm sorry, but I don't. I really don't understand. What difference does it make if I don't have a wedding planner? We already made all the arrangements and—"

"I understand your frustration, ma'am, but our policy is firm; we can't make exceptions."

I take a deep breath and try to compose myself. "What if I

were to hire a wedding planner right now? Would you reconsider?"

"I'm afraid our schedule is fully booked for the next few weeks, and we wouldn't have enough time to properly prepare for your wedding."

"Can I speak to your supervisor?" I ask, my voice shaking with anger and desperation.

"I am the supervisor, Miss Powell. I'm sorry, but there's nothing more we can do," she says firmly. "Goodbye and good luck with your wedding."

I hang up the phone, a heavy weight pushing down on my chest.

How could this be happening?

I'm pretty sure Elena asked them to cancel my contract with them. She's clearly intent on destroying my wedding.

I'm not giving up, though. No matter what, I'm going to have my perfect day with my perfect man.

Still, I can't help but fear I've met my match in Elena. I've never doubted myself like this before.

But how can I stop her?

TWENTY-FOUR

Later that morning I make an appointment with a doctor as Debbie suggested, because she's right, I haven't been feeling well. And I need to be operating at full capacity now more than ever. But beforehand, I meet Hannah for a coffee at Honeywood.

The place doesn't feel nearly as cheerful and inviting as it usually does. Suddenly, I find everything garish, the smell of the pastries too rich and sickly sweet, sending nausea into my stomach.

I'm really hurt that my best friend didn't tell me about Elena and Nathan. But I want to talk it out with her and give her a chance to explain. I need her right now; I don't want to lose her too. I couldn't bear it.

"So, you know," she says, looking down into her giant mug of chai. "About Nathan and Elena, I mean."

I clench my jaw, trying to hold back my tears. "Hannah, why didn't you tell me? I know I haven't known you for as long as you've known them, but we are friends. You're my maid of honor."

"I know, and I feel terrible for keeping it from you." Hannah reaches out and clasps both my hands with hers, transferring the warmth from her mug. "I've been feeling so guilty about it for ages. Elena made me promise not to say anything, and you know how convincing she can be. And I didn't want to do anything that could jeopardize your relationship with Nathan. You guys are just so good for each other. I've been really torn up about it, but the more time went by, the harder it seemed to tell you. And anyway, nothing's going on between them now. Will you ever forgive me?"

I force a weak smile. "I'm still pissed at you, but it's hard to stay mad forever."

"So, you will forgive me?" she repeats, her eyes wide and sincere.

"I'll think about it." I give her a small wink.

"Okay, and in the meantime, please, please let me help with the wedding. You must have so much on your plate now Elena isn't working for you. I know you keep saying you don't want to do this, but have you given any thought to buying yourself a bit more time, so you can process all of this?"

I groan and bury my head in my hands, then look back up at Hannah. "I don't want to postpone it, I really don't. But yeah, it's not easy. I just got off the phone with the photographers and they canceled our reservation. I'm pretty sure Elena had something to do with it."

Hannah gasps. "What? You really think she'd be so vindictive?"

"You know everyone has a dark side, Hannah," I say. "Sometimes the people we love are the ones who hurt us most."

When I see pain sweep past her features, I squeeze her hand. Hannah knows what it's like to experience hurt and betrayal better than most.

I know she was physically abused by her father as a child, and that one night when she was fifteen, he left the house saying he was going to buy groceries. But he never returned home. Two months later, Hannah found her mother still and lifeless on her bed, with divorce papers around her.

"Anyway, for once can we please talk about something other than my wedding? Let's plan your future flower business. It's going to be amazing, Hannah, I just know it. You make people so happy with your designs."

"Yeah, well, it's what I love. And I really hope I can make the business work, but it's so hard, Brynn. It could take years to build up enough savings. I had a good thing going before, and I lost it all. God, I hate Amanda Lane." Her face falls again. "I wish Elena never connected me with her. After she was arrested and that magazine feature trashed me as the Black Widow Florist, that was the end of things for my lovely shop. Now I have to start all over again."

"Hey, you'll get there. You're a fighter, Hannah—we both are."

Hannah nods, her eyes brightening up a bit. "You're right. I just need to stay positive and determined. And I'm grateful for the life I have, truly I am." She takes a deep breath and lays both hands on the table between us, her fingers splayed. "Now, come on, we can't avoid the wedding forever. What needs doing next?"

We quickly go through the list, and Hannah starts making suggestions and taking notes. When we're done, she puts down her pen and clasps her hands on the table. "Look, I'm really happy to help you out with anything. But now that I'll be taking on so much, I'm going to have to cancel some of my contract work to make time for this. Do you think you could give me some of the money you were going to pay Elena?"

When she sees the surprise on my face, she continues, "It's just that I won't have much time for anything else and I really need the money now, especially if I want to pay for that yoga teacher training."

I swallow hard and lean back in my chair, slightly taken

aback. I never thought Hannah would ask me for money. I guess I assumed she'd be happy to take on some extra tasks as my maid of honor, particularly since I've been helping her out with her contract work for free. It might seem harsh, but it's a rule of mine, never mix money and friendship. It's something Sam drilled into me a long time ago, and I always follow Sam's advice.

"I'm so sorry, Hannah. I wish I could, but I've pretty much depleted my wedding budget with all the cancellations and rebookings. I'm actually over budget already and I'm not even sure how much more money I'll still bleed before the wedding. Maybe I can manage—"

"No." She waves a hand. "It's fine. I just thought I'd ask. Seriously, don't worry about it."

She proceeds to drain the dregs of her chai and stands up. "I need to go. Good luck at the doctors. I hope you feel better soon."

"Oh, okay," I say, feeling guilty. "That's... Go ahead."

When she pulls out her purse, I stop her. "This is on me."

Before I can say anything else, she gives me a wave instead of a hug and walks off.

Feeling too exhausted and upset to go to the doctor's appointment now, I call ahead to cancel, and as soon as I get home, I crawl into bed with a tub of ice-cream.

I wish Sam was here.

TWENTY-FIVE

8 Days Before the Wedding

I step into my walk-in closet and stand there, staring into space and trying to steady my racing thoughts. Two days have passed since Nathan and Elena's secret came to light and I've been forcing myself to believe the worst is behind me.

It's not like me to feel so unstable and tearful, but my emotions have been in turmoil. I keep waiting for the other shoe to drop, certain that there's another blow coming. One that would shatter the last bit of hope that I'm holding onto.

I reach for the bag that holds my wedding dress and unzip it to reveal the delicate lace and tulle. As promised, Elena had it delivered yesterday morning along with my shoes and the rest of the things she's been keeping safe for the wedding day. I push down my simmering emotions and slip into the dress. And like every other time I've tried it on, I feel immediately as though I'm stepping into another world, a magical place where everything is going to be okay.

But as I twirl in front of the mirror, my reflection reminds me that, lately, things have been far from a fairy tale. My hair is a mess, my nose is red, and my eyes are still swollen from crying. Turning away from the mirror with a sigh, I pick up the box with my wedding shoes and place it on one of the white leather ottomans.

Pushing the paper stuffing aside, I take out the first pristine white shoe and slip my foot into it, relishing the touch of the smooth fabric against my skin and feeling immediately more confident, more myself. It's so elegant and detailed, with intricate beadwork and delicate straps that twine around my ankle.

But as I remove the second shoe from its paper stuffing, my breath catches in my throat. This one is covered in dark, blood-red splashes.

A sickening sensation takes hold of me, freezing the air in my lungs. Shock and anger surge through me in equal measure.

These shoes were really special to me, and someone has ruined them.

I searched through countless websites and boutiques before I found the website of Alessio Martino, an Italian shoe designer. For a high price, he agreed to custom-make a pair of heels for my big day. And when he sent me a drawing, I was smitten. They were exactly what I had been looking for.

What makes them so special is hidden away, a secret that only I would know unless someone was looking very closely. On each sole, there's a painting of a beautiful sunset scene, with vibrant oranges, reds, and pinks blending together in glorious harmony. It's the first painting I ever sold.

Yeah, they were special. One of a kind. And there's no way I can replace them now, not so close to the wedding, even if I could afford to spend that kind of money again.

It must have been Elena. She knew exactly how important they were to me, and she's the one who was looking after them at the store. And the fact that she'd do this and then just send them over to me knowing full well I'd know it was her? It shows how bold she's become. How dangerous.

That woman clearly thinks she can get away with anything.

I close my eyes and swallow the bitter taste at the back of my throat. Summoning all the restraint I can muster, I pull out my phone and dial Elena's number. She answers with a chilly formality in a voice that's a far cry from the warmth she used to show me.

"Brynn," she says, "how can I help you?"

"Elena, tell me the truth," I demand, my voice quivering with suppressed rage. "Did you ruin my shoes?"

"What? No, don't be ridiculous, of course not," she says calmly. "When I sent them to you, they were in immaculate condition. If something has happened after you received them, it has nothing to do with me."

"You did it, I know you did." Rage starts building up inside me, but I shove it down. "These shoes were special. You know that."

My accusation and her denial continue to bounce back and forth before she cuts me off, saying that since I've chosen to part ways with her as my wedding planner, I should stop contacting her altogether. Then she hangs up on me.

I'm apoplectic, and I send Nathan a message, telling him to call me immediately. An hour later, I'm staring out of my bedroom window at the glimmering ocean when the phone rings.

"Babe, I'm sorry I couldn't call you back sooner. The court session has been so intense."

Without wasting time, I tell him what happened, and when I'm finished, his silence is deafening. I twist a lock of hair around my finger. "Can't you see? Elena is sabotaging our wedding. She doesn't want you to marry me. She's still in love with you."

"So what? Even if that's true, no one can stop me from marrying you, my love. Not even her." He pauses. "But as I said before, I think you need to stay away from her. Please, Brynn, don't try to call her back. And listen, I also think you need a break, to get away from everything. How about you leave town for a few days?"

I shake my head. "No, I can't just drop everything and go away. There's so much left to do before the wedding."

"I know that, but it will all work itself out, and there's nothing more important than your health. Why don't you just go away for a day or two? Get some rest and pampering. You deserve it. I'll ask Hannah to help out with anything else that needs to be done."

I bite my lip. The truth is, I am exhausted, and I would dearly love a chance to clear my mind and recharge.

I flop onto the bed. "Well, I guess a couple of days away wouldn't hurt."

"Leave it to me. I'll book something for you. I need to go, babe. I'll call you back in a bit."

He calls back within the hour, while I'm nursing a chamomile tea out on my balcony and scrolling through the Safe Haven Sisters Facebook group.

"I've reserved a suite for you at the Serenity Crest Resort in Clearwater, from tomorrow night. It's a forty-minute drive, tops."

"And the wedding... Nathan—"

"Everything will be taken care of," he cuts in gently, his voice reassuring. "I called Hannah, and she has agreed to handle any emergencies. I just want you to have some time for yourself, to relax and de-stress over the weekend. Don't worry about a thing."

"You really are amazing, you know that?" I whisper, choking up.

"I just want to see you happy. Now pack your bags and go and enjoy yourself."

TWENTY-SIX

7 Days Before the Wedding

The next morning, I'm dragging a small suitcase down the stairs when I catch Debbie in the hallway and tell her that I'm going away for a few days.

She raises her eyebrows at me suspiciously and asks if everything is okay with the wedding. I reassure her that all is going well, I just need a break, and I tell her to make herself at home while I'm gone. As if she hasn't already done that.

But I give her a big hug before I leave, like we're the closest of friends. Because I've never been more vulnerable. My nerves have been so strained, it's been days since I felt in control.

And the last thing I need is for Debbie to flip and show her dark side, too.

After a pleasant drive I find myself standing outside the grand entrance of the Serenity Crest Resort. The sign upfront promises its guests tranquility and rejuvenation, and the sprawling estate comprises lush gardens, manicured lawns, and a lake that glistens under the morning sun.

It's bright and early, and the temperature is mild, the air carrying the faint scent of cut grass and blooming flowers. As I step through the wide wooden doors, I'm greeted by a warm melody played on a grand piano and the soft murmur of guests mingling in the lobby.

An elegant older woman with a gleaming smile approaches me and introduces herself as the receptionist. She takes my name, checks me in, and hands me a golden key card as well as a glossy brochure detailing all the services available to me during my stay.

"We have a complimentary massage scheduled for you," she says. "After you've settled in, just give the front desk a call to let us know when you'd like to book it."

I nod in gratitude and make my way toward the elevator, feeling a welcome sense of calm wash over me. As the doors open, I step into the plush interior and press the button for the third floor.

My suite is a spacious and elegantly furnished space, bathed in natural light that pours in through the large windows. The colors are muted and soothing, and fresh white roses grace the coffee table, infusing the room with a delicate fragrance. I take in the breathtaking view from the window, where I can see the cotton-white clouds reflected in the tranquil waters of the lake.

I deserve this. It's okay for me to be happy.

After unpacking my suitcase, I settle into a comfortable armchair, a cup of steaming coffee in hand, listening to the bird-song through the open window.

I always take time to pause and really appreciate the finer things in life because when I was a kid, we had very little. My parents constantly fought about money, sometimes to the point where it got ugly. Our house was always in a state of disrepair, and I remember the ever-present worry about whether we'd have enough to eat or if the electricity would be turned off again.

That was one of the reasons why I loved going to visit my Grandpa Moses. He didn't know how bad things were at home, but whenever I stayed with him, I knew I'd always get a proper cooked meal. And he'd teach me things that made me feel like I had more control over my life: like how to repair things around the house. When Grandpa died, the memories I cherished the most were of the times we spent together in his workshop, tinkering with his tools, and learning new skills. He was the one who taught me to take care of myself. Sam did too, of course, but Grandpa's lessons came first.

Now, as I sit here in this luxurious suite, I can't help but feel grateful. Because no matter what life throws at me, I know I'll always land on my feet. It's not luck; it's my absolute refusal to be defeated or to let anyone bring me down. But as much as I know how important it is to rely on myself, it's also so nice to be taken care of. I'm still angry with Nathan about Elena, but I know he loves me, and he genuinely wants to protect and take care of me.

We'll get through this.

After sitting in the armchair for a while, my phone dings with a text from Nathan.

Morning, my love. I hope you're enjoying your time at the hotel.

A smile tugs at the corners of my lips as I type out a quick response.

I'm already in love with this place. Thank you.

As I set the phone down, there's a knock at the door. I walk over and open it to a friendly hotel staff member pushing a trolley laden with a delicious spread of breakfast treats. Warm croissants, assorted fruits, yogurt, and a glass of freshly squeezed orange juice make for a delightful morning feast.

Nathan really is so sweet.

Time seems to slip away as I savor each bite and enjoy the luxury of having a day ahead of me full of self-care and nothing else. Away from all the wedding planning, Debbie's invasive presence and that persistent feeling of someone watching me, I find myself sinking into a state of relaxation I haven't experienced in some time.

I'm truly grateful Hannah agreed to take over everything for a few days, even after I hurt her by turning down her request for money. I feel so guilty about it, and I decide that before I leave, I'm going to buy her a voucher for a long weekend stay at this hotel, to thank her for everything she's done for me.

After a wonderful morning with a massage and a swim, I head back to my suite to freshen up and slip into a comfortable cotton blue dress, one I bought in Paris when Nathan took me there last Christmas. I'm about to go down for lunch when I open the door to find a waiter there, delivering once again a meal I had not ordered.

"Thank you," I say and step aside for him to place the food on the table. It's a thinly sliced steak with roasted potatoes, sautéed vegetables, a bottle of expensive-looking red wine, and a giant bowl of strawberries and cream for dessert. Nathan really wanted to make sure I ate today. And he knows me so well, this is exactly what I would have ordered. I take the meal out on the balcony and enjoy every mouthful.

Then I startle as I hear a deep, familiar voice behind me. "I hope I'm not interrupting, darling."

I turn around to find Nathan standing in the doorway to the balcony, a warm smile on his lips. My heart leaps in my chest.

"Nathan... I... what?"

"I wanted to surprise you," he continues, as he pulls me into his arms.

I'm at a loss for words. My eyes fill with tears as I tighten my arms around him, inhaling his scent deeply. Until right now, I didn't realize just how much I missed him.

"You're here," I whisper.

He nods as he pulls away to look into my eyes. "I needed to see you after our fight the other day. I'm so sorry I hurt you, baby." He hugs me again and his embrace is like coming home. Without warning, and surprising myself completely, I start sobbing against his chest.

He strokes my hair gently as he whispers soothing words in my ear. "I'm here, sweetheart. I'm here."

Eventually, my tears subside. "I can't believe you came, with the trial still going on."

A soft smile graces his lips as he brushes a strand of hair away from my face. "I wanted to make sure you're okay."

I lean in, capturing his lips with mine in a tender, heartfelt kiss. It's filled with unspoken emotions—the love we share, and the promise that we'll get through whatever challenges come our way, together.

When we finally pull away, I rest my forehead against his, our breaths mingling. "Thank you for being here, for doing this. It means so much to me."

He presses a gentle kiss to my forehead. "Of course, my darling. I'd do anything for you." Cupping my face with both hands, he gazes into my eyes. "I know you had a difficult childhood and my goal is to give you what you really deserve. I want to spend my life giving you all the things you never had. And our future kids will never lack anything. We will create a beautiful, happy family together." He takes a step back, a mischievous glint in his eyes. "I have one more surprise for you."

He reaches into his shoulder bag and produces an elegant

pale-blue box wrapped with a white satin ribbon. He holds it out to me, a smile playing on his lips.

"For you," he says softly.

Unwrapping it, my breath catches in my throat as I see an exquisite pair of ivory wedding shoes with sparkling crystals that catch the light.

"Oh, Nathan, they're... they're stunning," I manage to whisper.

Nathan slides a finger under my chin and tilts it up, so I can look into his eyes. "I'm just sorry your dream shoes got ruined. But aren't these even better?"

"Yes, these are so much better." I kiss him on the lips.

The shoes are not the custom-made ones of my dreams, but they are from Nathan. Even with everything he has going on, he took the time to find these for me because he wants me to know how loved I am.

I slip them on, and they fit perfectly. I'm amazed he was able to organize this and find them in such a short space of time. Touched beyond words, I wrap my arms around his neck in a tight embrace.

My heart is full of gratitude and love for him. It's not about the shoes, it's about his thoughtfulness, how determined he is to make me feel cherished.

"Thank you," I murmur again, and he kisses me hard.

After a little while, we start to talk about the trial, and I can see how much it's worrying him.

It's unlike Nathan to be so affected by anything; he's usually so centered and calm. I ask him if he still thinks someone else might have been involved in the murders Amanda Lane is accused of, and he tips back his head and sighs before meeting my eyes.

"Yes, I'm starting to think it was someone else. Or that maybe she had help."

I take a moment to find the right words to comfort him.

"Well, if that's the case, she's lucky to have you as her lawyer. If you can't get her to be completely absolved, you can at least negotiate for a lighter sentence."

He nods, but his eyes are clouded with worry. "I just hope I'm doing the right thing," he murmurs. The stress of the case is etched deeply into his features, and I reach out and place my hand on his cheek, rubbing my thumb gently over his stubble.

"You are doing the right thing. You are an amazing lawyer, and you're doing everything in your power to help Amanda. You can't control the outcome, my love, but you can control how hard you fight for her. And I know that you'll always fight until the very end."

He leans into me, closing his eyes for a moment. "Thank you, my future wife. Your words mean the world to me."

We stay in each other's arms for a while, the world around us fading. And in this moment, I realize that this is truly the happiest I have ever been.

But that thought terrifies me to the core of my being.

Because I have everything to lose.

TWENTY-SEVEN

THE WOMAN

It's a beautiful, fresh summer morning as the woman sits inside her car, watching the hotel entrance where Brynn checked in a few hours ago.

She had followed her all the way out of Stoneview, driving a few cars behind, blending in with the traffic. As they got further out of town, with little traffic on the road, it would have been so easy to just bump her car off the road and watch calmly as it careened into a ditch.

The woman had gripped the steering wheel tightly, taking deep breaths. Acting impulsively was not an option, not when she had so much to lose. She would not end up like Amanda Lane, on the fast track to prison.

She had to be patient.

Now, reaching into her bag, her hand wraps around a bottle of pills, and she washes down a few with a swig from her water bottle. She needs to calm her nerves and think clearly. She can't let her emotions get the best of her.

But as she sits there, she thinks about all her failed attempts to break up Brynn and Nathan. Frustration boils inside her belly, and she curses under her breath, feeling a very dangerous mix of powerlessness and desperation.

And then she sees him.

Nathan, her Nathan, getting out of a taxi at the entrance of the hotel with his confident gait and handsome features.

She watches him smile at the valet, and as he disappears through the rotating doors, she buries her face in her hands. She has put so much time and effort into trying to end their relationship. And now it seems like everything is falling apart. But for her, not for them. If anything, her attempts have only strengthened their bond.

But despite everything, she won't give up.

The wedding is only one week away.

Slowly, she gets out of the car and heads to the hotel.

By the end of the day, she will know what to do.

And this time, she will not fail.

TWENTY-EIGHT

BRYNN

Nathan and I head into the hotel gardens, where the vibrant colors and the soothing sounds of water features create the most romantic atmosphere. But a nagging feeling tugs at the back of my mind—a feeling that we're not alone.

Of course, there are plenty of other guests and hotel staff, but I don't think that's it. I look around, and nothing seems out of the ordinary. But I can't shake away the prickling at the nape of my neck and the tightening sensation in my chest.

As we stroll farther into the garden, Nathan's grip tightens on my hand. "You okay, love?"

I lean in to him and smile. "Yeah, I'm just enjoying the scenery."

He kisses my temple. "You're a terrible liar, you know that?"

I chuckle, my chest constricting. "Okay, fine. I've just been feeling a bit... watched, I guess."

He stops walking and turns to face me, his expression serious. "What do you mean, watched?"

I shrug, not wanting to make a big deal out of it and cause him any stress. He knows about the shoes and the wedding venue, but if he knew about the note, the wedding cake topper, the veil... I honestly think he'd freak out, call the police, and ruin everything. "It's probably just my overactive imagination."

His furrowed brows tell me he's not convinced, but he doesn't press further, and we get back to talking about our honeymoon.

"Sailing in the Caribbean is going to be just what I need after this trial." His eyes light up with excitement.

"It will be a dream come true," I say, squeezing into his side.

"I know it will be, I can't wait." He leans in for another kiss. "By the way, did I tell you that Justin and the other guys are driving up to Tallahassee to see me a couple of days before the wedding? They're going to throw me a bachelor party. It was meant to be a surprise, but of course Justin spilled the beans."

I laugh. "That's great! You deserve a fun night out with the guys before the wedding."

Justin is Nathan's best friend and his best man. I don't see him often because he doesn't seem to like me very much, and I know for a fact that he tried on several occasions to talk Nathan out of marrying me. He thinks our romance happened too fast, while Nathan was still recovering from a previous relationship, and he gets annoyed when Nathan cancels their plans to spend time with me. But I'm genuinely glad Nathan is going to let loose a bit with his friends before our big day.

He grins. "I'm pretty excited, actually. It'll be nice to just relax and not have to worry about anything for a night."

It's been a year and a half since Amanda employed Nathan as her lawyer after she was first charged with murder. Not long after, her charges were dropped due to lack of evidence. But the police kept digging and soon she was charged again. Since then, Nathan has been working tirelessly. The truth is, this trial has been looming over us for what seems like forever. It feels like we've been living in limbo, waiting for it to be over.

As the hours go by, I try to make the most of the time we have together and push away my paranoia. But no matter how hard I try, I still can't shake the feeling that we're being watched.

Later in the evening, Nathan surprises me with a new dress draped over the bed, and the promise of a romantic rooftop dinner. As I slip into the dress, I'm struck all over again by how thoughtful he is, and how well he knows me. It's breathtaking, in a deep shade of green with intricate lace detailing.

When we arrive on the hotel rooftop, my breath catches. The area is adorned with lanterns, creating an inviting and magical atmosphere. A table is set for two, covered in crisp white linen and flickering candles. The view of the skyline at sunset is spectacular, and for a moment, all my worries fade away.

Nathan pulls out my chair, and his eyes are fixed on mine as he takes his seat across from me. "You look stunning, my love."

"Thank you," I reply, feeling a flutter of true happiness.

The evening unfolds in warm conversation, as we discuss our exciting plans for the future and enjoy the delicious food. And whenever I start to feel anxious again, Nathan notices and reaches across the table to take my hand, his touch grounding me.

As we make our way back to our suite, his arm wrapped around my waist, I look forward to hiding away from the world with him, from whoever has been trying to frighten me.

If it's Elena, then she's just going to have to get used to the fact that she lost.

She'll never take Nathan away from me.

When we enter our room, Nathan pulls me to him, his fingers gently tracing circles on my back, and he speaks softly, breaking through the noise in my head. "Baby, I can tell there's still a lot on your mind."

I glance up at him, my heart a mix of emotions. "I want everything to go perfectly, that's all. Our wedding, our life together... I want it all to be beautiful."

He smiles. "Our journey together won't always be without challenges, but that's what makes it real. It's the ups and downs that will shape our story. As long as we're together, we'll find a way to conquer anything." His thumb brushes against my cheek. "I love you, Brynn. And no matter what happens, that won't change."

I lean in, pressing a soft kiss against his lips. "I love you, too. And I believe in us."

His smile widens, creasing the corners of his eyes, and then he scoops me up into his strong arms, carrying me toward the bed. "No more talking," he whispers.

Later, after Nathan falls asleep, I go over to the lounge area of the room and curl up on a sofa under a blanket, knowing I need to respond to Sam's many texts. I haven't been in touch for a little while. I've been busy. And honestly, I'm getting a bit tired of Sam's insistence on constant communication.

There's something a little tense about some of Sam's recent messages. We've always been close, but now that we haven't seen each other for a while, I feel like maybe Sam is getting jealous of the new people in my life. But it's just been so much easier to confide in people who are actually here. And since I've got to know Hannah and Elena so well, I've found their natural, open, mature friendship refreshing. Or at least I did, until I discovered the truth about Elena. That recent development aside, building these new friendships has shed light on just how controlling Sam has been.

It's not just that, though. If I'm honest, I'm increasingly feeling uncomfortable that Nathan doesn't know anything about Sam. I have very good reasons for keeping Sam from him. But the more I see how genuinely loving and trusting he is, the more I wish I didn't have to hide anything.

But what can I do? Beneath a veneer of love and loyalty, I

know Sam has a darker side. I've never allowed myself to put any boundaries between us, because I'm actually a little bit afraid of what would happen if I did.

Now Nathan has shown me just how bright and beautiful our future together could be. Can't I just put the past behind me?

With my eyes closed, I draw in a deep breath and respond to Sam's latest request for an update.

> *All fine on this end. Couldn't be better. I really love Nathan and I can't wait to spend the rest of my life with him. He's the one for me. Listen, things are very busy right now and I won't be able to message much. Thinking of you, though. Take care.*

I see the dots appearing that mean Sam is typing, but then they disappear.

And for the first time in I don't remember how long, Sam doesn't wish me goodnight.

TWENTY-NINE

5 Days Before the Wedding

After a lovely weekend away with Nathan, I come home feeling refreshed, determined, and grateful. I cannot wait for us to start our new life together in this beautiful home. Nothing is going to get in our way.

Standing in the hallway, for the first time in my life I find myself thinking of having children and watching them run down the stairs to greet me when I get home. I never thought I wanted to be a mother before. But now I can almost feel their tiny hands clutching at mine, their laughter echoing, their smiles contagious.

Sam has always said that kids are a huge responsibility, that they change everything. And having grown up as an only child, I never experienced the joy of siblings or the chaos of a full house. But as I stand here, putting down my suitcase and relishing that comforting feeling of being home, I realize that I want to build a family of my own with Nathan.

Memories of myself as a scared little girl crawling under the table when things got ugly flood back to me. With Nathan by my side, I can write a different story. I can create my own family, one full of love and happiness.

Inside my bag, I hear a beep as yet another text comes in. But I ignore it, and I head to the living room where I stand by the porch doors to enjoy my favorite view: the ocean at sunset.

Then on the path leading to the beach, I catch sight of Debbie and Hannah. They are engrossed in what looks like a heated argument. Debbie's hands are on her hips, and she's leaning forward, her face contorted in anger.

A breeze carries their raised voices through the open doors. I can't hear their words, but the tension in their postures is unmistakable.

Why would they be arguing? They barely know each other.

I take a deep breath and make my way outside, hoping to defuse the situation and find out what's going on. They see me at the same time and something resembling guilt flashes across their faces. Debbie quickly tries to compose herself, patting her hair and smoothing out her garish floral dress.

"Hi, dear. You're back already?" she says. "I thought—"

"Hello, Debbie. Yes, I'm back." I glance at Hannah. "Were you two arguing?"

Debbie clears her throat. "It was nothing, just a little spat."

"Oh, really?" I raise an eyebrow, waiting for an explanation.

Hannah shakes her head. "Brynn, can I speak to you in private, please?" Her voice is soft, but there's an edge to it that tells me this is serious.

A knot forming in my stomach, I shoot a glance at Debbie, wondering what she said to Hannah. Then I nod, and we make our way back into the house as Debbie lingers behind.

"Let's talk in my bedroom," I suggest.

We go upstairs to my room, and Hannah takes a seat on the chaise lounge while I throw open the balcony doors to replace the stale air and welcome in the sound of the waves.

I turn to her again, and her face is flushed with frustration, her jaw clenched tight. She takes a deep breath and rakes a hand through the tight curls in her hair.

"Sorry you had to witness that." Her tone is apologetic.

Sitting down opposite her, I wait for her to continue. "What's going on, Hannah?" I ask after a moment. "What was all that about?"

She closes her eyes and opens them again with a sigh. "You know what? Maybe I shouldn't bother you with this. It's nothing you need to worry about. Just some wedding planning stress."

"But Debbie is not involved in any wedding planning. What would she have to do with it?" I press. "Please, Hannah. I need to know what's happening."

"You're right." She sighs. "Look, I need to tell you something about Debbie. I know she's going to be your mother-in-law and everything, but—"

"What about her? What did she do?"

Hannah's eyes are fixed on her lap. "Earlier, when I came over with the caterers to show them how we want the tables to be set up on the porch, I heard a noise upstairs and I caught her going through your personal things, in here."

My eyes widen, and I shift uncomfortably, feeling suddenly nauseous. "Right, okay, I... I'll talk to her. Thanks for telling me."

Hannah places a hand on my arm, her expression dark. "There's something else. I know I said to let it go, but I've been thinking about the wedding cake tasting. Nobody else got sick, we all ate the same cakes. But Debbie made us coffee, remember? And she gave me yours to pass onto you, but I took that one myself because it had cream in it, and I know you don't drink it like that."

"Yeah, I remember. But—"

"Look, I don't want to meddle in your relationship with your future mother-in-law, but I'm worried. I think she was trying to poison you, not me. She's up to something. You can't let her stay here with you. I don't trust her." She takes a breath, having said all of this in a rush. "We both know she doesn't really have a relationship with Nathan, so what if she is so angry with him, so bitter that she is here to sabotage your wedding? Even if you aren't worried about yourself, she might really hurt him. There must be a reason why he's kept her at arm's length all these years."

Hannah's theory about the coffee is interesting, and she's right not to trust Debbie. Maybe Debbie did tamper with a drink intended for me, because she wanted to put me off Deli-cakes so she could make the cake herself. She's so controlling, I could see her doing that.

But after everything else that's happened? No, I'm pretty certain that was Elena. Debbie is just a bitter old woman with nothing better to do than get in my business.

"I'll talk to her," I say reassuringly, and go over to give Hannah a hug. "Thank you for steering the boat while I was away. You're the best maid of honor this girl could ask for. I've got something for you, by the way."

I hand her the voucher for a luxury stay in the hotel, and she squeals with pleasure. I tell her all about the gardens, the massage, the amazing food—and above all, Nathan's surprise visit to see me. But before long I notice her expression has changed. She looks worried, sad even.

"Hey, Hannah, are you okay?"

She shakes her head and forces a smile. "Yeah. It's just that I'm worried about you."

"Why? You don't need to be. Is this about Debbie? I can handle her, you know."

"No, it's about everything that has been happening lately. I know you make fun of me for being a little superstitious, but I find it hard to ignore so many bad omens. And, well, it's like everything is going wrong. I don't understand why you're not more worried about all these awful things that keep happening. That veil still creeps me the hell out, and I can't shake the feeling that maybe the universe is sending you a message, a warning."

"Well, I admit it's been a tough couple of weeks. But I just don't believe in bad omens or messages from the universe, Hannah. Someone has been playing games with me, yes, but the last thing I'm going to do is let them win. Sometimes life just throws you a curveball, you know? And what matters is how you respond to it. So, let's just hope that everything turns out all right in the end." I pat her arm.

"Okay. But please be careful around Debbie. That woman is trouble."

"I will, I promise."

Hannah declines my offer to stay for dinner, saying she's tired and needs to get home. And when she leaves, and I'm alone in the house with Debbie, I go into the kitchen where she is busy frying garlic and onions. As I help her chop vegetables, making quick work of an eggplant with my sharpest kitchen knife, I confront her about going through my stuff.

"I was just trying to help," she says, scattering a pinch of salt over the onions. "I know you have an address book dedicated to the wedding and I was looking for it."

"Why on earth would you need my address book?"

"I wanted to make sure everyone on the guest list was confirmed, especially with the change of venue. I thought I could help you out by making some calls."

"That's not your job, Debbie," I say, my throat tightening. "And going through my personal belongings without my permission is not okay."

She puts down the wooden spoon and presses a hand to her chest. "Oh, but we're family, dear. And I thought since you can come in and out of my room without permission, I could do the same."

My cheeks heat up immediately when I remember being caught red-handed after I left my keys in her room. But I put down the knife and push back my shoulders. "I think from now on, it's best if we respect each other's privacy."

Debbie nods. "Of course. I'm sorry if I overstepped. All I wanted was for you to have a wedding that doesn't end in disaster. You wouldn't want that, would you, darling?"

"Of course, I don't want that, Debbie," I say between gritted teeth. "And I appreciate you want to help. But please, just leave the wedding planning to me."

"All right then," she says calmly, but her face is thunderous. "I'll let you finish up in here, I'm not hungry anymore. For what it's worth, I really hope your wedding day is everything you dreamed it to be, and everything goes according to plan. Oh, by the way, dear," she adds as a parting comment, "you might want to know that I found Hannah dipping into that spare change container over there."

With that she hangs up her apron and disappears, leaving me reeling with anger. How dare she go through my things? And now she's accusing my best friend of stealing? I know Hannah wouldn't do that. Or at least if she'd needed cash for a wedding expense, she'd have told me afterwards.

I put a pot on to boil for the pasta, my movements mechanical as I try to calm down. But I'm starting to understand what Debbie's game must be.

She came here looking for something she thinks I have.

She has no idea that what she's looking for is long gone.

And I'm not going to tell her. Because the moment she knows, the power is all hers.

THIRTY

4 Days Before the Wedding

The next day, I'm reading on the sofa in the living room when I reach for my phone to check the time and see another message from Sam. Without even reading it, I press delete.

My wedding is just days away, and I'm doing my best to avoid anything that could ruin my mood. I've been exhausted, too, bone-tired in a way I've never been before. I need to rest as much as I can.

But I call Nathan, longing to hear his reassuring voice. When he answers, there's a sense of urgency in his tone, and he says he doesn't have long. My heart sinks a little; I had hoped for a few minutes of casual conversation.

"I love you so much, my darling," I tell him, a habit that now rolls off my tongue as easily as breathing.

"Oh Brynn. I love you, too. And the way you just said that... It feels different. Like I'm hearing it for the first time."

"You're being silly. It's the same 'I love you' I always say. We've just had a lovely romantic weekend together, that's all."

He chuckles. "That weekend was exactly what we both needed."

He's so right. Our romantic time together really has changed things. It feels like we're in the start of a new relationship. I'm experiencing those trademark nervous butterflies in my stomach and a constant longing for us to be together.

"I guess I'm just so grateful to be marrying a man as wonderful as you. I don't know what I'd do without you, Nathan."

"I feel the same way. You're the best thing that's ever happened to me and very soon, we're going to be husband and wife. I can't wait. Babe, I hate to end our call, but I really have to run."

"Quickly, before you go, how's it all going?"

"Everything is going really well," he says, sounding confident and energetic. "The evidence we have is strong, and our strategy is solid."

"Great. I'm so proud of you. I'll call you later."

Glancing over at the brooding ocean outside, I decide to catch up with the trial online. But first I head to the Safe Haven Sisters Facebook group and hit the "leave" button.

As much as I want to be supportive to my online friends, with everything else I have going on, I just don't have the time to dedicate to it anymore. And maybe my life has moved on now, too.

Then I click on one article after another about Amanda Lane's trial, and soon a knot begins to form in my stomach.

Nathan seems very confident that he will win. But almost the entire internet thinks Amanda is guilty.

Pursing my lips together, I read a post on a Facebook group about a protest in front of the courthouse yesterday:

Family members, friends, and their supporters gathered in front of the courthouse yesterday to demand justice for the victims of Amanda

Lane. Protesters carried signs and chanted, demanding that Amanda
be found guilty.

The case has gained national attention, and there's a growing fear
that if Amanda Lane walks free, riots will break out. It has been a
while since a murder case has stirred up such an intense reaction
from the public. What angers people the most is that Amanda seems
totally unmoved, sitting in court with a blank expression on her face
and never showing any remorse for the lives that were lost.

I sit back on the sofa, worrying about Nathan. I wish I could
help him, protect him somehow. But soon the doorbell jerks me
out of my thoughts, and I quickly go and answer the door before
Debbie can get there first.

"Elena?" I say, shocked to see her standing in front of me.
She's wearing a maxi dress in earthy shades with a stylish deep-
green scarf twisted around her head, and she's carrying a giant
box of luxury chocolates. I wish I'd thrown on something more
stylish this morning than my sweatpants and oversized t-shirt,
but I've been so tired, all I wanted was to be as comfortable as
possible. "What are you doing here?" I ask, trying to sound
stronger and more confident than I feel.

"I'm sorry I didn't call first." She hands me the box of chocolates. "I just wanted to talk. Please, Brynn."

My first instinct is to turn her away, but in that moment, she
looks so vulnerable and sincere that I can't help but invite her
in. And, honestly, I'm curious about what she has to say for
herself. I gesture her into the living room, and I offer her some
tea. When I come back in with it, she smiles nervously as I sit
across from her.

She only takes one sip before putting the cup down on the
coffee table and looking over at me. "I just came to say I'm really
sorry about everything."

"About smearing my shoes in red paint? Threatening me?
Trying to frighten me and destroy my wedding?" My anger

raises its head like a snake, but I manage to lower my voice. "Do you really think an apology is enough to make up for what you did? Do you realize how messed up all of this is?"

"Brynn." She reaches for my hand, but I pull away. Bringing her hands back to her lap, she looks down. "I know you don't believe me, but all of that wasn't me, I swear." She pauses. "I just came here to apologize again for not telling you about Nathan and me, and for losing my cool with you on the phone. I want to assure you that what we had is long gone. I'm not a threat. Believe it or not, I am happy for Nathan. He deserves someone who can give him what I couldn't."

"Why did the two of you break up?"

Crossing her legs, she stares into space. "We wanted different things, that's all." She meets my eyes again. "After me, he dated other women, and I honestly had no issue with it. I wished him the best. I was so happy that he found you, after what happened with his last relationship, with Lola."

"What? What happened with Lola?" Nathan did mention that his last relationship ended badly, but he didn't want to go into details. And I'm getting really sick of being kept in the dark.

"I'm not sure I'm the right person to tell you that." She looks hesitant, but then she seems to come to a decision. "Let's just say that Lola was... unstable. She had some serious issues that made it impossible for them to have a healthy relationship."

"Was she someone from this town?"

Elena nods. "Lola is the one that drove him out of Stoneview when he left for Tallahassee. She destroyed his reputation. That woman was totally obsessed with him. So, when he called it quits, she smeared his name all over local social media pages, saying he had physically abused her."

As she speaks, I rub my chest, finding it hard to breathe suddenly. "But it was all lies?" I murmur. *Poor Nathan.*

She shakes her head. "Nathan is one of the good guys.

When we were together, he never laid a hand on me. He would never raise a hand to a woman. He's a gentleman, always has been. He once punched a guy for disrespecting a girl in a bar, but he'd never be violent to a woman."

"But I don't understand. Why would Lola do such a thing to him? Who would go so far over a break-up?"

"She was dead set on making his life hell. If she couldn't have him, no one could. And most people believed her. In a small town like this, rumors and lies can spread like wildfire. It took ages for the gossip to die down."

I sit there in silence. "I honestly had no idea," I finally say. "Hannah never told me either. I guess she didn't want to cause any issues between me and Nathan. Where is Lola now?"

"I heard she moved away from Stoneview a little while ago, but I don't know where she went. Wherever she is, she's probably making someone else's life miserable."

I nod slowly. "Thank you for telling me all this."

"Of course," she says softly. "Please believe me when I say I really just want the best for Nathan. He's a great guy. I also really want to help you out again with the wedding. I kind of have a pet peeve with unfinished projects, they don't sit well with me. I would love to help you finish what we started."

"But I already told Nathan—"

"He doesn't have to know. He's still going to be away until the wedding, right?"

I nod. Elena seems genuine. Besides, it now seems like there's someone else who may have been behind everything.

And it's not someone I know and trust after all.

It's someone from Nathan's past, not mine.

That should scare me, I guess, but it doesn't. Instead, I'm relieved it's not someone I'm close to. And I'm certain I can take this Lola down if it comes to it. She's just a sore loser, that's all.

"I guess it wouldn't hurt to have an extra hand," I say with a small smile.

"Great!" Elena beams at me, and I am suddenly so relieved that I have her back. When the time comes, I'll just have to convince Nathan that this was the right thing to do.

"Now, how about we seal the deal with those chocolates?"

I nod, smiling. "Yes, please. They look delicious."

She reaches over to open the box and picks one up, holding it out to me.

But I only eat two before I start to feel queasy. I place a half-eaten chocolate back in the box and push it away.

"Is everything okay?" Elena asks, noticing my discomfort.

"I... I don't know. I..." My voice fades off as I grab my stomach and run to the bathroom.

I barely make it to the toilet before vomiting, and my body convulses as I empty my stomach into the bowl. Finally, the heaving stops, and I sit back, gasping for breath.

Elena comes to the door, knocking gently. "Are you okay in there?"

I wipe my mouth with a tissue before opening the door. "Yeah, I think so. I just felt sick, suddenly. I guess I didn't have breakfast yet, and then those chocolates were so rich..."

"Yeah. Maybe you're a little fragile. You've certainly had a rough time these last few days."

I nod weakly. "Yeah, I've not been feeling like myself lately."

Elena looks concerned. "You should take care of yourself. You don't want to be sick on your big day. Maybe you should go and see a doctor."

"I've been meaning to actually, but things kept getting in the way," I admit. "You're right, though, I should."

She nods, placing a comforting hand on my shoulder. "How about we do that today? I know a good doctor here; she's a friend of mine, so I'm sure she'll be able to fit you in for a check-up this afternoon. And I'm coming with you."

Tears prick at the corners of my eyes as I look up at her. "Thank you so much. I don't know what I'd do without you."

She gives me a small smile. "That's what friends are for. Now, let's get you some water, shall we?"

Elena keeps her promise of calling her doctor friend, but unfortunately, she can only fit me in tomorrow. So, Elena nips out and pops back half an hour later with some anti-nausea medication. Before I take anything, she hands me a box. "Can you do me a favor and do this first?"

"You can't be serious," I say when I read the words on the box. "A pregnancy test, really?"

"After hearing your symptoms, I'm just curious, that's all. Do it for me."

"I'm not pregnant, Elena." After a moment of hesitation, I take the box and head to the bathroom just to prove her wrong.

But the test shows two clear lines.

Positive.

My heart leaps into my throat and I stumble out of the bathroom.

Elena rushes over to me. "What does it say?"

I show her the test, and she gasps. "Oh my gosh, congratulations! This is amazing news."

I stare at it in disbelief, my mind reeling. "I don't know if I'm ready for this," I admit.

Elena takes my hand. "No one ever feels ready. But you have Nathan. And he will be so happy." Her smile wavers, and she sits me down. Her words sound kind and genuine, but I notice that her eyes are full of anguish. "One of the reasons why Nathan and I decided not to get married in the end was because I don't want kids. I'm too worried about passing on the recessive gene that led to my mother's illness, and he always wanted them. But now he gets to have a child. This is a beautiful gift, Brynn."

I nod slowly, feeling numb. "I know, I guess I just need some time to process. Can you promise me something?"

"Anything."

"Please don't tell Nathan or anyone else yet. Not even Hannah. I want to do that myself, but I need to figure out how I feel about this first. And I want them to hear it from me."

"Of course, Brynn. You have my word."

After she leaves, I rest in my room, only leaving a few times to grab some plain food.

As the hours pass, I find myself growing more and more excited at the idea of becoming a mother. It's a new beginning. A wonderful life stretches ahead, for all of us.

But I'm also terrified. When Elena told me about Lola, I didn't really take that threat seriously. I was just relieved to have an answer that didn't involve someone I know.

Everything is different now.

I know I can take care of myself. But if this unstable woman is out to get me, then she could hurt my child too.

THIRTY-ONE

3 Days Before the Wedding

It's the last day of Amanda Lane's trial, and Nathan calls me before he heads to court, confidence radiating from his voice as he talks about setting Amanda free, despite the entire country's belief in her guilt.

"Sweetheart, I'm so happy to hear that everything is going well." I swing my legs out of bed. "But are you sure it's okay that I'm not over there to support you today? I'd have loved to be there. I'm just not feeling so good, and I need to rest."

"My love"—his voice softens to almost a murmur—"I feel your support even from a distance. You've got so much on your plate with the wedding just days away. You need to relax." He pauses. "And once this is all over, we can finally start our lives together. Besides, the atmosphere around this case has become so toxic and I think it could get dangerous. I heard a large crowd is already gathered outside the courthouse right now. I don't want to put you in harm's way."

He's right, but not because of my own safety. I need to keep our baby safe. I decided not to tell him yet in case it's too distracting while he wraps up the case. And the thought of surprising him with the news on our wedding night fills me with excitement and joy.

"But you have to be careful as well, Nathan," I say. "It could be dangerous for you, too."

"Of course. Don't worry, I'll be careful. And as soon as I'm done, I'll call you and tell you everything, my beautiful bride."

"I can't believe we're getting married in three days."

"You better believe it, baby. But you're right. It's happened so quickly, but I wouldn't have it any other way. You've brought so much light into my life, Brynn. And I'm grateful for you every day."

Before I can respond, he continues, "Listen, I have to prepare for the showdown. But just remember, no matter where I am or what I am doing, you're always on my mind."

I lay a hand on my stomach, stroking it gently. "Okay. I'll be thinking of you, too. Good luck."

"Thanks, baby. I'll speak to you soon."

Lightness in my steps, I make my way to the kitchen for breakfast. Debbie hasn't prepared it this morning; in fact, she hasn't for a few days. Not that I'm complaining. To be honest, I'm relieved. All I want is a simple bowl of fruit and yogurt and nothing more. The last thing I'm in the mood for is sitting with her, engaging in meaningless small talk while she refills my plate with heavy biscuits and rich sausage gravy.

Without her around, the kitchen feels like mine again as I gather an apple and orange from the fridge and start slicing them up.

But then I hear the all too familiar sound of her clearing her throat behind me, that irritating little "ahem" she makes. I clench my jaw and turn to look at her standing in the doorway.

"Oh, dear." She cocks her head to the side and narrows her eyes. "You look very pale, Brynn. Is everything all right?"

I force a smile and answer, "I'm fine." But the truth is, a dull ache throbs in my skull, threatening to escalate into a full-blown headache.

Debbie continues to prod, suggesting we go out for lunch together later, that spending some time outside the house would do me a world of good. I quickly decline, explaining that I have a lot to do. She just nods and goes to pour herself a cup of coffee. As she sips it, she brings up Nathan's trial and says she's surprised that I'm not in Tallahassee to support him today.

"If it were me, I'd be at every single day of Nathan's trial, supporting him until the very end," she says, and her words are dripping with judgment and condescension.

I take a deep breath, trying to keep my voice steady. "Debbie, Nathan and I have discussed this. We agreed that it would be best for me to stay here and keep up with the wedding planning while he deals with the trial. It's what works for us."

"Well, I do apologize if I stepped out of line," she says, but her tone still holds a hint of disapproval.

"I understand where you're coming from, Debbie, but Nathan knows I support him. If he needed me at the trial, I'd be there in an instant."

She just nods, and I can still feel her judgmental gaze on me as she leaves the kitchen.

I lean against the counter, rubbing my temples as the headache intensifies. After gulping down a large glass of water, I finish making my fruit salad and take my time eating it, savoring each juicy bite as I try to calm myself down.

When I leave the room, Debbie is coming back across the hallway. She's wearing an almost neon yellow dress with a high neckline and short puffed sleeves, and it's cinched at the waist. Ruffles and lace decorate the hemline, and she has on a matching wide-brimmed hat and white gloves.

"I know the colors for your beach wedding are plain and pastel, but I thought I'd add a pop of color and sunshine to the mix," she says with a smile, twirling in her dress. "This dress is from my younger days, but I think it still looks quite lovely, don't you agree?"

To me the outfit looks ridiculous: excessive and overly bright, but I'm not about to say that. "It's very nice," I say in a cool tone, and I walk past her up the stairs to my room.

A while later, as I lie on my bed watching reruns of the trial so far, I force myself to focus on the present moment. To stay calm for the little life growing inside me. But a knock on my door startles me, and I sit higher up as Debbie enters, without even waiting to be invited in. She's changed out of that horrible yellow dress into a gray skirt suit.

"Brynn, I'm sorry to disturb your rest, but I wanted to let you know I'm heading out to run some important errands. I'll be home late, so please don't wait up for me."

Home. That irritates me, but I don't let it show.

"Okay. Thanks for letting me know."

The prospect of having some time without Debbie near me is a relief, and as soon as she's gone, I call Hannah and invite her over for lunch.

"Sorry, love. I'm going out on the ocean, fishing with Ed." Hannah's voice is apologetic, but I can hear the excitement as well. It seems to be going pretty well with this latest guy, but as usual I haven't met him. Hannah keeps putting that off. He's an outdoorsy type, and from what she says, he's just as responsible and kind as he is handsome. For generations his family has been providing fresh fish for local restaurants and markets, and she appreciates his practicality and straightforwardness. He sounds almost too good to be true, and I'm looking forward to finally meeting him when she feels ready.

"No worries at all. Have a great time." I hang up and sit back on the bed, feeling a sudden pang of loneliness.

As I head down to the kitchen again to get myself a glass of water, my eyes are drawn to Debbie's room and, without thinking, I walk over to it and turn the doorknob. It's locked.

The *audacity* to lock doors in someone else's house.

Fuming, I get my water and retreat back up to my room, heading out onto the balcony, where I curl up on the rattan chair and catch up with my phone messages.

Most of them are from Sam.

Are you really going to ignore me? After everything I've done for you?

I type out my response, emotions tangled in every word. My fingers move over the tiny keyboard as if they have a life of their own.

I can't help but wonder if I'm signing my own death warrant as I do this.

I'd be crazy to think that Sam would never hurt me. But I've been living in fear for so many years. I'm going to be a mother now, and I'm determined to set an example of courage and independence for my child.

It's time to break free.

I'm not ignoring you. I'm simply living my life. It's over, Sam.

THIRTY-TWO

THE WOMAN

She glances around the coffee shop in Tallahassee, just down the road from the courthouse, struck by the strange contrast between the professional attire and serious conversations of the many wealthy lawyers and the café's homey atmosphere.

The smell of coffee and frying bacon fills the air along with the sounds of steaming milk and the clink of glasses and mugs.

Taking a sip, the woman glances up at the small TV on the wall behind the counter and sees Amanda Lane pleading her innocence in a recent interview. She's seen this interview before, so she sits back and digs into her club sandwich, listening in to the conversations around her.

At the bar, two suited men are having an intense discussion while the female barista prepares their drinks with a practiced ease, pretending not to listen in to everything they say.

When the men look up at the TV screen, their conversation changes to Amanda Lane's murder case, and they begin to go over the merits of her defense. As the debate gets heated, they stand up from the bar and move their conversation to the street.

The woman drains her coffee cup and finishes her sandwich before heading out to the courthouse. It's the final day of the trial, and the atmosphere is electric. The building looms above her imposingly as she approaches. She pushes her way through the throngs of reporters and onlookers and into the courthouse.

The courtroom is packed, and the air is thick with tension and anticipation. She takes her seat in the gallery and waits until the trial continues. She hasn't been here for the whole thing, but today is the last day and she's pleased to be present. Supporting Nathan.

Unlike Brynn, who chose not to come.

As always, Nathan moves around the courtroom like he owns it, in absolute control. But as the trial wears on, she studies Amanda Lane, too. Her face is a blank slate, but she has to be terrified inside. She feels a little tug of sympathy for her.

Her focus moves to the jury box, where all eyes are riveted on Nathan.

"Ladies and gentlemen of the jury," Nathan declares at last, with a passionate voice that reverberates around the courtroom as he summarizes his defense. Finally wrapping things up, his voice becomes heavy with emotion that seems very real. "You have a responsibility to uphold justice and to ensure that an innocent woman is not punished for crimes she did not commit."

The woman looks over at the jury's faces, which are all utterly captivated. Not for the first time, she admires Nathan's skill, and as she continues to watch him in action, she has never been prouder.

When the trial draws to a close, the tension in the courtroom reaches its peak. The verdict is about to be read.

As the jury leaves to deliberate, a sense of discomfort grips her. Nathan is an incredible lawyer, but the evidence against Amanda is damning.

· · ·

An hour passes as the jury deliberate, and she is settling in for a long wait when the door to the courtroom swings open. The men and women who have been chosen to decide Amanda Lane's fate file back into the room. The woman's heart pounds as they take their seats.

Finally, the foreperson, a young woman with large hoop earrings, stands up to announce their verdict.

"In the murder of Charles Broadridge, we find the defendant, Amanda Lane, guilty of the crime of first-degree murder." She pauses before reading the verdict on the second, then the third husbands.

Guilty. Guilty. Guilty.

As the verdicts are read out, Amanda Lane breaks down in tears, her sobs echoing throughout the courtroom. It's the first time she has shown any emotion during her entire trial. Her makeup runs down her face, and she shakes uncontrollably.

The woman almost wishes she could comfort her. But her priority is Nathan, who looks crestfallen, disappointment etched on his face.

As the judge pronounces the sentence, a hush falls over the courtroom. "Amanda Lane, I hereby sentence you to life in prison without the possibility of parole."

Nathan covers his face with his hands.

The woman knows how much this loss, his first, in his biggest trial yet, will weigh on him. It will haunt him for years to come.

As if in slow motion, Amanda turns to him, her eyes spitting fire. "This is all your fault!" she screams, pointing a finger at Nathan. "You said you would get me off. You promised me. You will regret this, Nathan Howard. I will make sure of it."

Nathan doesn't react, and instead, he focuses on packing his brown leather briefcase. Amanda's outburst dies down as quickly as it started, and she sinks back into her seat, looking utterly defeated. But when the guards come to escort her out of the courtroom, the woman watches in horrified fascination as Amanda's fighting spirit returns. She struggles against them like a wild animal, her shoulder-length hair flying in all directions. Her face twists with rage as she tries to break free from their grasp.

As Amanda disappears with the guards, Nathan finishes packing his briefcase in silence, his face a mask of stoicism. The woman desperately wishes she could walk up to him, comfort him, but she can't.

He doesn't even know she is here.

As he finally walks out of the courtroom, she follows behind. He walks slowly through the building, with his head down.

From a distance, she watches him pause and talk to several other men in suits, all of them looking grave and concerned. Nathan's face remains inscrutable. But even from where the woman stands, she senses the tension in his body.

When he leaves the building, he is immediately mobbed by reporters, their cameras flashing as they thrust their microphones and recorders toward him.

"Mr. Howard, how do you feel about the verdict?" one of them shouts.

"Are you planning to appeal?" another asks, shoving a microphone closer to his mouth.

Nathan doesn't respond. He just walks straight ahead, his shoulders stiff.

Getting into a taxi, she follows him all the way to a seedy bar with a name she can't read because it's so faded and worn, and a sign that flickers on and off. She watches as he enters, then follows him inside.

The air is thick with smoke and the smell of cheap alcohol. Looking around her, she recoils at the sight of the shady characters in dimly lit corners. She hates to see Nathan in such a place. But after what he went through today, maybe he just needs to blow off some steam. He orders a drink and sits down at the bar, his eyes staring off into space.

The woman doesn't stay to see what happens next. She shouldn't be here anyway, spying on him like this. This is a small bar, and it would be all too easy for him to spot her. So, she heads back outside and hails another taxi.

More than ever, she needs to do something to protect him from any further harm.

From marrying the wrong woman.

THIRTY-THREE

BRYNN

2 Days Before the Wedding

Just two more days and I'll be Nathan's wife. From the moment I woke up this morning, thoughts of floral arrangements, seating plans, and a myriad of last-minute details have consumed my mind, alongside my worry about Nathan after he lost his case.

I'm exhausted, and I'm just about to start cooking dinner and looking forward to getting some rest when the doorbell rings and Hannah is standing on the doorstep in pink and white pajamas. She's carrying a wicker basket piled high with popcorn, chips, cookies, and champagne.

"Surprise!" she exclaims, her light-brown eyes dancing with excitement. "I know you didn't want a bachelorette party, but I also think you deserve a memorable celebration. So, as a compromise, how about a girls' night in with cheesy movies, snacks, and champagne? As your maid of honor, I can't possibly let you get away without a little party. And it will just be the two of us, I promise. Well, you, me, and all of these treats, of course. Anyway, I'm already here, so you can't back out now." She winks, holding up the basket as if it's a peace offering.

"Come on, Brynn. What's better than a slumber party with your best friend, right?"

I shake my head, laughing, but a smile spreads across my face as I step aside to let her in. "Fine, you win. Let's make this a night to remember."

As we head for the stairs, an "ahem" cuts through our conversation and we turn to see Debbie standing in the doorway from the hall to the living room.

"Oh, hello, Hannah. We were not expecting you this evening," she says in that cheerful but condescending tone that she's honed over time.

Hannah's smile wavers for a moment, but she recovers quickly. "Hi, Debbie. I'm just here to surprise Brynn. We're planning a quiet evening in to celebrate her upcoming wedding. It's a bachelorette party so to speak... without the strippers and the wild partying, of course." She chuckles.

I'm glad that she's still being civil toward Debbie despite their argument the other day. She hasn't pushed me about it, and I've told her my suspicion about Lola being behind everything, rather than Debbie. I know she still doesn't trust Debbie, but she's doing as I've asked and keeping the peace before the wedding, and I'm grateful for that.

Debbie nods. "Good for you, Brynn. It's nice to see a young woman who's sensible enough not to get caught up in all the crazy bachelorette party trends these days. Some of those parties are just an excuse for disrespecting your future spouses."

On one hand, I appreciate Debbie's rare approval, but on the other hand, I also can't help but feel like she's passing judgment yet again. Even so, I smile politely at her.

"Well, then, carry on," she says finally. "Have fun, dears."

As she goes back into the living room, I exchange a knowing glance with Hannah and she rolls her eyes, and both of us giggle.

"Great," Hannah says, rubbing her hands together. "Now that's over, let's get this celebration started, shall we?"

We head upstairs to my room, and she reveals all the goodies in the basket she brought with her, along with a collection of my favorite movies.

"I figured we could do a throwback night with some classics that never go out of style."

Laughing, I remove the DVD of *Grease*. "Hannah, you really are living in the past. Nobody uses DVDs anymore." I hold the disc up to the light. "Nathan and I don't even own a DVD player. Hell, the only person I know who still has one is Elena."

"Okay, Miss Technology. I'll have you know that I have a digital copy of every one of these movies on my laptop." She pulls out her MacBook from her oversized bag. "I just wanted to do something a bit nostalgic. Remember the days when people had to physically go to the video rental store and pick out a movie to watch? I kind of miss that."

"So do I," I say. "Things were so much simpler."

"I know, right? By the way, did I ever tell you that Elena still owns a Walkman? She says nothing beats the sound of a cassette tape."

I throw my head back with laughter. "Are you serious?"

"Yep. That's our Vintage Queen Elena for you. Now, what do we watch first?"

"*Grease*, of course."

As we settle in front of the laptop on the glass coffee table of my bedroom's lounge area, warmth spreads through my chest. This is exactly what I needed. Quality time with my best friend, in a setting that makes me feel safe.

I wish I could tell her my secret, that I'm about to have a baby. But I'm not telling her before Nathan; that wouldn't be fair. It's only Elena who knows for now.

She has been so much help to me in just the past few days,

and despite everything, I feel like she should be here now. I know Nathan distrusts her, but I think she's shown her true character to me recently. And right now, I could use all the friends I can get.

"Hey," I say to Hannah, "would you mind if I call Elena over? I think she would really enjoy this."

"Sure. That would be lovely. I would have brought her with me, but I wasn't sure if you were quite there with her yet. I didn't want to push it."

"I appreciate that," I say, grabbing my phone to text Elena. "But honestly, she's been an amazing friend to me lately."

"I agree," Hannah says with a smile. "And I'm sure she'll be thrilled to be included."

I call Elena and the phone rings a few times before she picks up.

"Hey, you," I say. "What are you up to?"

"I'm just finishing up some work," she replies. "Why, what's up, darling?"

"I was wondering if you wanted to come over and join Hannah and me for a movie night and a sleepover."

"Aah... Sure, that sounds fun! I'll see if the carer can stay on later for Dad, and then head over in a bit. See you in about twenty minutes?"

She soon arrives wearing soft gray sweatpants and a baggy sweater, looking relaxed and happy.

She greets us with a hug. "Thanks so much for inviting me." She holds up a bottle of sparkling white grape juice. "I recently discovered this, and I love it. I thought it would be great for tonight, particularly after the headaches you've been having lately, Brynn."

I know what she's doing, and it warms my heart. Within minutes, we all settle down on the couches with blankets and pillows, and Hannah starts the first movie. Through the open balcony doors, a cool ocean breeze streams in, carrying the faint scent of salt and seaweed. We're cozy and warm, relaxing with the movie as we indulge in our favorite junk food. It's the ideal celebration for me.

"Should I order us a pizza?" I offer when the movie ends, reaching for my phone after ignoring a call from an unknown number. It's probably Sam, hiding her number so I won't ignore her call.

"Yes, please!" Elena folds her feet underneath her on the couch. "I'm starving."

I make the call and then pick up the next classic on Hannah's movie list, *The Notebook*.

"Should we watch this next one on the porch?" she suggests, pointing over at the doors. "It's such a beautiful night, and this movie deserves a backdrop that matches its romantic theme."

I nod in agreement and pause the movie to set up some blankets and pillows out there, and we settle in after admiring the early evening stars. But the moment the opening credits start to play, the doors creak open again behind us, and I turn to see Debbie standing there.

"Would you ladies mind if I join you?" she asks, her tone pitiful.

I glance at Hannah and Elena. This is an evening reserved for our friendship, a precious time where I can be myself without any of Debbie's judgments or expectations. There's no way I can be myself with her around. But perhaps because I feel so happy tonight, my heart goes out to her, and I feel suddenly generous.

"Of course you can join us." I wave her over. "We're just about to start *The Notebook*."

Hannah looks annoyed, and I feel guilty. But it's too late to take back my offer now.

Debbie's face lights up with excitement as she wedges herself in between me and Hannah, her musky perfume overpowering the ocean breeze.

With Debbie among us, the whole dynamic of the night changes. The comfortable and carefree atmosphere we had cultivated is now stiff and awkward. As usual, she keeps interrupting the movie with inane comments and endless guesses.

I can feel Hannah's annoyance like a physical presence, and I can see on Elena's face that she just wants the evening to be over with.

In the end, Debbie is talking so much that we stop paying any attention to the movie, and we end up discussing Amanda's trial.

"Do you really think she killed all of her husbands?" Debbie asks, her tone hushed as she glances around, as if someone might be listening in.

Hannah frowns. "Honestly, the evidence against her was pretty damning. Nathan certainly had his work cut out." She glances at Elena. "You've known her longer than all of us. You're pretty much friends, aren't you?"

Elena looks away. "I wouldn't call us friends. I planned her weddings, but we were never very close. She always seemed like a sweet woman, but you never really know what someone is capable of. One thing I do know about the woman is that she was very controlling. She would micromanage every little detail of her weddings. I can only imagine how she was with her husbands. She must have wanted everything to go her way, and if it didn't, she probably got angry. Maybe that's what led her to do something so extreme."

"So, what you're saying is, maybe she didn't plan to kill her husbands for money as everyone believes," Debbie says slowly, "but rather out of rage?"

The thought sends a chill down my spine, and my grip tightens on my glass of fizzy grape juice.

"Maybe there's more than one side to this," Hannah says softly. "She could have been in abusive relationships. Being in controlling relationships can really mess with your head."

"Yeah. Until recently, I had a friendship like that," I offer. "Sam was so dependent and controlling in a way that I didn't even realize until I finally broke free."

"So, you're no longer friends?" asks Hannah.

"Nope. I don't need that kind of energy in my life. It's important to set boundaries and recognize when someone is toxic for you."

Debbie nods in agreement before taking a sip of her own drink. "I, too, once had a friend who had such a controlling character that we had to part ways, but I didn't *kill* them. Whatever Amanda's motives were, she's been convicted of murder and now she's getting the punishment she deserves. No matter what you think someone did to you, nothing gives you the right to take a life. We can't play God. Nathan gave Amanda a fighting chance, a fair trial, and that's all anyone could ask of him."

"True. I agree that people should face the consequences of their actions, Debbie," I say and push past her just a little more than necessary as I get up and head to the bathroom.

Nathan didn't tell me himself that he lost the trial yesterday; I found out about it on the news. I tried calling him several times since then, even at the law firm, but I have been unable to get hold of him.

I'm trying not to catastrophize about it. I just hope he's busy with his bachelor party, and that it's not that he's been driven into a state of depression after losing the trial.

I call him from the bathroom, but he doesn't answer, so I send him yet another text.

Are you okay, baby? Please call me. I'm here for you.

This time, he responds almost immediately.

I'm fine.

Nothing more comes after that.

Instead of responding to his terse message, I call again, since he obviously has his phone close by.

No luck. The call goes straight to voicemail.

Something is definitely going on. If he's upset from losing the trial, shouldn't I be the first person he'd want to seek comfort from?

Rather than going straight back to the group of women, I head down to the kitchen to make us all some hot cocoa, and I spot a pile of letters on the hall table. I flip through each envelope absentmindedly until I come across one that is handwritten in a familiar script.

I tear it open, my heart lodged in my throat.

There's just one page inside, with a message written in thick font:

> *Since you won't speak to me, you've left me with no choice but to do what I have to do. May your wedding day be one to remember. Sam.*

THIRTY-FOUR

1 Day Before the Wedding

We're getting married tomorrow, but all my attempts to reach Nathan have been met with silence. Needless to say, this morning my concern is now spiraling into full-blown panic.

I grab my phone from the nightstand to call him again. The first ring sounds out, then the second. Finally, it goes to voicemail and my voice trembles as I leave a message, trying to be casual.

"Hey, babe, it's me again. I can't reach you and I'm starting to get worried. Please, call me back when you get this. I just want to know you're okay."

As soon as I hang up, Hannah breezes into my room. She spent the night at my place after our impromptu girls' night in, sharing my bed since Debbie has the spare room and the third bedroom is still cluttered with unopened boxes and random furniture. Elena was happy sleeping on the living room sofa, but she had an early meeting with a potential client, so she must have left already.

After all the wine she drank last night, Hannah looks

surprisingly fresh-faced and chipper. Unlike me, even though I didn't touch a drop of alcohol. After reading Sam's letter last night, I didn't get much sleep.

"Morning, sleepyhead. I made coffee."

I force a small smile, grateful for her presence, but I'm unable to get rid of the worry squeezing my heart. "Thanks," I say and turn to stare out the window, my focus on a seagull slicing through the sky in the distance. It's getting hard to hide my mounting anxiety from Hannah.

"Are you okay?" she asks as she approaches the bed and hands me my cup.

"Yeah, I'm just tired." The heat warms my hands but does little to ease the icy fear that grips me from the inside. I take a few sips, knowing I shouldn't drink too much caffeine now. But I wish I could drain the whole thing and then have ten more.

"Poor love." Hannah perches on the edge of the bed and crosses her legs. "You should take it easy today. How about we have breakfast at Honeywood, and you can tell me all about what's bothering you? I can tell that something is definitely off, and I wouldn't be doing my job as your maid of honor if I didn't at least try to ease your troubles." She places a comforting hand on my bent knees.

"Yeah, that sounds good." Maybe getting out of the house will be a good distraction, so I don't spend the entire morning staring at my phone in the hope that Nathan will call.

"Great. I'll just go and have a quick shower." She twirls toward the door like a ballerina, her hair swishing behind her. "You might want to do the same. You look like you spent the night in a ditch."

I force a laugh and head to the ensuite bathroom to freshen up. As I splash cold water on my face, I catch a glimpse of myself in the mirror. My eyes are puffy, and my hair is a mess. Hannah is right, I look like a wreck. I need to pull myself together.

Half an hour later, we're both dressed and ready to leave. Hannah is wearing her usual tank top and jeans, while I have opted for my comfiest sweatpants and a white T-shirt.

Before we head out of the door, Debbie comes into the hallway. "Where are you two off to so early? I was just about to make you a lovely breakfast."

"Sorry, Debbie, but we already made breakfast plans. See you later." I can't have her crashing my downtime again.

Hannah and I get into our cars, and before pulling out of the drive, I quickly check my phone again to see if Nathan has replied, but there's nothing. His silence is deafening, and my anxiety is like a rock weighing down on my chest.

The streets of Stoneview are fairly quiet this early in the day, as we drive toward Honeywood and look for parking. Inside, we go to our favorite table and order our breakfast. I opt for avocado toast with scrambled eggs and a green smoothie while Hannah chooses a breakfast bowl filled with quinoa, tofu, and a variety of veggies.

Savoring the smells of coffee and fresh food, I try to forget about Nathan ignoring my calls, and that letter. But I can't.

While we wait for our food, Hannah notices the way I keep checking my phone.

"Hey, what's wrong? You seem really tense." Her worry is so strong that I can feel it radiating off her like heat from a fire.

I try to muster a reassuring smile, but it feels weak even to me. "I'm fine, Hannah. It's just... Well, I haven't heard from Nathan since he lost the trial, except for one brief text. I don't understand why he hasn't called me back."

Hannah's eyebrows raise. "That's unlike him. You guys speak several times a day normally, don't you? Did you try calling his office or leaving a message with his secretary?"

I nod, my anxiety building. "I did. They just said he's been in meetings and is unavailable."

Hannah reaches across the table and takes my hand. "Maybe it's genuinely just a really busy time for him. And you know how important this case was. Losing it must be so tough. I don't think there's anything for you to worry about."

I wish I could tell her that it's not just about Nathan's silence.

But I can't burden her with the letter I opened yesterday. I know how much it'll freak her out, and I can't cope with that. So, I just nod at her attempts to reassure me.

After breakfast, we part ways, and I'm sitting in my car outside Honeywood, hesitating for a moment before I make another attempt to reach Nathan. My fingers tremble slightly as I dial his number.

This time, he finally picks up, but his voice sounds quieter than usual, distant somehow. "Hello?"

Relief floods through me, and I nearly choke up. "Nathan, finally. I've been trying to get through to you. Are you okay?"

There's a long pause, and his voice is deep when he speaks again. "Yeah, I'm okay. I just had a lot to do after the trial."

"Okay," I say. "I'm so sorry you didn't win. But you did everything you could. It's not your fault, and I'm so proud of you."

"Thank you, Brynn. That means a lot to me. We'll see each other soon."

My heart leaps at the thought of seeing him waiting for me at the end of the aisle tomorrow. "I'm counting every second."

Later that day, I go to hang up a set of fairy lights around the living room porch where we'll be displaying the food for our reception. The palm trees on the beach where the ceremony will take place already have their lights strung like golden fireflies between their branches and trunks, but we have extra, and last night Elena suggested we use them here. It's a good idea, and right now I'm grateful to have something to keep me busy.

I climb up the ladder, securing the lights in place. Seagulls soar overhead, their screeches mingling with the sound of the waves.

I know it's indulgent, but I can't wait to show off our beautiful home. Most of the guests are Nathan's friends or colleagues, but that doesn't matter to me. I think it's better to have a few good friends than lots of fake ones. In school I was a loner by choice and preferred my own company over that of others. Decades later, that hasn't changed much. I prefer the company of only very few people.

With my forefinger and thumb, I tug on the string of lights to make sure they're secure.

But then, without warning, one of the rungs on the ladder gives way under my foot, letting out a loud snap. My foot flails in the air and finds nothing.

Shock causes me to fall completely off the ladder, and my heart leaps into my throat as I plummet toward the ground.

My back hits the porch floor with a thud, knocking my breath out of me, and I lay there for a moment, gasping for air.

After slowly stretching out my limbs to check for broken bones or strained muscles, I sit up, wincing at the ache pulsating through my lower back. I'm pretty sure I didn't sustain any serious injuries—just a few scrapes and bruises—but the fall leaves me shaken and, above all, scared for my baby.

As my trembling hand goes to my belly, tears spring to my eyes and I reach for my phone and dial Elena's doctor friend, Dr. Gonzalez, who arrives quicker than I could have hoped. She swiftly assures me that the baby is fine, but she takes me to the hospital to get checked, just to be sure, and I spend the time there being poked and prodded by nurses and doctors.

When I return home, my heart races as I stare up at the fairy lights, which are now swaying gently in the breeze.

I go over to take a closer look at the ladder, and a disturbing realization enters my mind.

Someone dislodged the screws in that broken rung.

THIRTY-FIVE

THE WOMAN

The Wedding Day

The kitchen is bustling with wedding preparations. Clattering dishes echo, the air is filled with the aroma of freshly cut white roses, and the atmosphere buzzes with anticipation.

Among the organized chaos, the woman finds herself standing near the centerpiece of it all—the towering, three-tier wedding cake adorned with delicate decorations.

Escaping to the bathroom, the woman looks at herself in the mirror and sees that her eyes are wild with fury. She breathes deeply, takes a moment to calm down, freshens up her makeup, and puts on a fake smile.

Heading back out there, she makes her way to the living room porch, where she looks out at the beautiful scene, with rows of white chairs and pale-blue ribbons, and an archway covered in pastel flowers. Grief hollows out her heart and leaves a gaping black hole inside.

She can't let it end like this. She won't.

Back in the kitchen, she sees a knife lying on the kitchen counter, glistening in the sunlight. Her eyes fixate on the sharp blade. In her mind's eye, she sees blood spilling out of Brynn's body, staining her pristine white dress. She sees the chaos and panic that would ensue. Of course, Nathan would be devastated, but he would soon forget about Brynn. He would move on eventually. He would have her to comfort him.

She'd never previously thought herself capable of such extreme thoughts. But she's only human, and there's only so much one person can handle. It just isn't fair, it isn't right, for Brynn to have Nathan.

But she can't just kill Brynn in front of everyone, with dozens of witnesses.

No, she needs a more subtle plan.

And this time, it has to work.

THIRTY-SIX

BRYNN

It's my wedding day, and my stomach is fizzing with excitement. I'm sitting at my vanity table inside my walk-in closet, wearing a cream dressing gown, surrounded by makeup brushes, perfumes, and everything else I need to make me look and feel fabulous. It feels like I'm inside a dream.

Outside the window, the ocean stretches as far as the eye can see, and on the sand in front of the house, there are rows of white chairs, separated by a pathway of white rose petals on top of a wooden walkway. I haven't seen Nathan yet; he's somewhere around but Hannah and Elena are keeping us apart so the first time we see each other today will be when I walk down the aisle. I can't wait to see his shining eyes and feel his lips on mine.

The arch where we will exchange our vows catches the sunlight, with a cascade of pastel-hued flowers and white roses down both sides all the way to the bottom.

Elena and Hannah have done such an incredible job. Everything is so beautiful. And the day is glorious; it's as if the sea, the sky, and all of nature have come together to bless our union.

I push away the memory of the ladder and that terrifying fall yesterday. Nothing is going to go wrong today. I can feel it. As I finish applying my makeup, butterflies continue to flutter in my belly, and I imagine my baby growing inside there.

I know that once I walk down that aisle, my life will change forever. I will become Mrs. Brynn Howard, a new woman. The old Brynn will no longer exist, and a new chapter in my life will begin.

Soon Hannah enters with a radiant smile, although her eyes look a little strained and tired.

"Wow, girl," she says, crossing the closet in graceful strides, "you look drop-dead gorgeous. What a lucky man Nathan is. Are you sure you don't want help with the makeup?"

"No, I'm good, thanks." I smile brightly as she enfolds me in a hug. Her presence is so soothing. "Thank you, Hannah. I couldn't have asked for a better friend and maid of honor."

"It's going to be the perfect day" she says, squeezing me tight.

Elena soon arrives as well, seeming very Zen, even though I know she's been working flat out to keep everything running smoothly.

I put on my wedding dress and sit down while Hannah fastens my shoes. When I stand up, the bodice sparkles in the light of the chandelier, creating a dance of rainbows across the closet. Outside, the beach has come alive with the arrival of our guests. I can see them taking their seats now. They're all here to witness me exchanging vows with the love of my life. The only man I have ever loved.

My attention shifts to the box Hannah has just pulled out of her bag. It's covered in the blush-pink wrapping paper that I used for some of the wedding favors.

"What's this?" I ask as she hands it to me.

"A gift from your future husband. He wanted me to give it to you before the ceremony."

I tear off the wrapping paper to find a small powder-blue hip flask, personalized with my name engraved on it and covered in tiny crystals.

"Looks like that's your 'something blue,'" Elena says, perching herself on the edge of a soft cream seat.

"I already have something blue," I reply, holding up my garter with a blue ribbon woven through it. "But this is so beautiful. I can't wait to test-drive it."

"Well, how about we do it now?" Hannah suggests with a mischievous glint in her eye. "I'll get the champagne."

Before I can protest, she's already out of the door. She comes back in after a few minutes, holding up a bottle and followed by Debbie who is carrying some champagne flutes. Debbie has clearly inserted herself in the situation again, but I choose not to let her steal my joy. Nothing can do that today, not even her.

"I'd rather not," I say, shaking my head. "I want to be clear-headed when I walk down the aisle."

"Don't worry," Hannah says with a playful wink. "Elena got us one with zero alcohol, the killjoy. I'd never normally touch fake alcohol, but honestly, this tastes close enough to the real thing. You'd never know the difference. It's totally deceptive."

"You're the best," I say with a grin. "And I'm sure it will taste even better when I drink it from my lucky new flask."

While Hannah opens a box of white chocolate truffles, I give my flask to Elena who sets it down on the dressing table and carefully fills it and the crystal flutes with the fizzy drink. Debbie fusses over my flask, wiping it with her napkin, and finally we raise our drinks in a toast to happy endings.

Afterwards, Debbie leaves to take her seat and Hannah sweeps my wavy hair into a beautiful braided updo.

"Brynn," Elena says, her voice filled with genuine admiration as she munches on a truffle, "you look absolutely breathtaking."

"Yeah, Nathan won't believe his luck when he sees you," Hannah adds, clasping her hands together. But I sense a hint of sadness in her voice, and I remind myself to ask her about Ed later on. Maybe something has happened between them.

A sense of calm washes over me as I stand before the mirror, my wedding gown cascading down to the floor. I know I will want to remember every moment of this day for the rest of my life.

Finally, it's time to leave the bedroom, to walk toward the beach, and to my future husband. Hannah and Elena go ahead of me, with Hannah clutching my beaded purse. My heart flutters with excitement as I go downstairs and out via the living room porch.

But as I walk toward the chairs, I scan the crowd nervously, remembering that note I received weeks ago. The note with the smashed figurine of a bride who looked just like me.

The very first sign I had that somebody wishes me nothing but harm.

It's going to be the perfect day. For me, anyway. For you, my darling, it will be your worst nightmare.

Is the person who wrote those words here today, among my wedding guests?

THIRTY-SEVEN

The guests are gathered on the beach under the setting sun as it sends bold brush-strokes of orange and pink across the sky. We've timed everything so well.

As I step forward, everyone lets out a collective gasp of admiration, and warmth spreads through my chest.

With every step I take, I know I'm walking toward love and the promise of a future filled with more happiness than I can hold inside my heart. Along with the hushed whispers of the guests, the soft murmur of the ocean lulls me into a strangely serene state. Each step feels like a small victory against anything —and anyone—who has tried to stop me from reaching this moment.

But then it happens, like a bolt of lightning.

My throat tightens and a small wheeze escapes my lips, my vision blurring at the edges.

My heart begins to race as I realize what's happening, the panic rising like a powerful ocean wave. It threatens to drown me, but I force myself to take deep breaths, as much as I can. The guests' voices seem to grow louder in my ears, their joyful chatter blending with the roar of the sea.

Everything is a jumble now, and my knees are starting to buckle slightly beneath me. Fear sets in, and I wonder if I'll be able to make it all the way down the aisle.

But somehow, I keep going, one step after the other.

I spot a flash of neon yellow among the guests on the right and my eyes focus enough for me to see Debbie sitting not too far away. I cannot allow her to see me falter, to see me fail on my wedding day.

With fresh determination flooding my veins, I force myself to continue on down the aisle, my eyes fixed on the man waiting for me under the archway. Nathan, my future husband.

Through the blur, I see his eyes locked on mine steadily, in what I'm sure is a beacon of unwavering love and support. Nothing will keep me from marrying the man of my dreams. Not when our future together is just within reach.

With the next step, I draw in a deep breath, ignoring the itchiness spreading across my skin. I hide my discomfort as best I can, but soon my legs feel unbearably weak.

Beads of sweat break out on my forehead, and my body starts to shake.

Another wave of fear threatens to engulf me, but I refuse to succumb to it.

As I continue walking, my abdomen twists as if a fist is clenching inside my belly.

I'm so determined to persevere, but my body is trembling even more now, and I almost stumble.

The guests' whispers turn into gasps, but I ignore them. Someone reaches out a hand to help, but I shake my head.

For strength, I keep my eyes locked on Nathan's. I want to reassure him, to let him know that I'm okay, but I don't think I can get any words out. My lips are swollen, and my tongue feels thick inside my mouth. I'm so close to reaching him, to beginning our life together as husband and wife. But it's getting harder to keep upright.

For a split second, I imagine myself as one of the guests, watching myself from the outside. Summoning every ounce of strength I have left, I take another step, then another, but the pain is unrelenting. Wave after agonizing wave crashes through me, each one stronger than the last. I'm close enough now to see the concern etched on Nathan's face, his arms reaching out to steady me.

"Brynn," he whispers, his voice hoarse, "are you okay? What's happening?"

I try to answer him, but I can only manage a strained, breathless sound.

"We should postpone," Nathan says, glancing helplessly at the minister. "She needs help."

"No," I croak and for a few seconds, I feel a bit better. "Let's... let's start." To prove to him that I'm fine, I push away and do my best to stand on my own two feet.

"But, baby, you're clearly not okay. We need to—"

"Am fine," I mumble. Swaying from side to side, I nod at the minister. "Please, let's begin."

As soon as the words leave my lips, the world around me swirls while the minister nods and clears his throat.

My insides are on fire and my face feels like it's swelling up, but there's only one thought in my mind: I must make it through this, long enough to say yes to Nathan.

I try to focus on the minister's words, but my mind is too clouded to comprehend anything. Another sharp arrow shoots through my chest and I gasp for air. It feels like my lungs are collapsing. And when we reach the moment when vows should be exchanged, my voice, which should be filled with steadfast love and devotion, is reduced to a weak and raspy whisper.

Then my world tilts on its axis, and, unable to pretend anymore, I grab the lapels of Nathan's suit jacket. His eyes, once filled with love and anticipation, now mirror my own terror.

With sudden clarity breaking through the fog, it comes to me. I know what this is.

"EpiPen," I manage to choke out.

My throat constricting even more, I gasp desperately for breath. To my left, I make out Hannah's slender figure as she springs into action, her hands searching frantically through my purse for my EpiPen. But each second that passes feels like an eternity as I struggle for breath, Nathan still holding me upright while Hannah looks for my lifeline.

To my horror, she comes up empty-handed and shakes her head, her face etched with anguish.

"The baby," someone shouts, and I recognize the voice as Elena's. "Nathan, Brynn is pregnant."

"What?" I watch as Nathan's eyes widen in shock, his hands trembling as he looks at me. My vision is slipping now, but I can see the tears welling up in his eyes as the realization dawns on him that he might lose not only me, but also our unborn child.

Acting quickly, he takes charge, his words clipped and concise as he urges someone to call 911. And our once idyllic beach wedding transforms into a scene of chaos and despair.

The guests, who moments ago were sharing in our joy, now bear witness to the nightmare unfolding before them.

Then my knees give way and I crumple to the sand, my wedding dress billowing around me. Nathan drops to his knees at my side, his hand reaching out to steady me. I feel a sharp jab in my thigh: *Thank God. He must have had a spare EpiPen, just in case.*

"We have to get her to the hospital now," he shouts. "We can't wait." He brings a hand to my cheek. "Brynn, please stay with me," he pleads, his voice thick with emotion.

That voice, the precious voice of the man I love, is the last thing I hear before everything fades to black.

THIRTY-EIGHT

I feel as though I'm rising from the depths of a dark, murky sea. My senses gradually awaken, but I'm suspended in a vast expanse of nothingness, with no sense of direction or time.

When consciousness fully returns and I remember what's happening to me, the first thing I notice is the jolting of the vehicle I'm in. I'm half lying down, sandwiched between two people, my head cushioned by a soft surface. The pungent scent of Debbie's heavy perfume fills my nostrils. *Is she driving me to the hospital?*

My throat feels dry and scratchy, as though I've been screaming for hours, and I try to move, but the pain is unbearable. Clearly the EpiPen was administered far too late. It may have saved my life, but my body feels wrecked.

As I teeter on the brink of opening my eyes, compelling my muscles to respond to my brain's commands, hushed whispers reach my ears. Nathan and Hannah are here on either side of me; I can hear them speaking softly to each other. Too weak to open my eyes or say anything, I keep them closed, listening to their murmured conversation.

"I can't believe this," someone says. It's Elena's voice now, shaking with sorrow and disbelief. "How could this happen on her wedding day? Nathan, I'm so sorry you're going through this."

Nathan didn't know that Elena would be at the wedding, but I suppose given this emergency, he must have put his doubts aside and let her join him in taking me to the hospital. Along with Debbie.

Hannah's voice is barely above a whisper. "I didn't mean for it to... I didn't want her..." Her voice trembles, tears straining her words. "Oh God, what if she doesn't make it? What if...?" Her voice trails off.

"What are you talking about?" Elena asks sharply, and I can hear a rustling sound as if she's turning in her seat to face them. "You didn't mean for what to do what, Hannah?"

"Nothing. It's nothing. I'm just rambling." Hannah blows her nose loudly.

Nathan clears his throat. "Well? Did you do this on purpose, Hannah? Did you—?"

"You can't be serious, Nathan," Hannah snaps. "You know me, you can't possibly—" her voice falters, then halts abruptly.

"Of course you didn't do this," Elena says firmly. "Now let's just focus on stopping whatever it is and pray that Brynn and the baby pull through." Her seat squeaks, and I'm guessing she's facing the road again.

"No, Elena. Hannah knows exactly what I'm talking about," Nathan says coldly. "I'll ask you again. Did you have something to do with this?"

I want to open my eyes, but I don't want them to stop talking. My heart thuds in my chest as I strain to catch every word they say.

I can feel Nathan's large hand on my forehead now, stroking my damp hair from my face, but despite his calming touch, all my senses are on high alert.

"Nathan," Elena scolds again, "we all know what you're

going through right now. You are scared about Brynn and your baby, but making accusations like this won't help anyone. Hannah had nothing to do with what happened back there. That's ridiculous."

"People do all kinds of terrible things." Nathan's voice grows lower, but still loud enough for me to hear the words. "In the foyer before the ceremony, I showed you the flask I had for Brynn and you offered to wrap it up, so I took you to the study where we keep our wrapping paper. Did you put something into it, Hannah? You know she's allergic to nuts."

"You don't know what you're saying, Nathan." The panic in Hannah's voice is unmistakable, but it comes disguised as anger. "I would never do something like that. Come on, it's Brynn... she's my best friend."

"Then why is it that when I came back to the study to give you the Scotch tape you got startled, so much so that you dropped the flask? And why did I see a packet of peanuts on the desk, when we never keep them in the house?" he whispers furiously. "Do you realize that if Brynn and my baby die, Hannah, that's murder?"

"Is this true?" Elena asks, her voice uncertain now. "Hannah, did you really put something in Brynn's flask? Did you really—?"

"And what would you call what you did, huh, Nathan?" Hannah says, her voice pitiful and shaking with emotion. "Brynn would never have died if someone hadn't removed the EpiPen from her bag. And I saw you do that before you left the study, when you thought I wasn't looking. If you suspected I'd put peanuts in her drink, then why did you take out the EpiPen, unless you..." She blows out a breath and says nothing more.

"Oh my God!" Elena says. "What the hell is going on with you two?"

While my heart threatens to break apart inside my chest, a pregnant pause hangs in the car. Then Nathan, Elena, and

Hannah continue in an escalating argument, their voices growing louder as if they have forgotten they are not alone in the car, that I'm here. It's as if the car itself has become a pressure cooker of emotions.

Why would either Nathan or Hannah want to hurt me? There's no way. They're the two people I trust most in the world. I can't be hearing correctly. My head is a mess right now; maybe I'm distorting their words.

My thoughts are interrupted by Hannah's sobbing, the sound so heart-wrenching and raw it makes me want to instinctively reach out and comfort my friend. But instead, pain worse than the one swirling in my belly slices through my heart.

If Nathan is right, she did this to me. She ruined my wedding day.

She tried to kill me.

And, unless she's lying, so did he.

"I just can't believe either of you tried to kill Brynn." Elena's voice sounds so distant and detached, like she can't quite process what's happening. "How could you do that to her and her baby? Who are you people?"

Then I hear Debbie laugh. "You speak of Brynn like she's some kind of saint, Elena. That woman is far from innocent. She's been playing you all for fools."

Silence descends upon the car.

"What do you mean? And who are you, anyway?" Nathan asks, his tone sharp.

Heat spreads like a virus across my entire body from my cheeks to my toes.

"What, don't you recognize her?" Hannah interjects. "She's your mother, Nathan. The awful woman who ran out on you and left you with so much pain."

"What? My mother?" he sputters. "No, she isn't. I haven't spoken to my mother in quite some time. She's not a part of my life and that would never change. I have no idea who this woman is."

"He's right. I'm not his mother, but I *am* Brynn's mother-in-law," Debbie says, her voice trembling, but the truth comes out in a burst, as if it's been killing her to hold it back all this time. "Years ago, Brynn married my son, Jack. She ruined his life. I only came to stay with her because there's something I need to find, a hold she still has over Jack. It's been infuriating to see her living this perfect life she doesn't deserve. Truthfully, I wanted to remind her that I could take her happiness away too. She knew I could ruin her if I told all of you who I really am, and what she did to Jack. I've tried not to push her too hard though, as I know how dangerous she can be, and above all I needed time to find what she's hiding. I'm not the one who has been sabotaging her wedding."

There's a long pause, before a loud exclamation of "WHAT?" from both Elena and Hannah at the same time. But Nathan remains silent.

"She hasn't always gone by Brynn," Debbie continues. "Her name was Sandy Stanton back then. She treated my son terribly, in fact she nearly killed him, and then she took so much of our family money, even though she earned plenty herself. She's a cruel, dangerous woman."

Nearly killed him? My ears ring with Debbie's words and shock cuts through me. Is Jack alive?

"Did you know about any of this, Nathan?" Elena asks, cutting through my thoughts.

"No, I didn't," he says, his voice heavy and full of pain. "But there's something else I found out about Brynn... *Sandy*... from Amanda Lane. Amanda told me a few days ago. I guess she wanted to hurt me, punish me for losing the case. I was going to expose Brynn at the altar, embarrass her as much as I could before having her arrested. Then when I saw the peanut packet, I guessed what Hannah had done even though I didn't know why. I know it was so wrong, but I just snapped. I saw an opportunity and I took the EpiPen away. It sounds stupid, but I honestly didn't realize the reaction would be this severe. I just wanted to punish her. I was going to give her the EpiPen with plenty of time. And I did; she'd be dead by now otherwise. I'm not a murderer. But I'm furious, and I'm hurt. I thought I knew her. I loved her, and all along she's been hiding her true self from me—from all of us."

"Amanda Lane?" Elena repeats, sounding utterly flabbergasted. "Why would she...? Nathan, how does she—?"

"Brynn is Amanda Lane's daughter."

THIRTY-NINE

In my mind, I'm no longer in this car, but back in the tiny, rundown house of my childhood. And I find myself reliving moments I'd rather forget.

I was just ten, a frightened and confused child caught in the crossfire of my parents' tumultuous relationship. Our house was a place of constant tension.

To protect myself, I learned to hide in the shadows, to become invisible when the shouting started. But on that fateful night, I couldn't escape the horrifying reality that unfolded before my young eyes.

My father, a volatile man with a hot temper, known for his violent outbursts, had been drinking heavily when he decided to take his frustrations out on my mother.

I watched from the dark hallway, powerless to intervene.

My mother, a fragile woman worn down by years of abuse, had endured his beatings for far too long, and had spent too many nights in the emergency room, pretending that she fell on something, while I was sent to spend a few days with Grandpa Moses.

But on that night, something snapped within her as she

grabbed a nearby lamp with a hard metal base and swung it at him with all her might. The metal connected with his head, and he crumpled to the floor, blood spilling from his temple.

I gasped, frozen in shock, as she raised the lamp again. And I watched in horror as she unleashed years of pent-up anger and frustration on his broken body, the metal base of the lamp crashing down on his skull over and over again.

I couldn't scream, couldn't move, and couldn't look away from the gruesome scene. My father, who once loomed large and terrifying, now lay lifeless on the floor, his eyes staring vacantly. Then my mother dropped the lamp and turned to me, her hands trembling, her eyes filled with sorrow.

"Oh, Sandy, I'm so sorry you had to see that."

I finally found my voice. "Is... is he...?"

My mother nodded, her face ashen. "He's gone, sweetheart. He won't hurt us anymore."

In that moment, my world changed forever. I'd witnessed my mother kill my father, and it was an act that would change the course of both our lives.

She approached me, her arms outstretched, and pulled me into a tight hug. I clung to her, seeking solace in her warmth. When she pulled away, she made me look up into her face.

"Listen to me, Sandy," she said, her voice suddenly hard and filled with a determination I'd never heard before. "Men are dangerous people. You should never let any man hurt you. You must always be one step ahead. Get what you can from them and get out."

I was just a child and still in shock, the weight of her words too heavy for me to comprehend fully. But her tone and the look in her eyes told me that what she was saying was important. So, I nodded.

"Promise me," she insisted, her eyes searching mine for confirmation. "Promise you will never let any man hurt you. Hurt him first if you need to."

I nodded again, solemnly. "I promise, Mom," I muttered.

She smiled then, a tender loving smile that made me feel safe and protected. "Good." She kissed the top of my head. "Our lives will be better from now on, darling. I'll make sure of that." She paused to wipe her eyes with her blouse. "But first, there's something Mommy needs to do."

I walked behind her to the garage and watched as she pulled a shovel from the corner, its metal blade glinting in the dim light. I was old enough to know what she was planning to do with it, and even though I felt a chill down my spine, I trusted her completely.

My legs heavy underneath me, I went to get my own bucket and spade, a gift from Grandpa Moses from a recent outing to the beach. And I followed my mother.

FORTY

"Well, I never!" Debbie exclaims, her voice trembling. "I had no idea Brynn was Amanda Lane's daughter. But I reckon I should have known after what she did to my—"

"What do you mean, Brynn is Amanda Lane's daughter?" The shock in Elena's voice is palpable. "Who told you that? It can't be true. She told us all that her mother died when she was a child. And Amanda never told me she had a daughter when I knew her."

"That's what Brynn said to me as well, about her mother," Nathan says. "But of course, she would never admit to her mother being Amanda Lane. I think they've been working together all along: they are con artists who marry men, then murder them for their money. It seems they found their targets in some Facebook group for abused women, and I think Brynn used to donate the money she gained to domestic abuse charities. I guess that's why I was picked, because of the lies Lola spread about me."

"Did you know about this, Debbie?" Hannah demands. "If you did, why didn't you say anything?"

"Like I just said, I had no idea she was that awful woman's

daughter. All I knew was that she's dangerous. And I felt sorry for Nathan, but I had to focus on protecting my son. I thought that if Brynn started a new life with someone else, she'd leave my son and my family alone."

"Dangerous woman is an understatement," Nathan says bitterly. "Amanda told me that Brynn was going to kill me on our honeymoon."

"I don't understand," Hannah says slowly. "Why would Amanda tell you all those things about her own daughter?"

"God knows." I feel his body tense. "But the question is, Hannah, why were *you* trying to poison Brynn? If you didn't know any of this, what on earth possessed you to do such a thing?"

Tears choke Hannah's voice. "Please don't think badly of me, Nathan. I just wanted to scare her. I was going to give her the EpiPen in the nick of time too... But I had to stop the wedding. I—"

"You're in love with Nathan," Debbie interrupts, her words cutting through the tension. "When you came over to the house, I saw how you looked at the photos of him. I even saw you steal one of them when you thought no one was watching."

Hannah says nothing, and my heart races. I feel sick. This is all too much to take in.

"Is this true, Hannah? Are you really in love with me?" Nathan asks, his voice low and incredulous. "And this entire time you just pretended to be Brynn's best friend?"

"I'm sorry, Nathan," Hannah sobs. "I should have just come forward and told you. What I did today was stupid. But you don't understand how hard it's been, watching her prepare for her wedding with you, all the while knowing that you should be with me. Nobody loves you like me, Nathan. It's always been you. You've only ever seen me as a friend, but my heart was yours a long time ago. I've tried to be a good friend to Brynn because I care about you, and I don't want to lose you. But it's been tearing me up inside."

"I don't believe this," Elena mutters under her breath. "Hannah... please don't tell me that you were responsible for all those things going wrong with the wedding." She gasps out loud. "The cake tasting, the veil... Did you actually poison yourself, so you'd never be suspected? Oh, my God, Hannah. What were you thinking?"

Silence descends on the car for a moment, punctuated only by Hannah's sobs. But then Nathan swears suddenly and his body shifts. "This can't be happening."

"What? What's going on now?" Elena asks.

"I just switched on my phone; there's a message from one of my colleagues. Amanda Lane escaped early this morning and they think she's after me, that I should be careful."

My breathing starts to quicken, but I'm still too dizzy and weak to open my eyes.

"That might explain why a black sedan has been behind us for a while now," Debbie informs them, her voice tense. "It's been following us since we left the house. I didn't think much of it until this minute. But could it really be Amanda?"

Nathan curses under his breath as his body twists under me. "I see it. Speed up and take the next right."

As Debbie steps on the gas pedal, the car lurches forward and turns sharply. I can feel the car swerve and my body jolts against the seatbelt. My head spins and I feel like I'm going to throw up any minute now.

"It's still following us!" Elena exclaims, her voice rising in panic. "What do we do?"

"Oh, no, Nathan!" Hannah cries out. "She's speeding up... getting closer."

"I know. Just stay calm," Nathan says, his voice steady. "If Amanda is there, she must have been at the wedding, somewhere hidden, to be able to follow us now. So, she will have seen us take Brynn. And there's no way she'd want to hurt her own daughter."

"How can we be sure of that?" Hannah counters. "She already betrayed her by blowing her cover and telling you everything. Maybe she wants to get rid of Brynn. Maybe she's angry with her for still wanting to marry you, after you failed to win her case."

Panic grips me, vice-like around my chest.

And then, it happens.

A loud bang rocks the car, sending it careening out of control.

My ears fill with tires screeching, the sound of metal crunching against metal, and screams. I think one of the screams might be my own.

Then, with a thunderous roar, our car slams into something solid and flips end over end through the air before finally slamming back down to the ground with a tremendous force.

The acrid scent of gasoline and burning rubber plugs my nostrils, and I can feel something wet dripping down my cheek. Once again, everything is fading into black.

I can't see it, but I know the world outside, which just a few hours ago was the fairy-tale setting for my dream wedding, has morphed into a nightmare of twisted wreckage and shattered dreams.

Others might be shocked that my mother would want to harm her own daughter, but it doesn't surprise me in the least.

I've crossed her, and this is my punishment.

Everyone else is collateral damage.

FORTY-ONE

I'm terrified of opening my eyes. I can't bear to see what's left of the car, of the others, of myself. But slowly, I force my eyelids open, compelling myself to take in the scene. A shattered windshield, deployed airbags, and a crumpled front bumper greet my eyes. But from where I am, pushed against the twisted metal of the car door, I don't see anyone else. Not Nathan, not Hannah or Elena, and not Debbie.

I try to call out for help, but my throat is parched, and my voice barely leaves my lips. My body is racked by pain, sharp and unrelenting. I can feel glass shards embedded in my arms and legs, and my skin feels bruised all over.

The cramps in my abdomen have reached a new intensity. Groaning, I try to move, but a stabbing sensation burns its way up my leg. It feels as though my bones have been shattered, my muscles torn apart.

Help! I call out inside my head. *Someone, please help!* Fighting to keep my eyes open against the dark waves that threaten to pull me under, I now see Nathan trapped between the back and front seats, face down. I can't see Hannah anywhere. She must have been thrown out of the car.

I somehow find the strength to utter a single word, my voice weak and trembling, "Nathan."

There's no response, and the panic that begins to take hold of me is worse than anything I've felt so far. I try to lift my leg from him, but my body is unresponsive. Tears stream down my face as I whisper his name again and again, hoping for some sign of life.

Finally, he lets out a low grunt and manages to turn his head to one side. His eyes meet mine, and I can see the agony and despair etched on his face. He mouths something, but I don't catch it. Unable to hold on any longer, I allow the dark to consume me.

I'm barely awake as EMT workers arrive on the scene, their voices muffled as they try to free us from the wreckage. I can feel their hands on my body, as they check for injuries and assess the damage. I'm vaguely aware of the sound of metal being cut and the sensation of movement as they lift me onto a stretcher and whisk me away to an ambulance, where I continue to slip in and out of consciousness.

In my brief moments of lucidity, I let them know about my peanut allergy.

"Sorry, I can't hear what you're saying." An older female EMT brings her ear closer to my mouth. "Can you repeat that for me, sweetheart?"

I swallow hard and murmur the words again like someone learning to speak for the first time. "I'm preg... nant," I say, my words slurring. "Allergy... peanuts... EpiPen." I know my words are a jumbled mess, but I pray she's able to piece it all together.

"You are allergic to peanuts? Are you having a reaction now, ma'am?" the EMT asks, scribbling something down on a clipboard.

I nod feebly, feeling the familiar tightness in my chest again and the itchiness spreading across my skin. I can barely breathe now.

"And you're pregnant?"

I nod again, tears flooding my eyes. "Please help my baby."

"Okay. Thank you for letting me know. You're in good hands now. Stay calm. We'll take care of you and your baby."

After a quick discussion with one of her colleagues, she springs into action, administering epinephrine to counteract the allergic reaction.

The rest of the journey to the hospital is a blur of flashing lights and muffled voices. I'm strapped securely to a stretcher, my body immobilized to prevent further injury.

The discomfort is still there, a constant companion, but it's becoming distant, like a fading echo in the background. As the ambulance speeds through the night, sirens wail in the distance, and I imagine the vehicle parting traffic like a knife through butter, as the paramedics work diligently to keep me stable.

The EMTs are a well-coordinated team, moving with precision and urgency. They tend to my injuries with practiced expertise, their faces masked by a mix of determination and compassion.

Betrayal, pain, anger, and confusion intertwine in my mind. I wish I could delete what was said in the car before the crash from my memory, and it's a relief when the meds take over, and I drift off into a hazy sleep.

As the ambulance pulls into the hospital, a team of medical professionals is ready and waiting. The doors swing open, and I'm soon transferred from the stretcher to a bed with gentle efficiency.

The bright lights overhead are almost blinding, and the beeping of machines and the bustle of activity are overwhelming as doctors and nurses move about, their voices a constant murmur in the background.

Not long after my arrival, I'm whisked away for tests. My body continues to ache, but it's a dull ache compared to the agony I felt before. In fact, I feel like I'm floating in a dream, disconnected from my body.

In my mental haze, I'm only able to catch snippets of their conversations.

Fractured ribs.

Head trauma.

Possible internal bleeding.

The weight of their words sinks in, and I feel a panic rising within me. Broken bones? Internal bleeding?

What about my baby?

I'm eventually moved to another hospital room, where I'm hooked up to machines that monitor my vital signs and administer medication. From what I hear, it seems this will be my room for quite some time.

No waking up to the sound of the waves sweeping the shore. No walking out onto my beautiful balcony to greet the morning with a cup of hot coffee. No leisurely strolls on the beach at sunset. At least not for a while.

Over the coming hours, I slip in and out of sleep as faces come and go.

"Brynn, can you hear me?" a doctor asks, snapping me out of my thoughts.

I nod my head weakly and say nothing more.

"Good." He goes on to explain all the damage that was done to my body during the accident. It will be a long road to recovery, but at least I'm alive.

"You're in a stable condition now, but we still need to keep you here for a while to monitor your progress."

"Thank you," I whisper, and he gets up.

"You're very welcome." He pauses before looking down at his clipboard.

"Doctor... My baby? How's my baby?" I lay a hand on my belly.

The doctor's face falls slightly before he turns to face me directly. "I'm afraid the impact of the accident caused a miscarriage," he says gently. "I'm so sorry for your loss. If you like, we can provide someone for you to talk to about it."

As I reel from the news, he goes on to tell me that Nathan and Hannah sustained only minor injuries, but Elena suffered such a severe concussion that she has no recollection of anything that happened in the last few months. Then he hesitates before saying, "Unfortunately, the driver... she didn't make it."

Debbie is dead?

For weeks, I wanted that woman out of my way. But I never thought in my wildest dreams that she would actually die.

Maybe I should feel something, but honestly, I just can't take it in. My baby is dead, and that's all I care about.

Clasping my hands over my stomach, tears prick at the corners of my eyes, and I choke back a sob. *My baby.*

Gone, just like that.

The grief is suffocating, and I can barely breathe. When the doctor leaves, I close my eyes and try to focus on the sound of the heart monitor, anything to distract me from the anguish tearing at my heart.

I cry until I have no tears left, then I do the only thing I know will help me escape for a little while: I slip into a deep sleep, where my dreams take me far away from the hospital room.

Hours later, I open my eyes and the room is dark except for the thin moonlight seeping through the window. Something or someone woke me, but I can't quite put my finger on what. I glance around the room, and my heart jumps when I see that the door is slightly ajar. I freeze, straining my ears to listen for any sounds. But it's eerily quiet, even with the beep of the machines monitoring my condition.

I tell myself it's nothing, that I'm freaking myself out for no reason. It could have been a nurse or a doctor checking on me. But the familiar smell of expensive perfume in the air tells me otherwise. It's a sweet and sultry scent that I know all too well.

My mother's perfume. She was here.

FORTY-TWO

A Week After the Wedding Day

It's been seven days since the accident, and I've endured more heartache than I ever thought possible. Today is the day I'll be discharged, but I'm not sure if I'm ready to face the world outside, knowing that my baby will not be a part of it. The memory of the crash still haunts me, as do the unanswered questions and gaping wounds in my heart. Nathan hasn't visited me, not once, nor have Hannah or Elena.

I know that since Hannah and Nathan made it out of the accident with only minor injuries, they were discharged a day or two after being admitted. And one of the nurses told me that Nathan had been informed about the baby. But he didn't bother to come see me at all. I've called him countless times, left voice-mail after voicemail, pleading for him to answer or return my calls. But he never answered or called back.

The only person who I'm certain paid me a visit, even if I didn't see her, is my mother, on the night I was admitted. I can't help feeling that her visit was some kind of warning, and that I should watch my back. I tried calling her number, but it was disconnected.

A soft knock at the door disrupts my thoughts, and I turn to see a doctor entering the room, a middle-aged woman with kind, compassionate eyes and dark hair pulled back in a neat bun. Her name is Dr. Stone, and I've been seeing her regularly since I was admitted to the hospital. She greets me with a warm smile and a gentle touch on my arm. Even though my mind is all over the place, her calm demeanor instantly puts me at ease.

"Brynn," she begins, her voice gentle and reassuring, "how are you feeling today?"

I offer her a weak smile, my voice hoarse. "Physically, I think I'm getting better. Emotionally... I'm not so sure."

She nods, pulling up a chair to sit beside my hospital bed. "That's entirely normal. You've been through a very traumatic experience. But I have good news for you. You've made remarkable progress, and you're ready to be discharged today. I'm sure the nurse already informed you about that."

I nod, feeling both relief and apprehension.

I have no idea what to do now, or where to go.

"Thank you, Doctor. Is there anything I should be careful about in terms of my recovery?"

Dr. Stone clears her throat. "As I'm sure you already know, you'll need to take it easy for a while. No strenuous activity and be sure to follow up with your primary care physician for regular check-ups. You should be just fine, Brynn." She leans back in her chair. "Now, is there someone coming to pick you up, a friend or family member, perhaps? You might want to give them a call."

I nod and swallow hard, but my heart clenches when I pull out my phone, my fingers trembling as I dial Nathan's number again. It rings, and the hope that he might finally answer surges through me. But my hope is dashed once more when it goes to voicemail.

"No," I say, my voice wavering, "I can't seem to reach my fiancé. I'll call a taxi."

Dr. Stone's smile falters as she gets to her feet.

"All right then. I wish you the best, Brynn. Please take care of yourself and come straight back in if any of your symptoms get worse."

My eyes are blurry with tears and my hands clutch the sheets as I watch her leave the room. Alone again, I sink back into the hospital bed and squeeze my eyes shut, trying to block out the confusion raging inside me.

A few hours later, my taxi pulls up in the driveway in front of my home, and I step out gingerly, still wearing the loose-fitting clothes the hospital gave me and carrying a bag containing my wedding dress.

Despite seeing Nathan's shiny Mercedes parked outside, I decide not to knock. Instead, I pull my key from my wedding purse and slide it into the lock. The door opens silently, and I step inside slowly. I make my way through the hallway, taking in the familiar decor that I picked out so carefully. It all feels foreign to me now.

I don't know how I'm going to patch things up with Nathan, but I'm determined to do so. I know the love we shared was real. If he will just hear me out, listen to my side, I know we can make it through this. I've even forgiven him for taking the EpiPen. He did give it to me in the end, and I understand better than anyone how easy it is to act rashly in the heat of the moment.

But Hannah? Her I'll never forgive.

I'm about to head upstairs when I hear voices coming from the living room. But when I look in, the room is empty. The two people talking are Nathan and Hannah, sitting out on the porch.

Hannah's head rests on Nathan's lap, her eyes closed.

And with the arm that's not in a sling, he strokes her hair.

Then to my horror, I watch as he leans down and kisses her lips.

I feel sick to my stomach. I never dreamed he would reciprocate Hannah's feelings. Especially so soon. Especially after what she did to me.

But while I was in the hospital grieving our baby, it seems a lot has changed.

Anger erupting inside me, I limp onto the porch. "What the hell is going on here?"

They pull apart in surprise, and Hannah's eyes are wide as she sits up. Nathan's expression is a mixture of shock and fear, but there's also a definite steeliness there. "Brynn, I—"

I cut him off, my voice simmering with rage. "How long? Tell me. How long has this been going on?"

Nathan and Hannah exchange a quick glance before Nathan finally speaks. "Brynn, it's not what you think. We're not—"

I interrupt him. "Don't lie to me!" I suddenly feel an ache in my healing ribs and press a hand to my side. "And don't think for a second that I didn't hear everything you said to each other in the car."

Their faces turn pale, and Nathan pushes himself to his feet. "Brynn, I need to talk to you, privately."

Reluctantly, I agree, and we move away from Hannah, who has her arms wrapped around herself, her head sinking onto her chest.

We step from the porch into the living room, and I close the doors behind us. Nathan takes a deep breath before he speaks.

"There's something you should know." There are tears in his eyes, and I realize I've never seen that before. "I found out who you really are days before the wedding, Brynn. I learned about your past, the terrible crimes you've committed." He shoves the hand of his uninjured arm into his pocket. "I couldn't believe that the woman I loved could be capable of such things. I still can't."

The room starts to spin around me, and my legs give way. Unable to stop myself, I sink to the carpeted floor. "Loved?"

Nathan just looks down at me, his eyes cold. "Yes, loved. I found out the truth about you and it shattered me. It destroyed everything I felt about you."

"That's why you didn't—"

"Answer your calls, yes. I couldn't bear to hear your voice, to see your face."

I open my mouth only to close it again. When he didn't visit me in hospital, I guess a part of me knew this was coming. But hearing him say he doesn't love me anymore still hits me like a freight train.

"Nathan," I say, struggling to my feet. "Please, just let me explain. I'm different now. You... you changed me. We were going to have a baby." I reach for him, but he yanks his hand away.

"But we're not anymore." I watch as sadness sweeps across his features and is soon replaced by anger. He shoves a hand through his hair. "You lied to me. You made me believe you were someone you weren't." His voice is totally devoid of any of the warmth that used to be there. I've never seen him this angry before.

"Nathan, you don't understand. It's not what you think. I really... I loved... I love you. I promise I didn't—"

"You have no right to use that word. You have no idea what love is." The lightning in his eyes threatens to strike me down and I flinch.

"Nathan, please," I plead, tears streaming down my face. "I know I messed up, but please don't give up on us. I'll do anything to make it right. Just give me one more chance."

"There is no us, and now I know there never was." Looking defeated, he sinks onto one of the sofas and drops his head.

When he finally looks up, the torment in his eyes is almost too much for me to bear. "I'll make you a deal, Brynn. Hannah and I won't turn you in for the crimes you committed with Amanda Lane. Elena can't remember anything, and that's unlikely to change. She's gone to stay with her sister in New York, and I doubt she'll return anytime soon, if at all. But Hannah and I will only keep your secret if you don't have us prosecuted for attempted murder at the wedding. Now I need you to pack your stuff and leave my house. I never want to see you again."

I stumble toward the door in shock. I never thought it would end like this. I really believed the two of us were meant to be, that nothing could ever tear us apart. I want to continue pleading with him, but his eyes tell me there's no turning back. He has made up his mind, and I know I should be thankful that he's not calling the police. I have no choice but to leave before he changes his mind.

I need to pack my things, so without saying another word, I walk out of the room and head toward the stairs, moving like a robot. But before I climb the first step, he calls my name.

"Brynn, there's one more thing," he says. "Even though I can never forgive you, I do believe you might have changed, or at least that you want to. But if I ever find out... if there's ever even a hint you might be up to your old ways, then I'm going to the cops, no matter what you tell them about me and Hannah." He pauses. "I'll be watching."

FORTY-THREE

The air in my motel room is stale and unpleasant as I sit on the bathroom floor, hunched over the cool tiles. The pitiful light overhead casts a sickly pallor on everything, making me dizzy. It's the cheapest place I could find. I'm going to have to be careful with every dollar I spend now.

When we got engaged, Nathan opened up a joint account and I put all my ample finances in there, too, and then I withdrew from it as I pleased. But on my way out of Stoneview I tried to withdraw some cash and found that the account was completely drained.

My mother's plan was that on our honeymoon, sailing around the Caribbean, I would get rid of Nathan and make it look like a scuba diving accident. We had planned everything. I was going to sabotage his equipment and pretend to be devastated at his untimely death, before taking all the money he left to me and using it, alongside my own hard-earned cash, to escape together and start afresh, if her trial went badly.

My mother figured it was foolproof, and I had no reason to doubt her as she had always been the brains behind our schemes. But as time went by, I realized that I was genuinely falling in love with him. So, I decided to ditch the whole plan, and to step away from my mother's control.

She was going to jail anyway, and I never thought she would manage to escape. I really believed I would finally have a chance to forge my own path. Nathan was the man I wanted to spend the rest of my life with. I thought I could have all the happiness, safety, normality, and love I'd never believed would be possible for me.

And now, all I have is the emergency cash I took from our kitchen counter a few hours ago, before leaving our home for the last time, with a suitcase full of clothes and a heart that's shattered in pieces.

I'm going to have to look for a job right away. A regular 9–5 to help tide me over until I can find something more suited to my talents and passions. For now, I can't bring myself to even think about returning to the art world. As if anything could ever be beautiful to me again.

The acidic taste of bile rises in my throat, and I crawl to the toilet bowl, barely making it in time. When I'm done retching, sobs rack my body, each one tearing through me like a jagged knife. The sound is raw and primal as my anguish echoes off the bathroom walls. Finally, I shuffle to the sink and turn on the faucet, letting the water run until it's cold. I splash my face and look into the mirror at the stranger staring back at me.

I'd come so far, changed so much, but now I'm back to being a woman fighting for survival.

Back inside the tiny bedroom, I unzip my suitcase and begin to unpack. Debbie's large, brown leather handbag is on top. Nathan asked me to take her things away with me as well, and to send them on to her family.

I have no idea what I hope to find in Debbie's handbag, but I can't stop myself from looking. And as I sift through the contents, I find her leather-bound journal tucked inside. I open it and begin reading.

Most of the entries are about me.

The last place I want to be is under the same roof as this woman. Brynn doesn't deserve the luxury that surrounds her, the charmed life she's been handed on a silver platter. But I have to be here, to pretend I want nothing more than for her to be blissfully happy even after everything she did to my boy. I would do anything for my son, and if this new relationship keeps her away from my family, then so much the better. And I need to find the evidence that she could use to destroy Jack's life and his reputation. He's a changed man and he deserves to be happy. But if Brynn finds out he's alive and well, I wouldn't put it past her to ruin everything for him. I can't let that happen, especially now that he has finally found true love with Alice, a woman who brings out only the best in him. In our phone call the other day, I don't think I've ever heard him so happy, so content. They're going to be married. I won't let Brynn take that away from him. It's killing me, but I'm going to do everything I can to make sure Brynn is married off happily and to put myself in her good books, as well as finding this evidence. It must be here somewhere.

Shock makes me reel as I read the words again and again.

He has finally found true love with Alice, a woman who brings out only the best in him.

He's alive. Jack is really alive. I didn't want to believe it when Debbie hinted at it in the car, but here it is in black and white.

How is that possible? For years I thought he was dead, that I had shot and killed him that night he struck me for the last time. I called 911, but I didn't stay for long enough to find out if he survived.

I fled and messaged Debbie, promising to disappear with my bruises and my broken bones, so long as she sent me a huge sum of her family's money. I didn't need the money of course, and I immediately gave it to a women's shelter for abuse survivors. And I warned Debbie that if she ever tried to report me for her son's death, I would reveal everything. She knew I had gathered plenty of evidence, including photos of the many injuries Jack gave me while we were together.

And that's what she came searching for. But she was wasting her time: the journal and photos were destroyed in a fire that consumed my apartment in Tallahassee. A fire caused by my own mother, to punish me when I was reluctant to go along with one of her plans.

As I reread Debbie's words, I'm furious at her. How could she have been so naive? Once an abuser, always an abuser. Jack doesn't deserve happiness after what he did to me and the women before me.

I wish I could do something about it, to stop him hurting Alice or any other woman. But I made a deal with Nathan, and I know he'd never let me get that far.

As I turn the page, a knock interrupts my thoughts. I quickly close the journal and put it away.

No one but the motel manager knows I'm here.

I can barely breathe as I slowly make my way to the door, squinting through the peephole to see who it is. Then my heart jumps to my throat and I step back.

"Let me in, Brynn. I know you're in there," a familiar voice calls out. "Don't make me use your real name."

I take a deep breath and turn the knob. The once-vibrant hair of the woman in front of me is now dull and streaked with gray, and her face is crisscrossed with deep lines. Without makeup and with her hair unkempt, she looks like a shadow of her former self.

"Hi, Mom," I murmur as she pushes her way through the door and shuts it before turning to me with a humorless smile.

"As far as I'm concerned, you can continue calling me Sam.

No child of mine would do what you did to me." She goes to the window and peers out, perhaps looking to see if the cops have followed her. Her words send shivers down my spine. I know I've betrayed her, but I had no choice.

"You destroyed my life," I retort, my anger surfacing. "You told Nathan—"

"The truth?" My mother shrugs, her indifference chilling. "Can you blame me?"

My anger turns to tears as I feel the weight of everything crashing down on me. "I had fallen in love with him, Mom. For the first time in my life, I actually fell in love."

"You have no idea what love is, my dear." She shakes her head. "You betrayed me."

Tears stream down my face as I try to explain, to make her understand. "I had no choice. I knew you would be angry if I told you that I wanted a future with him. You wouldn't have understood."

Following the death of my father, to whom she was never married, my mother no longer believed in love. But she still married eight years later. He was a rich businessman, and he was twice her age, but she didn't seem to care. All she wanted was the security and comfort that came with his wealth. She was willing to do whatever it took to get it, even put up with his temper that was dangerously similar to my father's. But one day, her new husband died in a car crash. And when she didn't shed one tear, my gut told me it was not an accident at all.

As the years went by, I watched as she transformed from a loving and caring woman to a calculating and conniving murderer. She managed to pull me in to work with her, telling me that we were doing a good thing by ridding the world of dangerous men who did not deserve to be alive. She did the killing and I helped cover it up. I was the keeper of her secrets.

Until Jack Stanton came along and my mother decided he would be my first kill.

After reading all about him in a social media group for abuse victims and survivors, I deliberately ran into him at a charity event.

The seduction was easy, and within a few short weeks, we were dating. Less than three months later, I talked him into marrying me. And six months after that, I shot him in what anyone should agree was self-defense. But I knew our justice system doesn't work that way.

After that, my mother and I decided to make a fresh start in Tallahassee. I had no desire to go through something like that again, but she was not done yet. And after she set fire to my apartment, the message was clear. I either went along with her plans, or I'd feel the full brunt of her fury.

We read about Nathan in the Safe Haven Sisters Facebook group. The story told by his ex-girlfriend Lola was all too familiar, as she depicted a man who everyone loved, but who had a cruel, dark side only she could see. But she left him, something many people are unable to do.

Then my mother was arrested for murder, and her wedding planner, Elena, recommended Nathan as a lawyer. Of course, my mother immediately remembered him as Lola's abuser. So, she decided that she would hire him, and that after he cleared her name, he would be my target. If he failed, I'd kill him and use his money to help us get away.

She checked in on me constantly of course, having sourced herself a phone even when she was in jail. Money can get you anything, and if anyone knows how to get what they want, it's my mother. We had our own little code just for an extra bit of security: she was called Sam, and we never mentioned the trial, referring to it only as hot weather when things got difficult.

But as I got to know him, Nathan didn't show any signs of being the monster Lola had described. In fact, he was charming and attentive, a total gentleman. And I fell for him, despite myself.

Then I found out that Lola had been lying all along.

"You chose a man over me," my mother is saying, bitterly. "You turned your back on me, after everything we've been through together."

"We made a mistake, Mom. We went after the wrong man. Nathan wasn't the man we thought he was," I insist. "All those things we read about him in the group, they were not true. Yes, Lola did date him, but he never abused her. She made it all up... She even hurt herself to make it look like he did it. She was obsessed with him."

After a tense back-and-forth, and with my mother piling on the guilt, I finally apologize to her for shutting her out and for betraying her trust.

After all, Nathan might not have been an abuser, but he did break my heart. "You were right," I say, wiping my eyes with the back of my hand. "Men can't be trusted. I should have never allowed myself to fall in love."

Her expression softens slightly as she lowers herself into a chair by the window. "Thank you for saying that, but I'm finding it very hard to forgive you."

"And I you," I shoot back. "You tried to kill me in that car accident."

She blinks several times, and I can see that my words have struck a nerve. "You're still alive, aren't you? That's all that matters." She smiles.

"Yes, I am, but I could have died. And I lost my baby in the accident." A sob escapes my lips. "Do you even care? My baby never got to come into the world because of you."

Her own face crumples then and her eyes widen. "You... you never told me you were pregnant. How could you keep something like that from me? I'm your mother."

"Well, Mom," I say between gritted teeth, "I didn't think you would approve. I was going to have a baby with a target."

Silence sits heavily between us, thick with unspoken words and emotions.

Finally, she speaks. "I'm sorry," she says, her voice low. "I wasn't thinking straight, in that car." She stands and turns to the window, her back facing me. "At first, I just wanted to scare all of you, but things got out of control. It's just that I felt so betrayed. I was furious with Nathan for losing my case, and with you for turning your back on me when we were supposed to escape together." She turns to face me again. "I felt terrible afterwards, I still do. But you can't put all the blame on me. For all we know, the person who killed your baby is the one who tried to poison you at your own wedding. That woman, Hannah, is it?"

"How do you—?"

"I was at the wedding, watching from a distance. It was clear you were having an anaphylactic reaction and I followed you and your friends as they rushed you away, before my anger got the better of me in the car. And at the hospital, I heard you talking in your sleep about what Hannah did." She sits back down. "It's her fault you lost your baby, not mine. But I'm sorry for the part I played in all of this. I know I can't make up for what happened, but I want to try."

"How?" I fold my arms.

"By helping you fix your life. I know things didn't work out with Nathan, but there are many men out there like him. I saw you left the Facebook group. You should rejoin because there are some women in there who really need our help. It will give you a sense of purpose."

"Oh, so just get back to business as usual, is that it?" More tears flood my eyes as I shake my head. "I can't do it anymore, Mom. I'm sorry, but I want a different life for myself."

Memories of my past life dance through my mind. With Nathan and Hannah's threat hanging over my head, I must step away from all that. I'm not going to risk ending up behind bars.

And I've tasted what it's like to imagine a different kind of future, one that isn't tainted by suffering and violence. I want that vision back.

My mother just laughs. "There's no point in trying to be someone you're not, darling. No matter how hard you try, you will always be my daughter." She shakes her head. "You and I, we are cut from the same cloth, and nothing can change that."

But I don't want to accept that this is all there is for me. I can't keep living a life of deception and fear, always looking for the next woman to avenge and the next man to punish.

Taking a deep breath, I wipe my tears away, and summon all the courage I have left to stand up to her. "Sorry, Mom. I'm done."

I wonder if I'll ever find a way to truly escape the shadows of my past. Maybe I can't, not fully. But perhaps, without my mother pulling the strings, I can start to build a life that's truly my own.

"You don't mean that, and we both know it. You just need some time to recover, and once you do, you'll come back to me. We'll be a team again, like we always were." My mother's voice drips with honey, but I can hear the venom underneath.

She pushes a hand into her handbag and pulls out a piece of paper. "When you're ready, give me a call. You're the only person with this number."

She presses the note into my hand and walks out into the night.

EPILOGUE

Six Months Later

Dressed in black jeans, a loose blue sweater, and a cap for disguise, I close the squeaking door behind me. As soon as I turn the corner, the motel manager, a balding, sweaty figure with a sour expression, blocks my way.

"Hey there, sugar," he grumbles, his voice thick with an accent I can't place. "You owe me for the last two nights."

He's right. I've been here for a week, but I only paid for five days. I've been avoiding him, hoping to slip away unnoticed.

"I'll pay you tomorrow," I say, trying to sidestep him, but he blocks my path again.

"You said that yesterday," he growls. "Pay me now or get out."

Until now, I've managed to sweet-talk my way out of it, but not this time, it seems.

If I had the money, I would pay him right away. But I'm broke, and I know I won't be able to pay him tomorrow either. Over the last few months, my crushing depression has made it almost impossible for me to hold down a job, any kind of job.

I summon all the charm I can muster, flashing a coy smile. "Come on, Joe. I'll make it worth your while." I take a step closer to him. "I just need a little more time, okay? I'll even add a little something extra for the trouble."

Joe's expression softens a little, and he looks me up and down. "Well, maybe we can work something out." There's a greedy glint in his eyes now.

I grit my teeth, nausea rising in my throat at the thought of him touching me. But I can't let him see my disgust. I need to play the game, just this once, and then I'll make my escape.

"Tomorrow night." I wink at him, feigning a sultry expression.

Joe nods, his eyes still glued to my body. "All right, doll." He finally steps aside. "But don't forget, I will be expecting that little something extra."

With a sigh of relief, I head toward my battered old Volvo. I drive through the familiar streets of Stoneview toward the rich part of town I used to call home, and I come to a halt a few blocks away from the beach house that was supposed to be mine.

Stepping out of the car, I approach the house and hide behind a nearby bush in the garden, looking through the windows. From here I can see the door that leads into the kitchen as well, and my heart aches when I imagine myself sitting there at the island or walking over to the fridge and pulling out a jug of iced tea. It was all taken away from me so quickly.

I had it all. And now I have nothing.

Nathan's car is parked out front, but I can't see him through any of the windows facing the garden. I move slowly around to the back of the house, facing the beach, and there I spot him on the master bedroom terrace. But he's not alone. He's with Hannah, and she has her arms around his neck, her body pressed against his.

They're laughing, kissing, wrapped up in their own world. And then, when they pull apart, I see it. Hannah's belly is swollen, a small bump visible even from where I'm standing on the shore.

Tears prick at the corners of my eyes, but I wipe them away, my sorrow quickly replaced by anger as I place my hand on my own stomach and remember the life I left behind in the crash.

For months I have wallowed in hatred for Nathan and Hannah.

Hannah spent weeks trying her best to frighten me into postponing my wedding, torturing me because she was jealous of my relationship with the man she loved. And somehow, all that time she was pretending so convincingly to be my friend. Then not only did Nathan fall into her arms just days after he was supposed to marry me, but he also did something that could easily have killed me, on purpose. Just like she did.

I survived. But my baby died, and it's all their fault.

I have tried hard to stay away from them, but I can't any longer. And as I watch them in their blissful state, all I feel is a burning desire for revenge. I can't tear my gaze away from them even if it's killing me to see the two of them together.

That life should have been mine.

As the waves crash against the shore, a storm brews within me. They will pay for what they've done. Revenge is what drove my mother to do everything she did. And now, for the first time in my life, I truly understand how she became the person she is. The need for retribution is a powerful force, one that can consume you completely.

And now it has taken over my mind.

Back inside my car, I reach into the dashboard and pull out the piece of paper my mother gave me when I last saw her. I stare at it for a moment, before unfolding it with a shaking hand.

Reaching for my phone, I dial the number, my heart pounding. It rings once, twice.

"Mom," I say when she picks up, "I need your help."

A LETTER FROM L.G. DAVIS

Dear reader,

I'd like to thank you so much for reading *The Woman at My Wedding*. It was such a joy to write this book, creating characters who became very real to me. I loved delving into their deepest hopes, dreams, and fears against the backdrop of charming Stoneview. I can't think of anything better than unveiling the secrets hidden beneath the surface of a seemingly idyllic home and town.

You'll be glad to know that this book has a sequel, where the characters will grapple with the aftermath of the betrayals they endured in this story. I promise you more intense emotions and thrilling adventures.

In order to be notified every time I have a new book published, please sign up at the link below. Your email address will never be shared and you can unsubscribe at any time.

www.bookouture.com/l-g-davis

If you experienced escapism, excitement or an electric thrill while reading *The Woman at My Wedding,* I kindly invite you to consider leaving a review. Reviews play a crucial role in helping others discover and connect with stories they might cherish. Thank you in advance for sharing your feedback.

I love hearing from readers, so please feel free to reach out to me anytime—whether to share your thoughts, discuss the story, or just to say hello. You can connect with me through Instagram, Facebook, X, or my website. Your messages are like treasures to me, and I look forward to each one.

Thank you again for taking the time to read *The Woman at My Wedding*.

Much love,

Liz xxx

www.lgdavis.com

facebook.com/LGDavisBooks

x.com/LGDavisAuthor

instagram.com/LGDavisAuthor

goodreads.com/lgdavisbooks

ACKNOWLEDGMENTS

I owe a debt of gratitude to everyone who played a role in turning yet another one of my book dreams into reality.

A special and heartfelt thank-you goes to my wonderful editor, Rhianna Louise. Rhianna, your brilliance, dedication, and great attention to detail have transformed this manuscript into something we can both be proud of. Your insights truly enriched the heart of the story. Working with you from the first spark of inspiration to the final punctuation mark was a privilege, and I'm in awe of your ability to bring out the best in every word and sentence. I'm so fortunate to have you as my editor.

I also want to extend my heartfelt thanks to the entire Bookouture team. Your professionalism, creativity, and unwavering dedication have made this publishing journey not only seamless but also enjoyable. Every member of the team has played a crucial role in the success of this book, from the stunning cover design to the strategic marketing efforts. Thank you for all that you do.

To my readers, your enthusiasm and support are the driving forces behind my writing. I'm incredibly grateful for each and every one of you who has embraced this story with open hearts, allowing it to come alive in your minds. You have no idea how much your kind words and encouragement mean to me. Your loyalty and passion for my work inspire me to keep writing, to keep creating stories that transport you to different worlds. I'm so excited to continue this journey with you.

This book has been a labor of love, and I extend my deepest

appreciation to everyone who has been part of this incredible journey, especially my husband, Toye, and our two children, who have been my constant pillars of support. Their unwavering belief in me, their patience during the many long nights spent hunched over my laptop, and their understanding when I had to lock myself away in the depths of my imagination, have made all the difference.

Thank you all from the bottom of my heart.

With heartfelt thanks,

Liz

PUBLISHING TEAM

Turning a manuscript into a book requires the efforts of many people. The publishing team at Bookouture would like to acknowledge everyone who contributed to this publication.

Audio
Alba Proko
Sinead O'Connor
Melissa Tran

Commercial
Lauren Morrissette
Jil Thielen
Imogen Allport

Data and analysis
Mark Alder
Mohamed Bussuri

Editorial
Rhianna Louise
Nadia Michael

Copyeditor
Donna Hillyer

Proofreader
Emily Boyce

Marketing
Alex Crow
Melanie Price
Occy Carr
Cíara Rosney

Operations and distribution
Marina Valles
Stephanie Straub

Production
Hannah Snetsinger
Mandy Kullar
Jen Shannon

Publicity
Kim Nash
Noelle Holten
Myrto Kalavrezou
Jess Readett
Sarah Hardy

Rights and contracts
Peta Nightingale
Richard King
Saidah Graham

Made in the USA
Monee, IL
06 July 2024

61367918R00152